Blubs from 1976 edition:

THE SPACE VAMPIRES

THE SPACE VAMPIRES

COLIN WILSON

Monkfish Book Publishing Company
Rhinebeck, New York

Printed in the United States of America
Book and cover design by Georgia Dent
Library of Congress Control Number: 2009939658

Originally published by Random House in 1976.

ISBN: 9780982324615

Monkfish Book Publishing Company
27 Lamoree Road
Rhinebeck, New York 12572
www.monkfishpublishing.com

For
June O'Shea,
my criminological adviser

Acknowledgements

THIS BOOK ORIGINATED, many years ago, in a discussion with my old friend A. E. van Vogt, whose story "Asylum" is a classic of vampire fiction. (Aficionados of the genre will recognize my indebtedness to it.) August Derleth, who published my first work of science fiction, offered warm encouragement; unfortunately, he has not lived to see the completion of our project. For the idea of the parallelism between vampirism and crime, I must acknowledge my indebtedness to June O'Shea of Los Angeles, who has kept me plentifully supplied with books and press cuttings on recent American crime. This book also owes much to the stimulus of discussions with Dan Farson— on vampirism in general, and on his great-uncle, Bram Stoker, in particular. I must also express my warmest thanks to Count Olof de la Gardie, both for his hospitality at Råbäck, and for allowing me to inspect family papers relating to his ancestor Count Magnus. Finally, I must thank Mrs. Sheila Clarkson for her careful work in retyping and correcting the dog-eared manuscript.

—C.W.

1

THEIR INSTRUMENTS PICKED up the massive outline long before they saw us. That was to be expected. What baffled Carlsen was that even when they were a thousand miles away, and the braking rockets had cut their speed to seven hundred miles an hour, it was still invisible.

Then Craigie, peering through the crystal-glass of the port, saw it outlined against the stars. The others left their places to stare at it. Dabrowsky, the chief engineer, said: 'Another asteroid. What shall we name this one?'

Carlsen looked out through the port, his eyes narrowed against the blinding glare of the stars. When he touched the analyser control, symmetrical green lines flowed across the screen, distorted upwards by the speed of their approach. He said: 'That's no asteroid. It's all metal.'

Dabrowsky came back to the panel and stared at it. 'What else could it be?'

At this speed, the humming of the atomic motors was scarcely louder than an electric clock. They moved back to their places and watched as the expanding shape blocked the stars. They had examined and charted nine new asteroids in the past month; now each knew, with the instinct of trained spacemen, that this was different.

At two hundred miles, the outline was clear enough to leave no doubt. Craigie said: 'It is a bloody spacecraft.'

'But, Christ, how big is it?'

In empty space, with no landmarks, distances could be deceptive. Carlsen depressed the keys of the computer.

Looking over his shoulder, Dabrowsky said with incredulity: 'Fifty miles?'

That's impossible,' Craigie said.

Dabrowsky punched the keys and stared at the result. 'Forty-nine point six four miles. Nearly eighty kilometres.'

The black shape now filled the port. Yet even at this distance, no details could be seen. Lieutenant Ives said: 'It's only a suggestion, sir…But wouldn't it be an idea to wait until we get a reply to our signal from base?'

"That'll be another forty minutes.' Base was the moon, two hundred million miles away. Travelling at the speed of light, it would take their signal half an hour to get there, and another half-hour to bring a reply. 'I'd like to get closer.'

Now the motors were silent. They were drifting towards the spacecraft at fifty miles an hour. Carlsen switched off all the cabin lights. Gradually, as their eyes adjusted, they could see the grey-black metal walls that seemed to absorb the sunlight. When they were a few hundred yards away, Carlsen stopped the *Hermes.* The seven men crowded against the port. Through its thick crystal, as transparent as clear water, they could look up at the side of the craft, towering above like an iron cliff as far as their eyes could see. Below, the same wall seemed to plunge into the gulf of space. They were all accustomed to weightlessness, but it produced a sensation of dizziness to look down; some instinctively drew back from the glass.

At this distance, it was clear that the ship was a derelict. The walls were grained and pitted. A hundred yards away to the right, a ten-foot hole had been ripped through the plates. The searchlight showed that the metal was six inches thick. As the beam moved slowly over the walls, they could see other deep indentations and smaller meteor holes.

Steinberg, the navigator, said: 'She looks as though she's been in a war.'

'Could be. But I think that's mostly meteor damage.'

'It must have been a meteor storm.'

They stared in silence. Carlsen said: 'Either that, or she's been here a very long time.'

No one had to ask what he meant. The chances of a spacecraft being struck by a meteor are roughly the same as the chance of a ship in the Atlantic bumping into a floating wreck. For this hulk to be so battered, it would have had to spend thousands of years in space.

Craigie, the Scots radio operator, said: 'I don't like this bluddy thing. There's something nasty about it'

The others obviously felt the same. Carlsen said, almost casually: 'And it could be the greatest scientific discovery of the twenty-first century.'

In the excitement and tension of the past hour, no one had thought of this. Now, with the telepathic intuition that seems to develop between men in space, they all grasped what was in Carlsen's mind. This could make each individual of them more famous than the first men on the moon. They had found a spacecraft that was clearly not from earth. They had therefore established beyond question that there is intelligent life in other galaxies .

The sound of the radio made them all jump. It was their reply from moonbase. The voice was that of Dan Zelensky, the chief controller. Obviously, their message had already caused excitement. Zelensky said: 'Okay. Proceed with caution and test for radioactivity and space virus. Report back as soon as possible.' In the silence, they could all hear it. They also heard Craigie's reply, dictated by Carlsen, Craigie's voice sounded cracked from excitement. 'This is definitely an alien spacecraft, approximately fifty miles long and twenty-five miles high. It looks like some damn great castle floating in the sky. It seems unlikely there is life aboard. It's probably been here for at least a few hundred years. We request permission to investigate.' This message was repeated half a dozen times at minute intervals, so that even if space static made most of them inaudible, one might get through.

In the hour during which they waited for the reply, the *Hermes* bumped gently against the unknown craft. They were all eating tinned beef and washing it down with Scotch whisky; the excitement had made them ravenous. Again Zelensky came on personally, and his voice was also thick with tension.

'Please take fullest possible precautions, and if any danger, prepare for return to moonbase immediately. You are advised not to attempt to board until you've had a night's sleep. I've talked to John Skeat at Mount Palomar, and he admits that he's baffled. If this thing's fifty miles across, it should have been discovered two hundred years ago. Long-exposure photographs show nothing in that part of the sky. Please complete all other possible tests before attempting to board.'

Although the message told them nothing they could not have guessed in advance, they listened intently and played it back several times. Life in space is boring and lonely; now, suddenly, they felt they were the centre of the universe. On earth, their news would now be on every television channel. Since two hours ago, they had entered history.

Back in London, it was now seven o'clock in the evening. The men of the *Hermes* regulated their lives by Greenwich mean time; it was a way of maintaining contact. The evening that lay ahead already sagged with a quality of anticlimax. Carlsen issued more whisky but not enough to produce intoxication; he didn't want to board the derelict with a crew suffering from hangover.

Together with Giles Farmer, the medical officer, Carlsen manoeuvred the emergency port of the *Hermes* opposite the ten-foot meteor hole; guided robots took samples of cosmic dust from inside the derelict. Tests for space virus were negative. (Since the *Ganymede* disaster of 2013, spacemen had been highly conscious of the dangers they might be bringing back to earth.) There was slight radioactivity, but not more than would be expected from dust exposed to periodic bursts of lethal radiation from solar flares. Flashlight photographs taken by the robot showed a vast chamber whose dimensions were difficult to assess. In his last bulletin before he retired to sleep, Carlsen said he thought the ship must have been built by giants. It was a phrase he would regret.

Everyone had difficulty in getting to sleep. Carlsen lay awake, wondering what the rest of his life would be like. He was forty-five, of Norwegian extraction, and married to a pretty blonde from Alesund. Understandably, she disliked these six-month-long expeditions of exploration. Now it looked as if he might return to earth permanently. He had the traditional right, as captain of the expedition, to produce the first book and magazine articles about it. This alone could make him a rich man. He would like to buy a farm in the Outer Hebrides, and spend at least two years exploring the volcanoes of Iceland...These pleasant anticipations, instead of making him drowsy, produced an unhealthy excitement. Finally, at three in the morning, he took a sleeping draught; even so, he spent the night dreaming of giants and haunted castles.

By ten A.M. they had eaten breakfast, and Carlsen had chosen the three men who would accompany him into the derelict. He was taking Craigie, Ives and Murchison, the second engineer. Murchison was a man of immense physique; somehow it gave Carlsen a sense of comfort to know he would be along.

Dabrowsky loaded the mini-camera with film for two hours' shooting. He filmed the men climbing into their spacesuits, then asked each of them to describe his feelings; he was already thinking in terms of television newsreels.

Steinberg, a tall young Jew from Brooklyn, looked ill and melancholy. Carlsen wondered if he was upset at not being included in the boarding party. He said: 'How you feeling, Dave?'

'Okay,' Steinberg said. When Carlsen raised his eyebrows, he said: 'I've got a creepy feeling. I don't like this. There's something creepy about that wreck.'

Carlsen's heart sank; he recalled that Steinberg had experienced a similar premonition just before the *Hermes* almost came to disaster on the asteroid Hidalgo; on that occasion, an apparently solid surface had collapsed, damaging the ship's landing gear and injuring Dixon, the geologist. Dixon had died two days later. Carlsen suppressed the misgiving.

'We all feel that way. Look at the damn thing. Frankenstein's castle...'

Dabrowsky said: 'Olof, you want to say a few words?'

Carlsen shrugged. He disliked the public relations aspect of exploration, but he knew it was part of the job. He sat on the stool in front of the camera. His mind immediately filled with commonplaces; he knew they were cliches, but could think of nothing else. To encourage him, Dabrowsky said: 'How's it feel to...er—'

'Well...ah...we don't know what we're going to find in there. We don't know a damn thing about it. Apparently...Professor Skeat at Mount Palomar points out that—that it's strange no one ever saw this thing before. After all, it's pretty big, fifty miles long. Astronomers have detected asteroid fragments two miles long by photo-comparators. The explanation may be its colour. It's an exceptionally dull sort of grey that doesn't seem to reflect much light. So...er...' He lost the thread.

Dabrowsky prompted: 'Do you feel excited?'

'Well, yes, of course I feel excited.' It was untrue; he was always calm and matter-of-fact when faced with action. 'This could be our first real contact with life in other galaxies. On the other hand, this craft could be old, very old, and it's—'

'How old?'

'How the hell do I know? But to judge by the condition of the hull, it could be anything from ten thousand to...I dunno, ten million.'

'Ten *million?*'

Carlsen said irritably: 'For Christ's sake, turn that thing off. This isn't a fucking film studio.'

'Sorry, Skip.'

Carlsen patted his shoulder. 'It's not your fault, Joe. It's just that I hate all this...posing.' He turned to the others. 'Come on. Let's move.'

He was the first into the airlock; for the sake of safety they would go one by one. The powerful magnets in the soles of his shoes produced an illusion of gravity. When he looked down at the chasm below he felt dizzy. He pushed himself very gently out of the hatch, then slammed it behind him. In the vacuum, it made no sound. With a push of his hand, he propelled himself across the five-foot gap and in through the jagged hole. The camera was slung across his shoulder. The searchlight he carried was no bigger than a large torch, but its atom-powered batteries could send a beam for several miles.

The floor was about fifteen feet below him. It was made of metal; but when he landed on it, he bounced six feet into the air. Clearly, it was nonmagnetic. He floated down gently, head-first, and landed as lightly as a balloon. He sat on the floor and shone the torch towards the opening, as a signal that all was well. Then he looked around.

For a moment he had an illusion that he was in London or New York. Then he saw that the vast, towering structures that had reminded him of skyscrapers were in fact giant columns that stretched from floor to ceiling. The scale was breathtaking. The nearest column, a hundred yards away, could have been the size of the Empire State Building; he guessed its height at well over a thousand feet. It was circular in shape, and fluted; the top, he could see, spread out like the branches of a tree. He shone the beam along the hall. It was like looking down the aisles of a giant cathedral, or into some enchanted forest. The floor and the columns were the colour of frosted silver, with a hint of green. The wall beside him stretched up without any visible curve for a quarter of a mile. It was covered with strange coloured shapes and patterns. He backed up gently towards the nearest column—in spite of his lightness, violent collisions could damage the spacesuit—then propelled himself into the air. He widened the beam of light so that it covered an area of twenty or thirty yards. His mind had become numb to astonishment, or he might have called out.

Craigie's voice said: 'Everything all right, Skip?'

'Yes. This is a fantastic place. Like a huge cathedral, with great columns. And the wall's covered with pictures.'

'What kind of pictures?'

Yes, what kind of pictures? How could he describe them? They were not abstract; they were *of* something; that was clear. But what? He was reminded of lying in a wood as a child, surrounded by bluebells, and the long whitish-green stems of the bluebells vanishing into the brown earth. These pictures could have been of some kind of tropical forest with strange vegetation, or perhaps of an underwater forest of weeds and tendrils. The colours were blues, greens, white and silver. There was a haunting complexity about it. Carlsen had no doubt he was looking at great art.

Other torches stabbed the darkness. The other three floated down gently, propelling themselves as if swimming under water. Murchison floated up to him, and drove him fifty feet further along with his weight.

'What do you make of it, Skip? Do you think they *were* giants?'

He shook his head, then remembered that Murchison could not see his face. 'I don't even want to guess, at this stage.' He spoke to the others. 'Let's keep together. I want to investigate the far end.' With the camera running, he moved gently down the hall. To the right, between the columns, he could see something that looked like a huge staircase. He kept up a running commentary for the benefit of those back in the *Hermes,* at the same time aware that his words conveyed nothing of this mind-staggering scale of construction.

A quarter of a mile further on, they passed an immense corridor leading off towards the centre of the ship; its roof was vaulted like a mediaeval arch. Everything about these surroundings was at once alien and curiously familiar. He heard himself telling Craigie: 'If earthmen had built this, they'd have made it all look mechanical—square columns with rivets. Whatever creatures built this had a sense of beauty.' Far in the air, on the left-hand wall, there was a circular grid that reminded him of a stained-glass window. He floated towards it. At close quarters, he could see that it was functional. It was a hundred feet high and five feet thick, and the holes in the grid were several yards wide. Carlsen alighted in one of these and shone the searchlight beyond. The camera, strapped to his chest now, was working automatically, recording everything he saw.

He said: 'Christ.'

'What is it?'

The space beyond had the appearance of a dream landscape. Monstrous flights of stairs stretched up into the darkness and down into the depths of the ship. There were catwalks between, and curved galleries whose architecture made him think of swallows' wings. Beyond these, stretching upwards and farther into the blackness, more stairs and galleries and catwalks. When Craigie's voice said: 'Are you all right?' he realised he had not spoken for several minutes. He felt dazed and over-powered, and in some way deeply disturbed. The place had the quality of a nightmare.

'I'm all right, but I can't describe it. You'll have to see it for yourself.' He launched himself outward, but the immensity made him feel weary.

Ives said: 'But what purpose could it serve?'

'I don't know that it serves a purpose.'

'What?'

'I mean a practical purpose. Perhaps it's like a painting or a symphony—intended to produce an effect on the emotions. Or perhaps it's a map of some kind.'

'A what?' Dabrowsky sounded incredulous.

'A map… of the inside of the mind. You'd have to see it to understand.'

'Any sign of the control room? Or of engines?'

'No, but they might be at the back, towards the jets —if that's how it's driven.'

Now he was hovering over one of the stairways. From a distance, it looked like a fire escape, but at closer quarters, he saw that the metal was at least a yard thick. It was the same dull silver as the floor. Each step was about four feet high and deep. There were no handrails. He followed them upwards, to a gallery supported by pillars. A catwalk, also without rails, ran across a gulf at least half a mile wide.

Craigie said: 'Can you see a light?' He pointed.

Carlsen said: 'Switch off your lights.' They were in blackness that enclosed them like a grave. Then, as his eyes adjusted, Carlsen knew Craigie was right. Somewhere towards the centre of the ship, there was a greenish glow. He checked his Geiger counter. It showed a slightly higher reading than usual, but well below the danger level. He told Dabrowsky: 'There seems to be some kind of faint luminosity. I'm going to investigate.'

It was a temptation to thrust powerfully against the stairs and propel himself forward at speed across the gulf. But ten years in space had made caution second nature. Using the catwalk as a guide, he floated slowly towards the glow. He kept one eye on the Geiger counter. Its activity increased noticeably as they drew closer, but it was still below the danger level, and he knew his insulated suit would protect him.

It was farther than it seemed. The four men floated past galleries that looked as if they had been designed by a mad Renaissance architect, and flights of stairs that looked as if they might stretch back to earth or outward to the stars. There were more immense columns, but this time they broke off in space, as if some roof they had once supported had now collapsed. When Carlsen brushed against one of these, he noticed that it seemed to be covered with a fine white powder, not unlike sulphur dust or lycopodium. He scraped some of this into a sample bag.

Half an hour later, the glow was brighter. Looking at his watch, he was surprised to see it was nearly one o'clock; it made him realise that he was hungry. They had switched off their searchlights, and the green glow was bright enough to see by. The light came from below them.

Dabrowsky's voice said: 'That was moonbase, Olof. He said your wife had just been on television with the children.'

At any other time, the news would have delighted him. Now it seemed strangely remote, as if it referred to a previous existence. Dabrowsky said: 'Zelensky says there are four billion people all sitting in front of the televisions, waiting for news. Can I send an interim report?'

'Wait ten minutes. We're getting close to this light. I'd like to find out what it is.'

Now at least he could see that it was pouring up from a chasm in the floor. The greeny-blue quality reminded him of moonlight on fields. He experienced a surge of exultancy that made him kick himself powerfully downwards. Ives said: 'Hey, Skip, not too fast; He felt like a swallow skimming and gliding towards the earth. The edge of the gulf lay a quarter of a mile below him, and he could see the full extent of the immense rectangular hole that was like a cloud-filled valley among mountains. The Geiger counter had now passed the danger point, but the insulation of the suit would protect him for some time yet.

The hole into which they were plunging was about a mile long and a quarter of a mile wide. The walls were covered with the same designs as the outer chamber. The light seemed to be coming from the floor and from an immense column in the centre of the space. He heard Murchison say: 'What in hell's that? A monument?' Then Craigie said: 'It's made of glass.' Carlsen stretched out his hands to cushion his impact against the floor, rolled over like a parachutist, then bounced for a hundred yards. When he succeeded in standing upright, he found himself at the base of a pedestal that supported the transparent column.

Like most things on this ship, it was bigger than it looked from a distance. Carlsen judged its diameter to be at least fifty yards. Inside, immense dim shapes were suspended. In the phosphorescent light, they looked like black octopuses. Carlsen propelled himself upwards until he was opposite one of them, and then shone his search-light on it. In the dazzling beam, he could see that it was not black, but orange. At close quarters, it looked less like an octopus, more like a bundle of fungoid creepers joined together at one end.

Close beside him, Ives said: 'What do you make of that?'

Carlsen knew what he was thinking. 'I don't think these things built this ship.'

Murchison pressed the glass of his space helmet against the column. 'What do you suppose they are? Vegetable? Or some kind of squid?'

'Perhaps neither. They may be some completely alien life form.'

Murchison said: 'My God!'

The fear in his voice made Carlsen's heart pound. When he spoke, his own voice was choked. 'What in God's name is it?

Something was moving behind the squidlike shapes. Craigie's voice said: 'It's me.'

'What the hell are you playing at?' The shock had made Carlsen angry.

'I'm inside this tube. It's hollow. And I can see something down below.'

Cautiously, Carlsen propelled himself upwards, braking himself by pressing his gloved hands against the glass of the column.' He was sweating heavily, although the temperature of the space-suit was controlled. He floated past the top of the column, made a twist in the air and managed to land. He could then see that, as Craigie had said, it was hollow. The walls containing the squidlike creatures were no more than ten feet thick. And when he looked into the space down the centre, he noticed that the blue glow was far stronger there. It was streaming up from below the floor.

'Donald? Where are you?'

Craigie's voice said: 'I'm down below. I think this must be the living quarters.'

Carlsen reached out to grab Murchison, who had propelled himself too fast and was about to float past him. Without speaking, both launched themselves headfirst into the hollow core. Since space-walking had become second nature, they had lost their normal inhibitions about this position. They descended gently towards the blue-green light. A moment later they were floating through the hole into a sea of blue that reminded Carlsen of a grotto he had once seen on Capri. Looking up, he realised that the ceiling—the floor of the room they had just left—was semi-transparent, a kind of crystal. The glow they had seen from above was the light that filtered through this. Down the wall to the right, another great staircase descended. But the scale here was less vast than above. This was altogether closer to the scale on the *Hermes*. The light came from the walls and the floor. There were buildings in the centre of the room, square and also semi-transparent. And at the far end of the room, perhaps a quarter of a mile away, Carlsen could see stars burning in the blackness. Part of the wall had been ripped away. He could see the immense plates twisted inwards and torn, as if someone had attacked a cardboard box with a hammer. He pointed. 'That's probably what stopped the ship.'

The fascination of violent disaster drove them towards the gap. Dabrowsky was asking for further details. Carlsen stopped at the edge of the gulf, looking down at the floor, which was buckled and torn under his feet. 'Something big tore a hole in the ship—a hole more than a hundred feet wide. It must have been hot: the metal looks fused as well as ripped. All the air must have escaped within minutes, unless they could seal off this part of the ship. Any living things must have died instantaneously.'

Dabrowsky asked: 'What about these buildings?'

'We'll investigate them now.'

Ives's voice said: 'Hey, Captain!' It was almost a shriek. Carlsen saw that he was standing near the buildings, his searchlight beam stabbing through transparent walls and emerging on the other side. 'Captain, there's people in there.'

He had to check the desire to hurl himself across the quarter of a mile that divided him from the buildings. His impetus would have carried him beyond them, and perhaps knocked him unconscious against the far wall. As he moved slowly, he asked: 'What kind of people? Are they alive?'

'No, they're dead. But they're human, all right. At least, humanoid.'

He checked himself against the end building. The walls were glass, as clear as the observation port of the *Hermes*. These were undoubtedly living quarters. Inside were objects that he could identify as tables and chairs, alien in design but recognisably furniture. And two feet away, on the other side of the glass, lay a man. The head was bald, the cheeks sunken and yellow. The blue eyes stared glassily at the ceiling. He was held down to the bed by a canvas sheet, whose coarse texture was clearly visible. Under this sheet, which was stretched tight, they could see the outlines of bands or hoops, clearly designed to hold the body in place.

Murchison said: 'Captain, this one's a woman.'

He was looking through the wall of the next building. Craigie, Ives and Carlsen joined him. The figure strapped to the bed was indisputably female. That would have been apparent even without the evidence of the breasts that swelled under the covering. The lips were still red, and there was something indefinably feminine about the modelling of the face. None of them had seen a woman for almost a year; all experienced waves of nostalgia, and a touch of a cruder physical reaction.

'Blonde too,' Murchison said. The short-cropped hair that covered the head was pale, almost white.

Craigie said: 'And here's another.' It was a dark-haired girl, younger than the first. She might have been pretty, but the face was corpselike and sunken.

Each building stood separate; it struck Carlsen that they were like a group of Egyptian tombs. They counted thirty in all. In each lay a sleeper: eight older men, six older women, six younger males and ten women whose ages may have ranged between eighteen and twenty-five.

'But how did they get *into* the damn things?'

Murchison was right; there were no doors. They walked around the buildings, examining every inch of the glass surface. It was unbroken. The roofs, made of semi-transparent crystal, also seemed to be joined or welded to the glass.

'They're not tombs,' Carlsen said. 'Otherwise they wouldn't need furniture.'

'The ancient Egyptians buried furniture with their dead.' Ives had a passion for archaeology.

For some reason, Carlsen felt a flash of irritation. 'But they expected to take their goods to the underworld. These people don't look *that* stupid.' Craigie said: 'All the same, they *could* hope to rise from the dead.'

Carlsen said angrily: 'Don't talk bloody nonsense.' Then, as he caught Craigie's startled glance through the glass of the helmet: 'I'm sorry. I think I must be hungry.'

Back in the *Hermes,* Steinberg had cooked the meal intended for Christmas Day. It was now mid-October; they were scheduled to leave for earth in the second week of November, arriving in mid-January. (At top speed, the *Hermes* covered four million miles a day.) No one had any doubt that they would be leaving sooner than that. This find was more important than a dozen unknown asteroids.

The atmosphere was now relaxed and festive. They drank champagne with the goose, and brandy with the Christmas pudding. Ives, Murchison and Craigie talked almost without pause; the others were happy to listen. Carlsen was oddly tired. He felt as if he had been awake for two days. Everything was slightly unreal. He wondered if it could be the effect of radioactivity, then dismissed the idea. In that case, the others would feel it too. Their spacesuits were now in the decontaminator unit, and the meter showed that absorption had been minimal.

Farmer said: 'Olof, you're not saying much.'

'Tired, that's all.'

Dabrowsky asked him: 'What's your theory about all this? Why did they build that thing?'

They all waited for Carlsen to speak, but he shook his head.

'Then let me tell you mine.' Farmer said. He was smoking a pipe and used the stem to gesture. 'From what you say, all those stairways couldn't serve any practical purpose. Right? So, as Olof said this morning, it's probably an impractical purpose—an aesthetic or religious purpose.'

'All right,' Steinberg said, 'so it's a kind of floating cathedral. It still doesn't make sense.'

'Let me go on. We know these creatures aren't from within the solar system. So they're from another system, perhaps another galaxy.'

'Impossible, unless they've been travelling for a hundred million years or so.'

'All right.' Farmer was unperturbed. 'But they could have come from another star system. If they could reach half the speed of light, Alpha Centauri's only nine years away.' He waved aside interruption. 'We *know* they must have come from another star system. So the only question is which one. And *if* they've travelled that far, then the size of the ship becomes logical. It's the equivalent of an ocean liner. Our ship's no more than a rowboat by comparison. Now...' He turned to Ives. 'If people migrate, what's the first thing they take with them?'

'Their gods.'

'Quite. The Israelites travelled with the Ark of the Covenant. These people brought a temple.'

Steinberg said: 'And it still doesn't make sense. If we all migrated to Mars, we wouldn't try to take Canterbury Cathedral. We'd build another on Mars.'

'You forget that the cathedral's also a home. Suppose they land on Mars? It's an inhospitable place. It might take them years to establish a city under a glass dome. But they've brought their dome with them.'

The others were impressed. Dabrowsky asked: 'But why the stairways and catwalks?'

'Because they're the basic necessities of a new city. Their size is limited. As the population increases, they have to expand upwards. It's the only direction. So they've built the skeleton of a multilevel city.'

Ives said with excitement: 'I'll tell you another thing. They wouldn't be alone. They'd send two or three ships. And they wouldn't land on Mars, because it doesn't support life. They'd land on earth,'

They all stared at him. Even Carlsen suddenly felt more awake. Craigie said slowly: 'Of course...'

They sat in silence. Murchison whistled.

Steinberg voiced their thought. 'So those creatures could be our ancestors?'

'Not our ancestors,' Craigie said. '*They* were the ones who reached earth. But the brothers and sisters of our ancestors.'

They all began to speak at once. Farmer's slow Northumberland voice emerged after a few seconds. 'So we've explained the basic problem of human evolution— why man is so unlike the apes. We didn't evolve from apes. We evolved from *them.*'

Carlsen asked: 'And what about Neanderthal man and all the rest?'

'A different line entirely.'

He was interrupted by the radio buzzer. Craigie switched it on. They all listened intently. Zelensky's voice said: 'Gentlemen, I have a surprise for you. The Prime Minister of the United European States, George Magill.'

They looked at one another in pleased surprise. If the world could be said to have one statesman who emerged head and shoulders above the others, it was Magill, the architect of World Unity.

The familiar deep voice came into the room. 'Gentlemen, I daresay you have realised this already, but you are now the most famous human beings in the solar system. I'm relaying this message immediately after seeing your film of the inside of the ship. Even with some truly infuriating interferences, it is the most remarkable film I have ever seen. You are to be congratulated on your extraordinary adventure. You will have...' At this point, his voice was drowned with static. When it again sounded clearly, he was saying: '...agrees with me that the first and most important task is to bring back to earth at least one of these beings, and if possible, more than one. Of course, we shall have to rely upon your judgement as to whether this is feasible. We realise that when you break into the tombs, they may crumble to dust like so many mummies. On the other hand, it should be possible for you to ascertain whether these tombs contain an atmosphere, or whether they are vacuums. *If* they are vacuums, then you should have no problem...'

Carlsen groaned. *'Why* does the idiot want to rush things?' He subsided as he saw the others straining their ears to catch the rest of Magill's message. He sat there gloomily for the next five minutes while Magill boomed on, spelling out the scientific and political implications of their discovery.

Then Zelensky came on again. 'Well, boys, you heard what the man said. I agree with him. If it's possible, we want one or two of these creatures brought back to earth. Cut your way into one of the tombs. Bear in mind they may not be dead, but only in a state of suspended animation. If you get them into the ship, seal them in the freezing compartment, and leave it sealed until you get back to moonbase. Leave them untouched.'

Carlsen stood up and left the room. He went to his own quarters and used the lavatory, then lay down on the bed. Almost instantly, he was asleep.

He woke up to find Steinberg standing over him. He sat up. 'How long have I been asleep?'

'Seven hours. You looked so tired we decided not to wake you.'

'What's happening?'

'Four of us have just got back. We've opened one of the tombs.'

'Oh, Christ, why? Why couldn't you wait until I woke up?'

'Zelensky's orders.'

'I give the orders while I'm captain.'

Steinberg was apologetic. 'We thought you'd be pleased. We've cut a doorway in the tomb, and it's a vacuum. The body didn't crumble to dust. There shouldn't be any problem getting him into the freezer.'

Five minutes later, rubbing the sleep from his eyes, he went down to the control room. Through the port, he could see the familiar blue-green glow. The ship had been manoeuvred opposite the chamber of the humanoids: he could see the tombs clearly.

Dabrowsky said: 'Did Dave tell you it *wasn't* made of glass?'

'No? What was it?'

'Metal. A transparent metal. We've put the segment in the decontamination chamber, but it doesn't seem to be radioactive. And there's no radioactivity in the tomb. It's a shield against radioactivity.'

'How did you get in?'

'The heat laser sliced straight through it.'

Carlsen said irritably: 'Next time, you wait for my orders.' He brushed aside an interruption. 'I meant to contact moonbase and suggest we leave the tombs untouched for a later expedition. Suppose that thing *was* in a state of suspended animation? And suppose you've now killed it?'

'There's twenty-nine more,' Murchison said.

'That's not the point. You've thrown away a life, just because the damn fools back on earth don't know the meaning of the word patience. It'd take a few months to get a fully equipped expedition here. They could tow this thing into earth orbit, and spend the next ten years learning all about it. Instead—'

Dabrowsky interrupted firmly: 'Excuse my saying so, Skip, but this is your fault. *You* got them into this state by talking about giants.'

'Giants?' Carlsen had forgotten what he said.

'You said it looked as if it had been built by giants. That's the story that went out on the television news last night: explorers discover spaceship built by giants.'

Carlsen said: 'Oh, shit.'

'You can imagine the result. Everyone's been waiting to hear about the giants. A spaceship fifty miles long built by creatures a mile high…They're all dying for the next instalment.'

Carlsen stared gloomily through the port. He picked up a mug of coffee from the table and absentmindedly took a sip. 'I suppose I'd better go and look . . .'

Ten minutes later he was standing beside the bed, looking down at the naked man. He had removed the canvas blanket by cutting it. Now he could see that the man was held by metal bands. The flesh looked shrunken and cold; when he touched it, it moved under his gloved fingers like jelly. The glassy stare made him uncomfortable. He tried to close an eyelid, but it sprang open again.

That's strange.'

Craigie, back in the ship said: 'What?'

The skin's still elastic.' He looked down at the thin legs, the sinewy feet. Blue veins showed through the marble-coloured flesh. 'Any idea how we get these bands off?'

'Burn them with the laser,' said Murchison, who was standing behind him.

'Okay. Try it.'

The wine-red beam stabbed from the end of the portable laser, but before Murchison could raise it, the metal bands retracted, sliding into holes in the bed.

'What did you do?'

'Nothing. I wasn't even touching it.'

Carlsen placed his hand under the feet and raised them. They floated into the air. The body remained at an angle, the head now floating clear of the canvas roll that served as a pillow.

Carlsen turned to Steinberg and Ives, who were waiting outside. 'Come and get him.'

The body was placed in a grey metal shell. It was cigar-shaped and had two handles in the middle, giving it the appearance of an overlong carpetbag. In the ship's inventory, this was known as a 'specimen collector'; but all knew they were intended to serve as coffins in the event of a death in space. Dixon's body now lay in a similar shell.

When Steinberg and Ives had left with the body, Carlsen examined every inch of the surface of the bed. It was in fact little more than a metal slab, and when he removed the canvas underlay, there was no sign of buttons or levers. He crawled underneath, but the underside was also smooth and unbroken.

Murchison said: 'Perhaps it responded to your thought.'

'We'll find out with the others.'

They spent half an hour examining and photographing the chamber; nothing of importance was revealed. Everything appeared to be purely functional.

He watched with interest as the laser cut through the wall of the next room. The spectroanalyser showed it to be of some unknown alloy; at least, the molecular patterns were typically metallic. In every other way, it resembled glass. It was about three inches thick. He had wondered why Murchison had carved a comparatively small entrance in the other chamber; now he saw why. The metal resisted a beam that could normally slice Corsham steel like soft cheese. It took twenty minutes to cut out a segment four feet high by two feet wide.

This was the room containing the dark-haired girl. After testing for space virus and radioactivity, Carlsen stepped over the threshold. He crossed to the bed, unsheathed the scoring knife, and sliced through the canvas where it vanished into the metal. He threw back the sheet. She lay as if on a mortuary slab, the feet together. The breasts, unflattened by gravity, stood out as if they had been supported by a brassiere.

'Incredible,' Murchison said. 'She looks alive.'

It was true; the flesh of the body had none of the flabbiness associated with death.

'Could be blood pressure. If she was placed in here immediately after death, there'd be enough pressure to make the body swell slightly in the vacuum.'

'Shall I start with the laser?' The eagerness in his voice made Carlsen smile. Without taking his eyes off the girl, he said: 'Okay. Go ahead.' As he spoke, the metal bands slid back, leaving marks on the naked flesh of the belly and thighs.

'It *must* be some form of thought control. Let's see if I can make them go back.' He stared at the bed, concentrating, but nothing happened. He turned and beckoned to Steinberg and Ives. 'Okay. Take her back to the freezer.'

Steinberg said: 'If there's no room in the freezer, she can share my bed till we get back to earth.'

Carlsen grinned. 'I don't think you'd find her very responsive.' He turned to Murchison. 'Let's get back,'

'Is that all we're taking?' Murchison sounded disappointed.

'Two's enough, don't you think?'

'There's plenty of room for more in the freezer.'

Carlsen laughed. 'All right. Just one more.'

He let Murchison lead the way. As he expected, Murchison went to the Chamber containing the blonde girl. He stood and watched while the laser turned the metal-glass into red-hot globules that splashed on the floor. When the last link had been cut through, the segment fell inward; Murchison stumbled forward and the laser bounced against the floor, searing a small crater.

'Hey, careful. Are you all right?'

'Sorry, Skip.' His voice sounded laboured. 'I'm suddenly damn tired.'

Carlsen peered through the glass of the space helmet; Murchison looked exhausted and pinched. 'You go on back to the *Hermes,* Bill. Tell Dave and Lloyd to get back here with another shell.'

He moved to the bedside. This time, instead of using the scoring knife, he tried an experiment. He stared hard at the canvas sheet and mentally ordered it to retract. For a moment nothing happened; then the metal bands under the sheet slid away. A moment later, the sheet itself slid across the body and into a gap that opened in the edge of the slab. He said: 'Of course.

What's of course?' Craigie had overheard him in the *Hermes.*

'I just made the bands retract by willing them to move. You realise what that means?'

'High-power technology.'

'I don't mean that. It means these creatures are probably still alive. The bands are made to respond to their thought-pressure when they wake up. I wonder if I can...' He stared at the table, mentally ordering the bands to go back, but nothing happened. He said: 'No. That makes sense. They wouldn't need to make the bands go back, once they'd awakened. But how the hell were they supposed to get out of here?'

'Out of the ship?'

'No. Out of this glass chamber.' As he said this, he stared at the end wall and mentally ordered a door to open. Instead, the whole wall slid smoothly aside. At that moment, he saw Ives and Steinberg floating along the hallway, carrying the coffin shell. He said: 'You don't have to squeeze in through the door. Come on through the wall.'

'How the hell'd you do that?'

'Like this.' As he stared at the wall, he knew it would move. As he concentrated, it clicked into place. 'This whole thing's designed to respond to telepathic orders. But only from inside.'

'How do you know?'

'Look.' He walked to the wall, willing it to open; it slid aside to let him past. Outside, he ordered it to close. Nothing happened. 'You see. It was designed only to be operated from the inside.'

The men were staring down at the body of the blonde. She was slimmer than the other girl, and a few years older; but the flesh was as firm and unwrinkled.

'Come on. Let's get back to the *Hermes.*'

As they removed their spacesuits in the airlock, he observed that Ives and Steinberg looked ill. Ives massaged his eyes with his hand. 'I think I need a sleep.'

'Me too,' Steinberg said.

'Both of you go and lie down. You deserve it. Leave the girl, though.'

Steinberg said: 'Believe me, I feel so bushed I wouldn't be any use to her even if she was alive.'

As he went into the control room, Craigie said: 'We've just had our orders from moonbase. We're to spend a day filming the ship from end to end, then proceed back to earth.'

In Hyde Park the daffodils were beginning to flower. Carlsen lay stretched out in a deck chair, his eyes closed, his skin soaking in the April sunlight. He had been back three months now, and he still found everything on earth almost painfully beautiful. The earth's gravity still exhausted him after a few hours of being awake, so that he usually felt a pleasant fatigue, like convalescence.

A voice said: 'Excuse me, but aren't you Captain Carlsen?'

He opened his eyes wearily. This was one of the penalties of notoriety; strangers accosted him in the street. A powerfully built young man standing against the sunlight, his hands in his pockets. Carlsen's stare was unwelcoming.

'Don't you remember me? I'm Seth Adams.'

The name meant something, but he could no longer recall what it was. He said noncommittally: 'Ah, yes.'

'You were a friend of my mother's—Violet Mapleson.'

'Of course.' Now it came back.

'Do you mind if I talk to you?'

He indicated the empty chair beside him. 'Please sit down.'

A girl's voice called: 'Seth. Are you coming or not?' A pretty girl in a white dress came across to them. She had a Pekingese on a lead. The young man glared at her irritably. 'Yes, in a moment. I—' He glanced with embarrassment at Carlsen. 'This is Captain Olof Carlsen, a very old friend of my mother's.'

Carlsen heaved himself to his feet and held out his hand. The girl's blue eyes were very wide. 'Oh, *you're* Captain Carlsen! How absolutely marvellous! Oh, I've so wanted to meet you... Queenie, do be quiet!' The dog had begun to yap furiously at Carlsen. Seth snorted, 'Oh, Christ,' and raised his eyes to heaven.

'That's all right,' Carlsen said soothingly. He knelt down and held out his hand.

The girl said: 'Do be careful. She'll bite.' But the dog stopped barking, sniffed his hand, then licked it. The girl said gushingly: 'Oh, she adores you. She *never* does that to strangers.'

Seth said firmly: 'Look, Charlotte, do you mind making your own way home? I've got something I want to say to Captain Carlsen.' He took her by the elbow. The dog began to yap at him. He snapped, 'Quiet, you little monster,' and the dog ran behind the girl's legs. Seth turned to Carlsen with a charming smile. 'Would you excuse us just a moment?' He drew the girl aside. Carlsen made a half-bow to her and sat down.

He sat there, watching them ironically. Yes, he was Violet's son, all right—totally ruthless when he wanted something. Twenty-five years ago Carlsen had been engaged to Violet Mapleson, the daughter of Commander Vic Mapleson, the first man on Mars. When he came back from his first three-month trip in space, she had married the television star Dana Adams. That had lasted only two years; then she'd left him for an Italian shipping magnate. Now, after her third divorce, she was a very rich woman.

Carlsen heard the girl say: 'How mean!' Obviously, she wanted to stay and talk to Carlsen; Seth was equally determined that she should go. He struck Carlsen as the sort of young man who was accustomed to getting what he wanted. A few moments later the girl walked off without looking back. Seth came and sat down, a faint smile on his lips.

'You must get pretty fed up with adoring females gaping at you?'

Carlsen suppressed his annoyance. 'Oh, I don't mind. She seemed rather sweet.'

Seth said magnanimously: 'Oh, yes. Nice girl. But look, I really had to talk to you. I was furious when mother told me you'd taken her to dinner and she hadn't introduced me.'

'Er...no. We just had a quiet little meal.' In fact, Violet had contacted him the moment he got back to earth, and asked him to dinner. He knew her well enough to know that it would be a big dinner party, and that he was to be the showpiece. He had quickly countered by explaining that he was exhausted—which was true—but had asked her to dinner at the Savoy. She had accepted with a fairly good grace, and they had spent a pleasant evening talking about old times. Ever since then, he had been inventing excuses to avoid going to dinner at her house.

Seth leaned forward. 'Look, I think I'd better put my cards on the table. I'm working for a newspaper.'

'Ah, I see.'

That probably surprises you. But the fact is that my father's broke, and mother's as mean as hell. All she thinks about is her rotten weekend parties. Now I'm getting paid a lousy hundred a week on the gossip column of the *Gazette.'*

Carlsen made sympathetic noises. Ten years ago he would have taken a violent dislike to this spoilt young man with his wavy black hair and sensual mouth. Now he listened detachedly and wondered how he could escape. He said: 'You want to interview me?'

'Well, that *would* be marvellous, of course . . ,' His tone indicated that he had something more in mind. He glanced quickly at Carlsen, assessing his sympathy. 'Would that be possible?'

Carlsen smiled. 'I dare say. But there *is* a problem. The S.R.I.'s called a press conference for ten o'clock tomorrow morning. I shall be there. I don't think your editor would care for two interviews.'

'I know. That's why I want to interview you first'

'You think your story would be given preference?'

'It might, if I had some more interesting stuff than the other man.'

'Of course. What had you in mind?'

'Well, look, what really *would* be a tremendous scoop' —he had adopted the tone of an admiring schoolboy speaking to a football hero— 'and I don't mind if you tell me to go to hell—but what would be *really* terrific is if I could get into the lab and get a look at those creatures.'

Carlsen chuckled. 'Well, you've got ambition.'

'I suppose.' Seth's face darkened; he took it as criticism. 'But Oscar Phipps of the *Tribune* has seen them.'

'He happens to be an old friend of the director.'

'I know. And let's face it, you're an old friend of my mother's.' Seth's smile said more than his words; Carlsen realised, with mild astonishment that the boy thought he and his mother were lovers. In fact, for all he knew, Seth thought Carlsen was his real father. Playing for time, he said: 'It's hardly gossip-column material.'

'Of course it's not. That's the whole point. Let's face it, a gossip columnist's a nobody. But if I could get an exclusive interview with you *and* see the space lab, I'd be writing features tomorrow.'

Carlsen looked out over the park, reflecting on how much he detested people who said, 'Let's face it.' On the other hand, he felt guilty about Violet; if he gave her son this opportunity, he'd feel he'd discharged his obligation. He said: 'So you want to do your features writer out of a job?'

'I don't want to. But if it happens that way...' Seth's eyes were bright; he sensed he had won.

Carlsen sighed. 'Okay.' He looked at his watch. 'Let's go.'

'What, now?' Seth was testing his luck as though it were thin ice.

'It'd better be now, if you want to get that article written.'

As they walked towards the cab rank at Marble Arch, Seth asked: 'Any chance of getting a photograph of you in the lab?'

'No, I'm sorry. That's strictly against regulations. No cameras in the S.R.I. Security and all that.'

'Yes, of course.'

By the time their cab had crawled in a traffic jam from Park Lane to Whitehall, it was almost five o'clock, and the sky was darkening. As Carlsen expected, most of the office staff had left. The old doorman saluted him.

'Is this young man with you, sir?'

'Yes. We're just going up to the club.'

The doorman should have asked to see Seth's S.R.I. card, but he had known Carlsen for twenty years. He let them past.

Carlsen used his electronic computer card to summon the lift. There were no stairs in the S.R.I. building, so no one could get past the ground floor without a pass. Seth asked: 'Are we going to the club?'

'I think so. I need a drink.'

'Could we see the lab first?'

'I don't see why not.'

As they walked down the corridor, Seth said: 'I can't tell you how grateful I am for all this.' Carlsen wished he could have believed him. He had the feeling that Seth regarded the satisfaction of his own desires as a law of nature.

At first sight, the laboratory was empty; then a young lab assistant came out of the specimen room. Carlsen recognised him as one of his admirers.

'Oh, hello, sir. Come to see the film?'

'What film?'

'From the *Vega.* It arrived this morning.'

The *Vega* was one of two big space cruisers that had set out for the derelict a month ago. They could achieve up to ten million miles a day.

'Good. What's the news?'

'There's another hole in the *Stranger,* sir.' The *Stranger* was a name the popular press had invented for the derelict.

'How big?'

'Pretty big. Thirty feet across.'

'Christ! That's unbelievable.' His immediate impulse was to rush upstairs and find out more; then he remembered Seth. He introduced the two young men. 'Seth Adams, Gerald...I've forgotten your other name.'

'Pike, sir.'

'When are you leaving, Gerald?'

'In about ten minutes, sir. Why? Can I help you?'

'No, it doesn't matter. I wanted someone to show Mr. Adams the lab while I go upstairs.'

Seth said: 'If you're in a hurry, perhaps I could just see the aliens?'

'Sure. Come on.' He led him into the specimen room. Against the wall at the far end, a row of mortuary cabinets had recently been installed. He said: 'Do you know where they are, Gerald?'

'Yes sir. I'll show you.'

He pulled out a drawer that opened like a filing cabinet. The man's body lay inside. His eyes still stared blankly upwards.

Carlsen said: 'Strange. He looks more alive than when I last saw him.'

Gerald said: 'Well, of course, he *is* alive.'

Seth asked quickly: 'Is that certain?'

'Quite,' Carlsen said. 'If he wasn't, he'd be rotten by now.'

'Can he be wakened?'

'If he can, we don't know the secret. His body's life field is still strong—that means he's alive. It drains away completely after death. He's in some kind of a trance, and we don't know how to bring him round.'

Gerald Pike opened the other two drawers. The naked bodies looked much as Carlsen remembered them, but the faces were no longer corpselike. They might have been asleep.

Seth was looking at them with fascination. When he spoke, his voice caught, and he had to start again. 'They're beautiful.' He bent over, stretching out his hand. 'May I. ..'

'Go ahead.'

He laid his hand lightly on the breast of the dark-haired girl, then ran it down over the stomach, brushing the pubis. He said: 'Incredible!'

Gerald said: 'Yes, they are rather pretty.' He had seen the bodies every day. 'I think the man has the most interesting face.'

Seth asked: 'Any idea of their age?'

'None at all.' It was Gerald who answered. 'They could be older than the human race.'

'And what methods do you use to try to bring them back to life?'

'Well, it's rather complicated. It's a matter of trying to build up the lambda field by nondirect integration.'

'Could you explain that in words of one syllable?'

Carlsen said: 'Listen, I'll leave you two together for five minutes, if I may.'

In his own office, he dialled the projection room. It appeared on the telescreen. Every seat was taken, and people were standing in the aisles. On the big screen at the end of the room he recognised the *Stranger,* its vast bulk scarcely illuminated by the sunlight. The camera was evidently pulling back for a final shot. A moment later, the screen went blank, and people began to stand up.

He rang the director's office; he knew Bukovsky would have seen the transmission earlier. Bukovsky's rasping voice said: 'Who is it?'

'Carlsen, sir.'

'Olof! I've been trying to get hold of you all afternoon.' The tone was reproachful.

'Sorry, sir. I fell asleep in Hyde Park.'

'Well, thank God you're here now. Listen, you know what's happened?'

'Not really, sir.'

'Then listen and I'll tell you. The *Vega* reached the *Stranger* at half past ten this morning. The first thing they discovered was an enormous hole in the roof. A meteor had gone through it like a cannonball What do you think of that, eh?'

'You astound me, sir. An incredible coincidence.'

'That's what I think. You didn't report any meteor showers, did you?'

'There weren't any, sir. Meteor showers are always associated with comets, and there wasn't a comet within forty million miles.'

'Yes, yes.' Bukovsky hated to be told anything. "Then how could it happen?"

'It must have been a sporadic meteor. But the chances against that are about a million to one.'

Bukovsky grunted. 'Just what I said. But of course, there'll be pressure to act quickly as soon as the news gets out. You realise that, don't you? Would you be able to appear on television tonight and explain that it's a million-to-one chance?'

'Of course, sir. If you think it necessary.'

Bukovsky's door opened, and half a dozen people came in; he recognised them as advisory staff. Bukovsky said: 'I think you'd better get up here right away. How soon can you be up?'

'In five minutes, sir.'

'Make it two.'

He hung up. Carlsen looked at his watch and said: 'Hell.' That meant leaving the interview with young Adams until later. He pressed the button that would connect him to the laboratory telescreen. The lab was empty. He reconnected with the specimen room. There was no telescreen in there, but there was an observation camera and a speaker system.

Seth Adams was alone. Carlsen was about to speak; then something made him pause. Adams was crossing the room furtively, like a cat stalking a bird. Carlsen switched back to the lab, looking for Pike, but he was nowhere to be seen. He switched through to the doorman.

'Have you seen Gerald Pike, the young man from electronics?'

'Yes, sir. He went out a few minutes ago.'

So Seth Adams had been alone for at least five minutes. He switched back to the specimen room. As he expected, Seth had opened one of the drawers. It was the one containing the man. He reached into his pocket, and took out a small object—a pen. He unscrewed the end, placed it close to his eye and pressed a button. It was a pen camera, of the type perfected in the twentieth century for spying. Carlsen should have remembered that no gossip columnist was ever without one.

He was disappointed. He did not like Seth Adams, but he had been willing to help him. In fact, he had even begun to feel a kind of sporting excitement at the prospect of his sensational scoop. Didn't the young idiot realise that it was stupid to do this kind of thing? Now he wouldn't get his damned interview, and if Bukovsky found out, he'd get kicked off the paper. He watched Adams close the drawer and open the next one. He was tempted to clear his throat and give him a fright. Or would it be simpler to pretend he didn't know what had happened and let him get away with the photographs? It would be easy enough to stop the newspaper from using them.

Adams photographed the blonde girl, closed the drawer, then moved on. He pulled open the remaining drawer and sighted down the pen. A moment later, the pen was back in his pocket, and he had straightened up; his sigh of relief was audible over the telescreen. He tiptoed to the door and peered out, to verify that the laboratory was still empty. He looked carefully around the room, but failed to notice the disguised camera lens that followed him. Then he went back to the drawer and stood looking down at the girl. She was on a level with his knees. He bent over and touched the breast, then ran his hand slowly down over the body. Then he reached up and stroked the face, caressing the lips with his fingertips and pulling the lower one down. The other hand was resting on the thigh. Carlsen could gauge his increasing excitement by the sound of his breathing, which was clearly audible. When Adams dropped on his knees beside the drawer, Carlsen felt it was time to interrupt. He crossed to the door, intending to slam it; the sound would carry over the loudspeaker. With the door open, he paused. He could see the shoulders bent over the drawer, but there was something unnatural about them; they were tensed, and the body was writhing. Fascinated and touched by sudden foreknowledge, he crept back to the telescreen. Seth's head was inside the drawer, his face against the girl's; but his body was jerking, as if in agony. Carlsen called out, and the body seemed to twist more violently. Then it became frozen again. It seemed to last for a long time. Then, very slowly, Seth Adams crumpled backwards, and fell. A hand appeared on the edge of the drawer. Unsteadily, as if waking from a deep sleep, the girl sat up. She looked around, ignoring the man's body, then swung her legs over the side of the drawer, as if getting out of bed.

The other telescreen buzzed; Bukovsky's voice said: 'Carlsen, are you still there?'

Carlsen ignored it, running for the door. The lift stood open. Seconds later, he was in the corridor below, running to the laboratory. There was no thought of danger in his mind. He was thinking of Violet Mapleson, and hoping that Seth was merely unconscious.

The lab was empty. He ran to the specimen room, expecting to see the girl at the door. To his surprise, she was not there; then he realised she was lying down again. Her eyes were closed. He looked at Seth's face and stepped back involuntarily. This was no longer the same man. Something had happened to the face. The lips had shrunk back, exposing the teeth, and they were cracked and grey. At first, it seemed that the face was covered with a grey cobweb; then he saw that it had also shrunk. The cobweb effect was produced by wrinkles. It had become an old man's face. As Carlsen watched, he realised that the black hair was turning grey. The hands that protruded from the sleeves had also become wrinkled, and their flesh was shiny, as if turned to grey celluloid.

He noticed the movement from the drawer. Her eyes were open, and she was looking at him. There was no doubt that she was alive. The whole body seemed to radiate a soft glow. She smiled gently, like a child waking from sleep. He stared at her, experiencing an amazement that seemed to expand in waves. It was something he had never expected to see, some distant memory of childhood that had left no trace on his consciousness. It had something to do with trees and running water, and a fairy or water spirit who was also his mother. Beside this woman, all women in the world were crude, half-masculine copies. He felt his face twitching with a desire to burst into tears. His eyes wandered over her naked body, without lust, only with amazement at her beauty.

She smiled and held out her arms, like a child asking to be picked up. He reached out to take her hands, then stumbled over the body. He looked down and saw the grey, shiny face and the white hair; the clothes now looked several sizes too big. With sudden total certainty, the same certainty he had known when he saw Seth's body stiffen on the television screen, he knew she had just sucked the life from a human being. He looked back at her, still feeling no horror. He said: 'Why did you have to do that?'

She said nothing, but he seemed to feel her reply in his head. It was not clear; she seemed to be excusing herself, saying that it was necessary. Her hands were still held out; he shook his head, backing away. The girl sat up and climbed gracefully out of the drawer. She moved quickly, with total control, like a ballet dancer. Then she came and stood in front of him, and smiled.

At close quarters, even a beautiful woman shows defects. This girl had none; she was as beautiful as when she was at a distance. She reached up and started to put her arms around his neck. Inside his head, she was saying: 'Make love to me. I know you love me. Use my body.' It was true; he loved her. He backed away, pushing aside her hands. The flesh was warm, slightly warmer than human flesh. He was not rejecting her; he wanted her with a greater intensity than he had wanted any woman, but he had always been a man of self-control; he attached importance to behaving like a gentleman. It would have been against all his instincts to make love to her where they were, in the specimen room.

He looked down again at the body, and it struck him that she had sucked out the man's life, sucked out the results of twenty years of growth and organisation, as gluttonously as a hungry child drinks an ice cream soda. He said: 'You murdered him."

She took his hand, and he felt a glow of delight at the contact. Suddenly, all inhibitions vanished. She was urging him to go with her, somewhere where they could make love, and he wanted to do it. Still looking at the body, he knew that it would probably mean his death, but this seemed unimportant. He understood something he could not put into words. But his masculine training still resisted.

She put her arms round his neck and pulled his mouth down to hers. He kissed her, feeling the warmth of her naked body against him, his hands pressed against her waist and her buttocks. Now he understood more consciously what he had known since she opened her eyes. She could not take his life unless he gave it. She was offering to surrender to him; while he still held back, she had no power to take him. But he was aware that it was only a matter of how soon his gentlemanly self-control would dissolve.

Bukovsky's voice said irritably: 'Carlsen, where the hell are you?' It came from the laboratory. He stiffened and stopped kissing her. She released him unconcernedly and looked through the door. He felt her say: 'I must go. How can I get out?'

His thoughts told her she needed clothes. She looked down at the body. He said: 'No. They are men's clothes.' She reached into his pocket, took out his wallet, and extracted his pass card. He made no effort to prevent her. Then she turned and walked out of the door. He followed her to the doorway. He could see Bukovsky on the lab telescreen talking to someone on the other side of his desk, saying: 'I know he's on that floor.' He looked up and saw Carlsen. There you are.' The girl went out. Suddenly, Carlsen grasped his danger. It hit him with delayed shock; the realisation that this girl had been about to drink his life—with his full consent. All his strength went out of his body. He felt his knees buckle. He grasped the door for support and sank to the floor, still fully conscious, but utterly, completely weary, drained as if he had exhausted himself with some tremendous physical effort.

Bukovsky was bending over him. He had no recollection of becoming unconscious, only of dozing pleasantly. 'What's happened, Carlsen?' He said sleepily: 'They're vampires. They suck life.' He was on the couch in Bukovsky's outer office. Harlow, in charge of Security, was sitting on a chair, bending over him. 'Who's the old man on the floor?'

He made an effort and sat up. He had the warm, woolly sensation he had experienced coming round from anaesthetic. 'He's not an old man. He's a boy of twenty.'

Harlow evidently thought him delirious. He said: 'Where's the woman gone?'

'She woke up. She came to life. I saw it through the telescreen in my office.'

He found he had some difficulty in speaking, as if his coordination had gone. Stumbling over words, feeling as if he had some large, uncomfortable object in his mouth, he began to tell his story.

Bukovsky snapped: 'You brought a reporter back here? You know that's against all the regulations.'

He said, wearily but stubbornly, 'No, it's not It's my decision. It's my press conference tomorrow. He was the son of an old friend. I just wanted to help him.'

'Well, you certainly helped him.'

Harlow was at the telescreen giving orders. He heard him say: 'If you see her, don't try to approach. Just shoot.'

The words brought a twist of pain. Then it struck him that she had his card; she could be anywhere in the building, or perhaps out of it.

Gradually, under the influence of black coffee, he was, beginning to feel better. To his astonishment, he was hungrier than he had been since he arrived back on earth. He said: 'Do you think I could have a sandwich? I'm ravenous.'

Bukovsky said: 'Okay. Go on. What happened after you rang me?'

'I watched her kill him—over the telescreen. Then I went down.'

'Was she still there?'

'Yes.'

'Why did you let her escape?'

'I couldn't stop her.'

The doctor came in. He made Carlsen take off his coat and shirt, then checked his pulse and blood pressure. He said: 'You seem to be perfectly normal to me. I think you're suffering from shock—nervous exhaustion.'

'Have you got a lambda meter?'

'Yes.' He looked surprised.

'Would you mind taking my lambda-field reading?'

The doctor connected up the galvanometer to his left wrist and placed the other electrode under his heart

'It's higher than it should be. Quite a lot higher.'

'Higher?' He sat up. 'Are you sure you've connected it the right way round?'

'Quite. It makes no difference anyway.'

Higher…It was true that he felt a strange, warm glow inside him, in spite of the fatigue. Yet he was certain she had taken some of his life. He also recalled how exhausted he had felt on the day they explored the derelict. And Steinberg and Ives had slept for twelve hours. These creatures had been sucking their life energy: of that he was certain. Yet his lambda reading was higher. In some way, she had given him energy, as well as taking it away.

The sandwiches came. When he washed them down with beer, he felt better.

Harlow came on the telescreen. 'She's definitely not on this floor—probably not in the building. We've searched everywhere.'

That's impossible. She couldn't get off this floor without a pass card.'

'She had my pass card,' Carlsen said.

'God, now he tells me!' Bukovsky turned back to Harlow. 'So she can get to other floors. But not out of the building. For Christ's sake, Robert, a naked girl can't get far.' He turned back to Carlsen. 'How in hell did she get your pass card?'

'She took it.'

'How did she know about it?'

'She read my mind.'

'Are you *certain* of that?'

'Absolutely.'

That complicates things. Do you think she can read the minds of the security guards?'

'Probably.'

Bukovsky went to the cabinet and poured himself a Scotch; Carlsen nodded when he held out the bottle. Bukovsky came back with the drink. Carlsen took a long pull and experienced relief as the smoky liquid burned his throat.

Bukovsky sat down. He said: 'Listen, Olof, I'm going to ask you a straight question, and I want a straight answer. Do you believe this girl is dangerous?'

He said: 'Of course. She killed a man.

"That's not what I mean. I want to know: Is she evil?'

He tried to answer, and the conflict built up inside him. His strongest impulse was to say no, but his reason told him he would be lying. Oddly enough, he felt no resentment about her, although he knew she wanted to drain his life force. Was she evil? Is a man-eating tiger evil?

As he stared at the floor, trying to find a reply, Bukovsky said: 'You know what I'm asking. That man intended to rape her. She destroyed him. Was it basically self-defence?'

He knew the answer. He said wearily: 'No. It wasn't self-defence. She needed his life. She took it.'

'*Deliberately?*' As Carlsen hesitated, he said: 'She was unconscious. I've seen her a dozen times. Her lambda field was .004. That's as low as a fish frozen in the ice. Is it not possible that she had no control over what happened?'

He took his time to answer. Finally he said: 'No. She had control. It was deliberate.'

'Okay.' Bukovsky stood up and went to the telescreen. He said: 'Give me George Ash…George, those two space creatures in the specimen room. I want them destroyed. Tonight. Now. Then get a message to the *Vega*. They're not to approach the *Stranger*. Stay at least a hundred miles from it.'

Ash headed the S.R.I. police; he was directly subordinate to Harlow. He said: I'll get them to the incinerator.'

Bukovsky came back. He said: 'Now all we have to do is to find that girl. I wish I knew she was still in the building. A general alert's going to cause panic' He plunged his face in his hands; he was obviously tired. 'Thank God there's only that one.'

'Inspector Caine is here, sir.' It was Bukovsky's secretary. Caine looked like a policeman: bulky, sad-faced, grey-haired.

Bukovsky introduced himself and Carlsen. Caine said: 'Ah, yes, I recognise you, sir. You found them in the first place, didn't you?'

Carlsen nodded. 'If that's what you can call it,'

Caine was about to go on, but Bukovsky interrupted him. 'What do you mean by that?'

Carlsen shrugged, smiling tiredly. 'Did we find them? Or did they find us? Had the *Stranger* really been there for a million years? Or was it planted so we'd find it?'

Caine obviously found this speculation futile. He said patiently: 'Excuse me, sir, but I'd like you to tell me in your own words just what happened this evening.'

Carlsen went through it again, and Caine recorded it. He listened without interruption until Carlsen described running into the specimen room and finding the body.

'You say she opened her eyes. Then what happened?'

'She sat up…and held out her arms…like this. Like a baby asking to be picked up.'

'And how did you respond?'

He shook his head. It would have sounded stupid to say, 'I fell in love with her.' Bukovsky was watching him closely. He said: 'I did nothing. I just stared.'

'You must have been pretty shaken. Then what?'

'Then she got up—very lightly. And she tried to put her arms round my neck.'

'She wanted to drain you too?'

'I suppose so.' It was incredible how difficult he was finding it to answer their questions; an immense inner resistance was building up like a wall.

The telescreen buzzed. Ash came on. He said: "These creatures, sir…They're dead already.'

'How can you be sure?'

'Come and look for yourself.'

Bukovsky went, out. They followed him without speaking.

There were three policemen in the specimen room; one of them was measuring it with a tape; another was taking photographs. Adams's body lay undisturbed. The police surgeon knelt beside it. The drawers containing the aliens were open. Carlsen saw immediately what Ash meant. There was no mistaking death. As he came closer, the faint odour of decay reached his nostrils.

When he looked at Seth Adams's body, he was shocked. Now it was like a mummy. The flesh had shrunk tight on the bones.

Caine said incredulously: 'Did you say the victim was about twenty?'

He nodded, experiencing a wave of depression. He asked Bukovsky: 'I don't suppose his mother's been contacted?'

'No. We don't know her address.'

'I suppose I'd better do it.' He asked Caine: 'Will you be needing me again tonight?'

'I don't think so. Are you in the telescreen book?'

'No. I've had to go ex-directory recently.' He gave Caine his number.

Bukovsky and the police doctor were looking down at the aliens. Bukovsky said: 'Well, that only leaves one.'

Carlsen started to speak, then changed his mind. He preferred not to let them know what he was thinking.

The buzzing of the telescreen brought him out of a deep, exhausted sleep. He heard Jelka say: 'Who is it?…I'm afraid he is asleep…' She was using the earphone. He asked thickly: 'Who is it?'

'The police.'

'Give it here.' He took the earphone. 'Hello.'

'Mr. Carlsen? Detective Sergeant Tully, sir. Chief Inspector Caine asked me to ring you. He'd like you to come immediately, if you can.'

'Is it urgent?'

'Yes, sir.'

'Where?'

'If you could be ready in five minutes, sir, we're sending a Grasshopper for you.'

As he dressed, Jelka said: 'Why do you have to go? Don't they know you're exhausted?'

'He said it's important.'

She switched on the light between their beds. Her cheek was marked where the pillow had pressed. He pulled on his trousers over the pyjamas, then a woollen sweater. He ruffled her hair playfully, touched by protectiveness. 'Go back to sleep. Lock the door, and don't open it to anyone.'

As he walked out into the road, he switched on his homing device. He could see the blue light of an aircraft overhead. Thirty seconds later, the Grasshopper swept down silently, hovered for a moment, then landed on the road. The door opened. The uniformed policeman helped him up the steps. Only one of the three seats was empty. The man who sat behind the pilot's cabin wore evening dress. He turned and said: 'I'm Hans Fallada. How d'you do.'

Carlsen took the hand he proffered over his shoulder. In spite of the German name, Fallada's accent was British upper class; the voice was throaty and rich.

He said: 'I'm delighted to meet you.'

Fallada said: 'And I too. It's a pity it had to be on business.'

Carlsen watched the Thames recede underneath them. In the east, the grey line of the dawn was already showing; below, the lights of the suburbs glowed yellow and orange.

Both started to speak at once. Then Fallada answered the question Carlsen had started to ask. 'I've just flown back from Paris. It was rather appropriate really. I was addressing the annual dinner of European criminologists when they sent for me. Now it looks as if the trip was wasted.'

'Why?'

'Haven't they told you? They think they've found her body.'

He was too tired to experience the full shock. He heard himself say: 'Are you sure?'

'No, they're not sure. That's why they want you to identify her.'

He sat back in his seat, and tried to assess his reactions. His feelings seemed numb. He was certain of only one thing: that some instinctive part of him refused to believe it.

Within five minutes, the lights of central London were below them. Fallada was saying: 'Amazing things, these Grasshoppers. I'm told they can do four hundred miles an hour, and land on a two-foot space in the middle of a traffic jam.' He recognised the green light on the S.R.I. building near Piccadilly. They planed down towards the black expanse of Hyde Park. The searchlight caught the still waters of the Serpentine.

The Grasshopper hovered, then landed without a bump. He let Fallada climb out first. Caine advanced to meet them; he saw Bukovsky and Ash behind him. Twenty yards away, they had erected canvas screens.

Caine said: 'Sorry to bother you, sir. But it won't take more than five minutes.'

'What makes you think it's her?'

Bukovsky said: 'It's her, all right. But they need you to identify her. You were the last to see her.'

They led him behind the screens. The body was covered with a blanket. He could see the legs were spread apart, the arms outflung.

Caine pulled back the blanket, shining the torch. For a moment, he was doubtful. The left eye was blackened; the lips were swollen and bruised. Then he saw the shape of the chin, the teeth, the high cheekbones. 'Yes, that's her.'

'You've no doubt?'

'None whatever.'

Fallada pulled back the rest of the blanket. She was naked except for a green nylon smock and an overcoat; both were open. The body was smeared with blood from the neckline to the knees. In the light of the torch, he could see teethmarks in the flesh. One nipple was missing. Rubber shoes lay within a few feet of the body. When Fallada touched the head, it rolled sideways.

Caine said: 'She found the clothes in a cleaner's cupboard.'

Fallada asked: 'How long has she been dead?'

'About nine hours, we think.'

'In other words, she was murdered about an hour after escaping from the Space Research building. What an incredible thing to happen. Do we know if there's a sex maniac on the loose in this area?'

'We've no record of one. The last murder of this type was in Maidstone a year ago.'

Carlsen straightened up from his knees. His trousers were wet. He asked Fallada: 'But why do you think he bit her?'

Fallada shrugged and shook his head. It's a familiar sexual perversion. It's known as vampirism.'

He woke up in darkness. The luminous dial of his watch showed two-thirty, A.M. or P.M.? He reached out and flicked down the switch of the soundproofing mechanism; immediately, he could hear the laughter of his children. That answered that question; it was afternoon. He pressed the switch that controlled the blinds; they slipped upwards, flooding the room with sunlight. He lay still for another five minutes, disciplined to move. Jelka came in with a tray.

'Here's some coffee. How are you feeling?' He yawned. 'I'll tell you when I wake up.' He struggled into a sitting position. 'I slept well.'

'You certainly did.'

Seeking the significance of her words, he looked again at his watch, and noticed the day: Thursday. He said: 'My God, how long have I been asleep?'

'I make it...nearly thirty-three hours.'

'Why didn't you wake me?'

'Because you looked worn out.'

The two children came in and climbed on the bed. They were both girls and both blonde. Jeanette, the four-year-old, got into bed and asked for a story. Jelka said, 'Daddy wants to drink his coffee.' She led them firmly out.

He stared out of the window, and wondered whether the grass was really greener or whether it was some trick of his eyes. He tasted the coffee and experienced a flood of sensual delight. For the first time since he returned to earth, he felt no residue of tiredness. Outside, the gardens and houses of the Twickenham Garden Suburb looked peaceful and beautiful in the sunlight. Now, as he rubbed the sleep out of his eyes, he knew there could be no doubt about it: he *was* feeling more alive. Everything seemed more vivid and exciting than he had known it since childhood.

Jelka came back as he was drinking his second cup. He asked, 'What's the news?'

'None.'

'None? Didn't they mention what had happened on the television news?'

'Only that the aliens had all died.'

'That's as well. No sense in causing a panic. Any messages for me?'

'Nothing very important. Who's Hans Fallada?'

'He's a criminologist. Don't you remember? He used to appear on the series about famous murder cases.'

'Ah, yes. Well, he rang you. He wants you to call him back. He says it's urgent.'

'What's his number?'

When he was dressed, he rang Fallada. A secretary answered. 'He's at Scotland Yard at the moment, sir. But he left a message to ask you to come here as soon as possible.'

'Where are you?'

'The top floor of the Ismeer Building. But we'll send a Grasshopper for you. When will you be ready to leave?'

'A quarter of an hour?'

He ate his scrambled eggs sitting in the garden, in the shade. Even there, the heat was uncomfortable. The sky was a clear, deep blue, like water. It made him want to strip off his clothes and plunge into it.

He was drinking iced orange juice when the Grasshopper arrived. There was a policewoman at the controls. As he waved goodbye to Jelka and the children, Jelka called: 'Don't go too near the edge.'

She was referring to the roof of the Ismeer Building. Occupying a square quarter-mile in the City of London, this was the highest building in the world. It had been built in the days of overcrowding, by a Middle East consortium. Their solution to the problem of lack of office space in London was to build a skyscraper a mile high, with five hundred floors. They had intended to build a similar skyscraper in every capital city of the world, but devolution planning had made the idea obsolete. The Ismeer Building remained unique: the greatest concentration of offices in the world. Now the Grasshopper was climbing steeply upwards through the smokeless air, and the sides of the building already loomed above them. Carlsen was suddenly reminded of the *Stranger,* and his heart contracted.

He asked the policewoman: 'Where are we going?'

The Psychosexual Institute, sir.' She seemed surprised that he didn't know.

'Is that run by the police?'

'No, it's independent. But there's a great deal of cooperation.'

As he stepped out onto the roof, he was surprised by the coolness. Above him, the sky looked as distant and blue as it had from the ground. He walked to the parapet; this was surmounted by a steel fence. From where he was standing, he could follow the curves of the Thames, down through Lambeth and Putney to Mortlake and Richmond. If Jelka used the astronomical telescope, she could probably see him standing there.

The policewoman said: 'I expect this is Mr. Fallada.'

Another Grasshopper was hovering above the roof; it dropped silently, landing as gently as a moth within six inches of the other vehicle. Fallada climbed out and waved to him.

'Good, it was kind of you to come so promptly. How are you feeling now?'

'Fine, thank you. Never better in my life.'

'Good. Because I need some help from you. I need it urgently. Come on down.'

He led the way down a flight of stairs. 'Excuse me one moment. I must speak to my assistant.' He pushed open a door labelled Lab C. They were met by a smell of chemicals and iodoform. Carlsen was startled to find himself looking at the naked body of a middle-aged man; it lay on a metal trolley near the door. A white-coated assistant was bent over a microscope. Fallada said: 'I'm back now. Sometime over the next half-hour, the Yard will be sending another body. I want you to drop everything to work on it. Call me as soon as it arrives.'

'Yes, sir.'

He closed the door. 'This way, Mr. Carlsen.'

He led the way into an office on the other side of the corridor; the card on the door read: 'H. Fallada, Director.' Carlsen said: 'Who was the man?'

'My assistant, Norman Grey.'

'No, I mean the dead man.'

'Oh, some idiot who hanged himself. He may be the Bexley rapist. We have to find out' He opened the drink cupboard. 'Is it too early to offer you a whisky?'

'No, I think I'd like one.'

'Please sit down.' Carlsen took the reclining chair near the immense bow window; it moulded itself to his body. From up here, the world looked sunlit and uncomplicated. He could see clear to the Thames estuary and Southend. It was difficult to believe in violence and evil.

On the metal bookcase a few yards away, Fallada's face stared at him from the jacket of a book called *A Primer of Sexual Criminology.* The thick lips and drooping eyelids gave it a curiously sinister appearance in photographs; in fact, there was something humorous, almost clownish, about Fallada's face. Behind the thick lenses, the eyes looked as if he was enjoying some secret joke.

'Your health.' The ice clinked as he drank.

Fallada sat on the edge of the desk. He said: 'I have just been examining a body.'

'Yes?'

'A dead girl. She was found on a railway line near Putney Bridge.' He reached into his pocket, and handed Carlsen a folded paper.

It was a typewritten sheet, headed *Deposition of Albert Smithers; address, 12 Foskett Place, Putney:* 'At about 3.30, I realised my wife had forgotten to pack my tea flask, so I asked the foreman's permission to return home for it. I took the shortcut along the line, a matter of about five hundred yards. About a quarter of an hour later, at ten minutes to four, I made my way back along the same stretch of line. As I approached the bridge I saw something on the tracks. It had definitely not been there twenty minutes earlier. Approaching closely, I saw that it appeared to be the body of a young woman lying face downward. Her head was across the inner line. I was about to run for help when I heard the approach of the goods train from Farnham. So I grabbed the body by the ankles and pulled it onto the side of the track. My reason for doing this was that I thought she might be alive, but on feeling her pulse I realised she was dead...'

He looked up. 'How was she killed?'

'Strangled.'

'I see.' He waited.

Fallada said: 'Her lambda count was only .004.'

'Yes, but...but surely that doesn't mean much? I thought that anyone who died by violence—'

'Oh, yes. It *could* be a coincidence.' He looked at his watch. 'We should know for certain in less than an hour.'

'How?'

'By means of a test that we have developed.'

'Is it a secret?'

'It *is* a secret. But not from you.'

Thank you.'

'In fact, that is why I asked you here today. This is something that you have to know about.' He opened the drawer of his desk and took out a small tin box. He opened the lid and placed it on the desk. 'Can you guess what they are?'

Carlsen bent down and peered at the tiny red globules, each the size of a pinhead.

'Electronic bugging devices?'

Fallada laughed. 'Right the first time. But not the kind you've ever come across.' He closed the tin and dropped it into his pocket. 'Would you like to come this way?'

He led the way through an inner door and switched on a light. They were in another small laboratory. The benches were lined with cages and glass fish tanks. The cages contained rabbits, hamsters and albino rats. In the tanks, Carlsen recognised goldfish, eels and octopuses.

Fallada said: 'What I am going to tell you now is known to no one outside this institute. I know I can rely on your discretion.' He stopped in front of a cage that contained two tame rabbits. 'One of these is a buck, the other a doe. The doe is now in heat.' He reached out and pressed a switch. A television screen above the cage was illuminated with a green glow. He pressed another button, and a wavy black line began to undulate across the screen; it might have been the path of a bouncing rubber ball.

'That is the lambda reading of the buck.' He pressed another button; a second, white line appeared, this one achieving higher peaks than the first. 'That is the doe's.'

I don't quite understand. What is it measuring?'

'The life field of the rabbits. Those small red objects were tiny lambda meters. They not only measure the intensity of the animal's life field; they also emit a radio signal, which is picked up and amplified on this screen. What do you notice about these two signals?'

Carlsen stared at the wavering lines. 'They seem to run more or less parallel.'

'Precisely. You notice an interesting kind of counterpoint—here, and here.' He pointed. 'You have heard the phrase. "Two hearts beating as one." This shows that it is more than a piece of literary sentimentality.'

Carlsen said: 'Let me make sure I understand you. You've planted these tiny red bugging devices inside the rabbits, and we're now watching their heartbeats?'

'No, no. Not their heartbeats. The pulse of the life force in them. You could say that these creatures are in perfect sympathy. They can sense one another's moods.'

'Telepathy?'

'Yes, a kind of telepathy. Now observe this doe.' He moved to the next cage, in which a solitary rabbit was listlessly gnawing a cabbage leaf. He switched on the monitor above the cage. The white line appeared, but this time it had fewer peaks, and its movement seemed sluggish.

'The doe is on her own, and she is probably bored. So her lambda reading is much lower.'

'In other words, their lambda reading is increased by the intensity of their sex drive?'

'Quite. And you ask if the meters are placed near the hearts. No. They are placed close to the sexual organs.'

'Interesting.'

Fallada smiled. 'It is more interesting than you realise. You see'—he switched off the monitor—'not only does the rabbit's life field intensify when it is in a state of sexual excitement. As you can see, their life fields *interact.* And I will tell you another interesting thing. At the moment, as you see, the buck's field is weaker than the doe's. That is because the doe is in heat But when the buck mounts the doe, its life field becomes stronger than the doe's. And now the doe's peaks move in obedience to the buck's, instead of vice versa.' Fallada laid a hand on his arm. 'Now I am going to show you something else.' He led the way to the far end of the room, to a bench that contained only glass tanks. He rapped on the side of one of these. A small octopus, whose total width was about eighteen inches, started up from the rocks at the bottom of the tank and glided gracefully towards the surface, turning gently with a movement that made it resemble drifting smoke. Fallada pointed. 'If you look carefully, you can see where we have planted the meter.' He switched on the monitor above the tank; the line that appeared had a slow, undulatory motion, without the sharp peaks that characterised the rabbits' graph.

Fallada moved to the next tank. 'This is a moray eei, one of the most unpleasant creatures in the sea. They regard the Mediterranean octopus as a rare delicacy.' Carlsen peered in at the devilish face that looked out from a gap between rocks; the mouth was open, showing rows of needle-sharp teeth. 'This one is hungry—he hasn't been fed for several days.' He switched on the monitor; the graph of the eel was also sluggish, but it had a surging forward motion that suggested reserves of power. Fallada said: 'I am going to introduce the moray into the octopus's tank.'

Carlsen grimaced. 'Is that necessary? Couldn't you just *tell* me what happens?'

Fallada chuckled. 'I could, but it wouldn't convey much.' He slid back a bolt on the metal lid that covered the octopus tank. 'Octopuses love freedom, and they're adepts in the art of escape. That's why they have to be kept in closed tanks.' From under the bench he took a pair of transparent plastic pincers; they resembled coal tongs, but the handles were longer. He dipped them cautiously into the eel's tank, reached down cautiously, then suddenly made a lunge. The water churned as the eel lashed violently, trying to bite the invisible jaws that gripped it. Carlsen said: 'I'm glad that's not my hand.'

With a swift movement, Fallada raised the moray clear of the water and dropped it into the octopus tank. It swam down like an arrow through the green water. Fallada gestured at the monitor. 'Now watch.'

Both graphs were visible: the octopus's, still sluggish but intensified by alarm; the moray's, surging now into peaks of anger. As Carlsen peered into the tank, Fallada said: 'Watch the graphs.'

For the next five minutes, nothing seemed to change. In the tank, the moray had blundered around for a moment, blinded by the mud and vegetable particles churned up by its movements. The octopus had vanished completely; Carlsen had seen it slide between the rocks. The moray swam in the far corner of the tank, apparently unaware of its presence.

'Do you see what is happening?'

Carlsen stared at the graphs. He now observed a certain similarity in their patterns. It would have been difficult to put into words, but there was a sense of counterpoint, as if the graphs were bars of music. The octopus's graph was no longer sluggish; it was moving with a jerky movement.

Slowly, as if taking a stroll, the moray idled its way across the tank. There could now be no doubt about it; the two graphs were beginning to resemble each other in a way that reminded Carlsen of the courting rabbits.

Suddenly the moray slashed sideways, driving into a crack in the rocks. A cloud of black ink darkened the water in the tank; the moray brushed the glass, its cold eyes staring out for a moment at Carlsen's face. There was a lump of the flesh of the octopus in its jaws.

He looked up again at the graphs. The moray's had surged upwards: it moved forward with a series of peaks, like a rough sea. But the octopus's graph had now changed completely. Once again, it had subsided into gentle undulations.'

Carlsen asked: 'Is it dying?'

'No. It has only lost the end of a tentacle.'

'Then what has happened?'

'I am not certain. But I think it has accepted the inevitability of death. It senses that nothing can save it. That graph is actually characteristic of pleasure.'

'You mean it's *enjoying* being eaten?'

'I don't know. I suspect the moray is exercising some kind of hypnotic power. Its will is dominating the will of the octopus, ordering it to cease to resist. But of course I could be wrong. My chief assistant thinks that it is an example of what he calls "the death trance." I once talked to a native who had been seized by a man-eating tiger. He said he experienced a strange sense of calm as he lay there waiting to be killed. Then someone shot the tiger, and he became aware that it had torn off most of his arm.'

The moray had returned to the attack. This time it gripped the octopus, trying to tear it away from the rock; the octopus was clinging with all its tentacles. The moray made a half turn, then dived in to attack. This time it went for the head. There was more ink. On the monitor screen, the octopus's graph suddenly leapt upwards, wavered and then vanished. The moray's graph showed an upward sweep of triumph.

Fallada said: 'That shows that the moray is very hungry. Otherwise, it would have eaten the octopus tentacle by tentacle, perhaps keeping it alive for days.' He turned away from the tank. 'But you have still not seen the most interesting part.'

'God, don't tell me there's more!'

Fallada pointed to a grey box between the tanks. 'This is an ordinary computer. It has been registering the fluctuations in the life fields of both creatures. Let's have a look at the eel's.' He touched several buttons in quick succession; a slip of paper emerged from a slot in the computer. Fallada said: 'You see, the average is 4.8573.' He handed Carlsen the paper. 'Now the octopus's.' He pulled out the slip of paper. 'This is only 2.956. It has little more than half the vitality of the eel.' He handed Carlsen a pen. 'Would you add those figures together?'

After a moment, Carlsen said: 'It's 7.8133.'

'Good. Now let us check the reading of the moray during the past few minutes.' He pressed more buttons, and handed Carlsen the paper without even looking at it Carlsen read the figure aloud: 'Seven point eight one three three. That's astonishing. You mean the moray's actually *absorbed* the life field of the…Christ…' He felt the hair on his scalp prickle as he understood. He stared down at Fallada, who was smiling happily.

Fallada said: 'Precisely. The moray is a vampire.'

Carlsen was so excited that he could hardly speak consecutively. 'That's incredible. But how long does it last? I mean, how long will its field be so high? And how can you be sure that it's really absorbed the life field of the octopus? I mean, perhaps the triumph of getting food sends its vitality shooting upwards.'

'That is what I thought at first—until I saw the figures. It always happens. For a short period, the life force of the aggressor increases by precisely the amount it has taken from the victim.' He looked into his glass, saw that it contained nothing but melting ice cubes, and said: 'I think we deserve another drink.' He led the way back into the office.

'And does it apply to all living creatures? Or only to predators like the moray? Are we all vampires?'

Fallada chuckled. 'It would take hours to tell you all the results of my researches. Look.' He unlocked a metal cabinet and took out a book. Carlsen saw it was a bound typescript. *The Anatomy and Pathology of Vampirism,* by Hans V. Fallada, F.R.S. 'You are looking at the result of five years of research. More whisky?'

Carlsen accepted it gratefully. He dropped into the chair, turning over the pages of the typescript. 'This is Nobel Prize stuff.'

Fallada shrugged. 'Of course. I knew that when I first stumbled on this phenomenon of vampirism six years ago. In fact, my dear Carlsen, there is no point in being modest about it. This is one of the most important discoveries in the history of biological science. It places me in the same category as Newton and Darwin. Your health.'

Carlsen raised his glass. 'To your discovery.'

'Thank you. So you see why I am so fascinated by *your* discovery—these space vampires? It follows logically from my theory that there must be certain creatures who can completely drain the lifeblood of fellow creatures —or rather, their vital forces. I am convinced that is the meaning of the old legends of the vampire—Dracula and so forth. And you must have noticed very often that certain people seem to drain your vitality—usually rather dreary, self-pitying people. They are also vampires.'

'But does this apply to *all* creatures? Are we all vampires?'

'Ah, there you have asked the most fascinating question of all. You observed the rabbits—how their life fields vibrated in sympathy? This is because there is a sexual attachment. When this happens, one life field can actually reinforce another. And yet my researches prove beyond all doubt that the sexual relation also contains a strong element of vampirism. This is something I first came to suspect when I studied the case of Joshua Pike, the Bradford sadist. You remember—some of the newspapers actually called him a vampire. Well, it was true, literally. He drank the blood and ate parts of the flesh of his victims. I examined him in prison, and he told me that these cannibal feasts had sent him into states of ecstasy for hours. I took his lambda readings while he was telling me these things—they increased by more than 50 percent.'

'And cannibals too.' Carlsen was so excited that he spilled whisky on the typescript; he mopped it with his sleeve. 'Cannibal tribes have always insisted that eating an enemy enabled them to absorb his qualities—his courage and so on . ..'

'Quite. Now, that is an example of what I call negative vampirism. Its aim is total destruction of the victim. But in the case of sex, there is also positive vampirism. When a man desires a woman, he reaches out towards her with psychic forces, trying to compel her submission. And you know yourself that women can exert that same kind of power over men!' He laughed. 'One of my lab assistants here is an ideal subject. She is literally a man-eater. It's not her fault. She's basically quite a sweet girl—tremendously generous and helpful. But a certain kind of man finds her irresistible. They hurl themselves at her like flies on flypaper.' He pointed to the typescript. 'Her lambda readings are in there. They reveal that she's a vampire. But this kind of sexual vampirism is not necessarily destructive. You remember all the old jokes about ideal marriages between sadists and masochists? They are basically accurate.'

The telescreen buzzed. It was the lab assistant they had seen earlier. 'The body's arrived, sir. Do you want me to go ahead with the tests?'

'No, no. I'll come across now.' He turned to Carlsen. 'Now you can see my methods in action.'

In the corridor, they stood aside to let past two ambulance men who were wheeling a stretcher. Both saluted Fallada. In Lab C, the assistant, Grey, was examining the face of the dead girl through a magnifying glass. A middle-aged, bald-headed man sat on a stool, his elbows on the bench behind him. When Fallada came in, he stood up. Fallada said: 'This is Detective Sergeant Dixon of the Crime Lab. Commander Carlsen. What are you doing here, Sergeant?'

'I've got a message from the Commissioner, sir. He says not to go to too much trouble. We're fairly certain who did it.' He gestured towards the body.

'How?'

'We managed to get fingerprints off the throat.'

Carlsen looked down at the girl. Her face was bruised and swollen. There were strangulation bruises on her throat. The sheet had been pulled far enough back to reveal that she was still clothed. She was wearing a blue nylon smock.

Fallada asked: 'Was he a known criminal?'

'No, sir. It was this chap Clapperton, sir.'

'The racing driver?'

Carlsen asked: 'You mean Don Clapperton?'

'That's right, sir.'

Fallada turned to Carlsen. 'He disappeared in central London on Tuesday evening.' He asked Dixon: 'Have you found him?'

'Not yet, sir. But it shouldn't be long.'

The lab assistant asked: 'Do you still want to go ahead, sir?'

'Oh, I think so. Just for the sake of a routine check.' He asked Dixon: 'Now, let me see, Clapperton was last seen at what time?'

'He left his home at about seven o'clock, on his way to a children's party in Wembley. He was supposed to give away the prizes. He never arrived there. Two teenagers say they saw him at about seven-thirty in Hyde Park with a woman.'

Fallada said: 'And this girl was killed by him about eight hours later, in Putney?'

'Looks like it, sir. Suppose he had some kind of brainstorm. Probably lost his memory and wandered around for hours...'

Fallada asked Carlsen: 'What time did your space vampire escape from the S.R.I. building?'

'About seven, I suppose. You think—'

Fallada raised his hand. 'I'll tell you what I think when we've examined the body.' He told Grey: 'I want to show Commander Carlsen how we test for negative life energy. So could you set up the apparatus on the man over there?'

Dixon said: 'I'll leave you now, sir. The Commissioner says he'll be in his office until seven o'clock.'

'Thank you, Sergeant. I'll tell him the result.'

The body of the dead man was still lying on the trolley near the door, now covered with a sheet. Carlsen guided the other end of the stretcher as they wheeled it to the other end of the laboratory. Grey said: 'In through that door.'

It was a small room that contained only one bench. Suspended above this was a machine that reminded Carlsen of an X-ray apparatus. Carlsen helped the assistant transfer the body to the bench. Grey pulled off the sheet and dropped it onto the trolley. The man's flesh was yellow and rubbery. The line made by the rope was clearly visible in the flesh of his neck. One eye was half open; Grey closed it perfunctorily.

Attached to the wall behind the bench was a large L-field meter, the scale calibrated in millionths of an amp. Next to this was a television monitor. Grey attached one lead to the man's chin, clamping the other to the loose flesh of his thigh. The needle on the meter swung over. Grey said: 'Point nought four. And he's been dead for nearly forty-eight hours.'

Fallada came in. He looked at the reading, then said to Carlsen: 'You see, this man also died by violence.'

'Yes, but by his own hand. That's not like being beaten and strangled.'

'Perhaps. Now what we are going to do is to induce an artificial life field with this Bentz apparatus. Watch.' He pressed a switch; a faint blue light glowed down from the apparatus above, the corpse, accompanied by a rising sound that soon passed beyond the range of audibility. After about a minute, the needle of the lambda meter began to climb steadily. Seven minutes later, it had climbed to 10.3, slightly lower than that of a living body. The needle wavered there. Fallada said: 'I think that's as high as it will go.' He snapped off the switch, and the light slowly died. Fallada indicated the meter. 'Now it should take about twelve hours before the life field leaks away. And that is in spite of the decomposition that must have started in his intestines.'

Grey unclipped the leads. This time, Fallada helped him to transfer the body back onto the trolley. Grey wheeled it out. A moment later, he returned with the body of the girl. He removed the sheet and they lifted it onto the bench. She was wearing a tweed skirt under the nylon smock. A pair of tights hung loosely around one foot.

Carlsen asked: 'Who was she?'

'A waitress from an all-night transport cafe. She lived only a few hundred yards from her work.'

Without ceremony Grey pulled up the skirt. Underneath, the girl was naked. Carlsen observed the bruises and scratches on her thighs. Grey clipped one electrode to the soft flesh inside her thigh, and the other to her lower lip. Fallada leaned forward. Suddenly, Carlsen was aware of his tension. The needle of the meter climbed slowly and stopped at .002. Grey said: 'It's dropped two thousand milli-amps in seven hours.'

Fallada reached out and pressed the switch; the blue light came on. When the hum faded, there was absolute silence. As slowly as the minute hand of a watch, the needle climbed to 8.3. After another minute, it was clear that it would stay there. Fallada said: 'Now,' and switched off the machine. Almost immediately, the needle of the lambda meter began to drop. Fallada and Grey looked at one another, Carlsen noticed that Grey was sweating.

Fallada turned to Carlsen. He said quietly: 'You understand?'

'Not quite.'

'It will take only about ten minutes for her artifical life field to disappear. She cannot hold a life field.'

Grey was watching the needle. He said: 'I've seen ruptured life fields before, but never anything as bad as this.'

Carlsen said: 'But what does it *mean?*'

Fallada cleared his throat He said: 'It means that whoever killed her sucked the life out of her so violently that it destroyed her capacity to hold a life field. You could compare her to a tyre with a thousand punctures, so that it can no longer hold air.'

Carlsen found he had to overcome a strong inner resistance to ask his next question. 'Are you sure there's no *other* way it could have happened?'

Fallada said sombrely: 'I know of none.'

There was a silence. Grey said: 'What happens now?'

Fallada said: 'Now, I think, the hunt begins all over again.' He laid a hand on Carlsen's elbow. 'Let us go back to my office.'

Grey asked: 'What do you want me to do?'

'Continue the tests. I would like to know whether the pressure on her throat was enough to kill her.'

Back in the office, Carlsen took up his half-finished drink. Fallada dropped into the chair behind his desk. He pressed the switch of the telescreen. A girl's voice said: 'Yes, sir?'

'Get me Sir Percy Heseltine at Scotland Yard.'

He turned to Carlsen. 'This is what I expected. I must admit to feeling a certain grim satisfaction to know that I am right'

'But are you *sure* you're right? Look, I saw what happened to young Adams. She drained all the life out of him, and he turned into an old man. Did you see the. body?' Fallada nodded. 'Now, this girl doesn't look in the least like that. She looks to me like the victim of an ordinary sex attack. Surely there could be some other explanation for this ruptured life field?'

Fallada shook his head. 'No. You do not understand.'

To begin with, it is not a question of a ruptured life field. What is ruptured is whatever *holds* the life field. No one knows exactly what that is—I even know biologists who think that man has a nonmaterial body as well as a physical body, and that the life field is a function of the atoms of this body—as magnetism is a function of the atoms of a magnet. Think of the flesh of an orange. The juice is held in tiny cells—'

The telescreen buzzed. He said: 'Hello?'

The secretary said: I'm afraid the Commissioner isn't in at present, sir. He's in Wandsworth. He should be back in about half an hour.'

'Very well. Tell his secretary that I'll be coming over there in half an hour. Say it's urgent.' He rang off. 'Now, where was I?'

'An orange.'

'Ah, yes. I was saying that if you allowed an orange to dry out, and then left it to soak in water for a day, it would regain its old shape, would it not? But if you crushed the juice out of the orange in a vice, nothing could make it return to its old shape. All the cells would be ruptured. It is the same with a living body. If it dies normally, the life field takes several days to disperse. Even if death is due to violence, it still takes a fairly long time, because most of the cells remain intact. The body is like an orange with a bad bruise, but dehydration still takes a few days. Now, *that* girl's cell structure had been destroyed like the orange in the vice. And there is no normal way in which this could happen. Unless she was burned to a cinder, or fell from the top of this building.' He paused to empty his glass. 'Or was cut into pieces by a train.'

'But *would* a train have destroyed the structure?'

"No, I was joking. But it would have made sure that no one bothered to take a lambda reading.' He crossed to the cupboard. 'Would you like another drink? It is early, but I think I deserve it.' Carlsen emptied his glass and held it out. For several moments, neither of them spoke. Carlsen observed that although he had drunk two whiskies, he still felt cold sober, without even a glow of exhilaration.

Fallada said: 'Tell me something. Did you really *believe* she was dead?'

Carlsen shook his head. 'No, I didn't believe it. And if you want to know the truth, I didn't want to believe it.' He felt himself flushing as he said it. Again, it had cost an effort to force himself to say the words.

If Fallada was surprised, he showed no sign of it. 'Was she so attractive?'

The desire not to go on was so strong that he was silent for almost a minute. He said finally: 'It's difficult to explain.'

'Would you say, for example, that she had some hypnotic effect?'

Carlsen felt angry with himself for feeling so embarrassed. He said, stumbling over the words: 'You know, it's…difficult…I mean it's strange how hard it is to talk about it.'

Fallada said quickly: 'But it's important to talk about it. This is something I want to understand.'

'Okay.' Carlsen swallowed. 'Did you ever read a poem called "The Pied Piper of Hamelin" when you were at school?'

'No, but I know the legend. My mother was born in Hamelin.'

'Well, in the poem, the piper leads all the kids away into the side of a mountain. And they all follow him willingly. Only one gets left behind because he's lame. And he describes what the music seemed to promise…something about…I can't remember the words exactly, but a joyous land where everything is new and strange. A marvellous, ideal kind of place where mince pies grow on trees and the rivers are made of ice cream soda.' He swallowed a drink, feeling the dry heat burning his cheeks and ears. *'That's* what it was like.'

'And can you describe what *she* seemed to promise?'

'Well…nothing. In that sense. But it was the same kind of thing—a kind of vision—of an ideal woman, if you like.'

'The *Ewig-weibliche?* '

Carlsen looked blank; Fallada explained: 'Goethe's eternal-feminine principle. He ends his Faust: "The eternal feminine draws us upwards and on." '

Carlsen nodded. He was now experiencing a strange sense of relief. 'That's it. That's true. I suppose Goethe must have met a woman like this. The kind of thing you dream about as a child. You look at your sister's friends, and you think they must be goddesses. When you're older, you get more realistic and you think women aren't like that at all.'

Fallada said softly: 'But the dream remains.'

'Yes, the dream. And that's why I couldn't believe it. Dreams don't just die like that'

'There is only one thing you must remember.' He waited until Carlsen looked up from his glass. 'This creature was not a woman.' As Carlsen made an impatient gesture, he went on quickly: 'I mean that these creatures are totally alien to everything we mean by human.'

Carlsen said stubbornly: 'They're *humanoid.*'

Fallada said sharply: 'No, not even that. You forget that the human body is a highly, specialised piece of adaptation. A quarter of a billion years ago, we were fishes. We developed arms and legs and lungs to move about on land. It is a million-to-one chance that creatures from another galaxy could have evolved along the same lines.'

'Unless conditions on their planet were similar to earth.'

'Possible, but unlikely. We now have a pathologist's report on the bodies of the three aliens. Their digestive systems are identical to those of human beings.'

'So?'

Fallada leaned forward. 'They live by draining the life of other creatures. They don't need food.'

Carlsen shook his head. 'I suppose so. But…I don't know. We just don't *know,* do we? We don't really know a damn thing—not one single definite fact.'

Fallada said patiently, like a professor coaching a backward student: 'I think we have a few facts. For example, we are fairly certain that the girl on the railway line was killed by one of these creatures, whatever they are. We also know that the fingerprints found on her throat belonged to a man called Clapperton.' He paused; Carlsen said nothing. 'That suggests two possibilities. Either that Clapperton was acting in obedience to the vampires, or that one of them had gained possession of his body.'

It was what Carlsen had known he was going to say; nevertheless, it made his scalp prickle, and a wave of coldness ran over his body. He started to speak, but his voice stuck in his throat. His heart was suddenly beating painfully.

Fallada said gently: 'We both recognise this as a possibility, in which case it is also possible that these things are indestructible. But that doesn't mean they are incapable of making mistakes. For example—'

The sharp buzz of the telescreen interrupted him. He pressed the reply key.

'The Commissioner of Police to speak to you, sir.'

'Put him through.'

Carlsen was sitting on the far side of the desk, so could not see the Commissioner's face; the voice was clipped and military.

'Hans, glad I caught you. There's been a new development. We've found the suspect.'

The racing driver?'

'Yes. I've just been to see him.'

'Alive?'

'Unfortunately not. In the Wandsworth mortuary. His body was fished out of the river this afternoon.'

'So there had been no post-mortem yet?'

'Not yet. But I'd say it's a clear case of suicide after committing a murder. So from our point of view, the case is closed.'

Fallada said: 'Percy, I want to see that body.'

'Yes, of course. Any…er…particular reason?'

'Because I'd like to take a bet he didn't die by drowning.'

'Then you'd lose it. I watched them pumping the water out of his lungs.'

Fallada shook his head incredulously. 'Are you sure?'

'Quite certain. Why? I don't understand you.'

Fallada said: 'I'm coming over there to see you now. Will you be there in half an hour?'

'Yes.'

'I'm bringing Commander Carlsen too.'

Fallada rang off. He stood up, sighing and massaging his eyes. 'That is unbelievable. I would have staked a thousand pounds that he was dead before he entered the water.' He crossed to the window and stared out, his hands deep in his coat pockets. 'When the screen rang, I was about to say that they had made a mistake in choosing Clapperton. He is too well-known. Consequently, he is of no use to them. So he has to die.'

'Well, you were right.'

Fallada grunted. 'Perhaps…We must go now.' He pressed the communication button and told his secretary: 'Order a cab to pick me up in front of the Ismeer Building in five minutes. And tell Norman to expect another body for examination.'

The high-speed elevator took twenty-five seconds to carry them to the ground floor, a mile below. There was no sensation of movement; only a momentary lightness. Fallada stood without speaking, his head sunk on his chest.

As they left the air-conditioned coolness of the Ismeer Building, the air of the city poured over them like warm water. The spring day was as hot as midsummer. Many of the dark-suited men had removed their jackets. Women had taken advantage of the sun to try out the latest fashion: transparent dresses over brightly coloured underwear. There was a gaiety about the crowd that made it hard to believe in vampires.

The tiny battery-powered cab was waiting by the pavement. Carlsen was about to climb in when he heard the voice of the robot news-vendor: 'New *Stranger* sensation. New *Stranger* sensation...' The changing neon sign in front of it read: 'Spaceman describes *Mary Celeste* of space...' Carlsen slipped a coin into the machine and took the *Evening Mail*.

There was a photograph on the front page that he recognised as Patricia Wolfson, wife of the captain of the *Vega*. She was holding two children by the hand.

In the cab, Fallada leaned forward, trying to read over his shoulder. Carlsen said: 'It looks as if Wolfson went aboard the *Stranger* after all.'

Fallada leaned back. 'Read it aloud, would you?'

' "Only one hour before receiving an order forbidding all further exploration of the *Stranger*, Captain Derek Wolfson and a three-man team entered its control room. This was revealed today in an exclusive interview by Mrs. Patricia Wolfson, the spaceman's wife. Mrs. Wolfson talked to our reporter at the London International Spaceport.

' "On Tuesday afternoon, Mrs. Wolfson, together with her two children, spent five hours in the signal room at moonbase, and exchanged messages with her husband, who was more than a quarter of a billion miles away, in the explorer-ship *Vega*.

' "In a televised message lasting eight and a half minutes, Captain Wolfson described how his team entered the derelict through a massive new hole torn by a meteor since the *Stranger* was discovered last November. 'If the hole had been a few yards higher, it would have totally destroyed the control deck,' Captain Wolfson told his wife.

' "According to Dr. Werner Hass, the physicist who accompanied Wolfson, the instruments in the control room revealed a technology far ahead of anything on earth.

' "Captain Wolfson told his wife that the control room showed no sign of damage, but that papers and star maps were scattered over the floor. "The cabin looked as if it had been abandoned half an hour earlier,' commented Wolfson. But there was no sign of the living creatures who had been on the control deck. Wolfson told his wife: 'It made me think of the mystery of the *Mary Celeste*.'

' "The documents in the cabin were printed on a material resembling thick paper impregnated with wax. This could provide a clue to the galaxy in which the *Stranger* originated.

' "Wolfson and his team were still aboard the *Stranger* when the *Vega* received the message from moonbase forbidding exploration of the derelict on account of radiation hazards.

' "Our space correspondent comments..." '

Carlsen lowered the newspaper and held it over his shoulder. 'Here, read it for yourself.'

Fallada said: I wonder who gave him permission, to explore?'

'Probably nobody. Wolfson's the sort who does things without permission.'

The cabdriver said: 'Rather have my job than his.' It reminded them that they could not speak freely. They sat in silence for the next ten minutes, each absorbed in his own thoughts. Carlsen was thinking again of the disturbing beauty of the underwater paintings of the *Stranger*, and of its vast, cathedral-like spaces, and wondering how he could convey these to Fallada.

Fallada said: '*Mary Celeste* of space. Another journalistic cliche.'

'Let's hope it doesn't stick.'

At New Scotland Yard, the duty sergeant recognised them. 'The Commissioner wants you to go up right away, sir. You know the way, don't you?'

In the lift, Fallada said: 'I wonder what that means?'

'What?'

'Sounds like a new development. He knew we were coming anyway, so there was no reason to leave a message.'

'This *Mary Celeste* story, I suppose.'

The big, bald-headed man was waiting for them as they stepped out of the lift. He wore civilian clothes but carried himself as if they were a military uniform.

Fallada said: 'Sir Percy Heseltine, this is Commander Carlsen.'

The big man's grip was powerful. 'Glad you've come, Commander. There's a message for you, by the way. Bukovsky from Space Research wants you to contact him right away.'

'Thank you. Is there a telescreen I can use?'

'In my office.'

They followed him into the big, anonymous office that overlooked the helicopter landing port on the roof. Heseltine pointed. 'Use the one in my secretary's office. It's empty.'

Carlsen left the door open. He had a feeling that whatever Bukovsky had to say would be for all of them. When he asked for Bukovsky, the operator said: 'I'm sorry, sir. He isn't available.' But when he gave his name, she said: 'Oh, yes. He's waiting for a call from you. We've been trying to contact you for the past hour.'

A moment later Bukovsky appeared. He looked harassed and irritable. 'Olof, thank heavens we've got you finally. We tried to get your home for an hour, but your wife was out.'

'I've been with Dr. Fallada.'

'So I gather. Have you seen the papers?'

'I saw that Captain Wolfson had been into the *Stranger.*'

'Captain!' Bukovsky said grimly. 'He'll be lucky if he's a second lieutenant by the time I've finished with him.

As to that moronic wife of his...I can't imagine what Zelensky was doing letting her into moon-base. And now on top of everything else, we've got a new problem. The Space Minister's just been on to me, saying he wants every inch of the *Stranger* explored immediately.'

Carlsen said: 'Tell him to get screwed.'

'All right Why?'

'Because Dr. Fallada thinks the three aliens aren't dead after all.'

'What! Not dead? What the hell are you talking about? We *saw* them.'

Carlsen said quietly: 'And I think he's probably right.'

Bukovsky suddenly became quiet and concentrated. 'What makes you think so?'

'What I saw in his laboratory this afternoon. If you saw it, I think you'd be convinced.'

'If they're not dead, where are they?'

I don't know. You'd better ask him.' He beckoned to Fallada, who was standing in the doorway, Heseltine beside him. Fallada came in and leaned forward so his face was within camera range.

'Hello, Bukovsky. Carlsen's right. By the way, is it safe to talk like this? Are you sure we can't be overheard?'

'Yes. This screen has an A.C.M. But how can these things still be alive? You mean they can exist without bodies?'

'For a limited time, yes.'

Bukovsky asked quickly: 'How do you know it's a limited time?'

'Deduction.'

'Will you explain it?'

'Certainly. When I heard Carlsen's tape describing his encounter with the girl, I couldn't believe she was dead. If she was as dominant as he says, she'd be a match for any sex maniac' Bukovsky nodded; he had clearly thought the same thing. 'I wondered then if she could have lured some man into the park and somehow taken over his body. So I tested her body to see if the life field was still intact. It wasn't. It hadn't been drained —like the body of young Adams. But it was still abnormally low. So it struck me as a working hypothesis that the girl was alive, in a man's body. But then there was the problem of what happened to Clapperton. You know about that?' Bukovsky nodded. 'He disappeared about half an hour after the girl escaped from the Space Research building, and at about the time you discovered the other two creatures were dead. Clapperton was last seen in Hyde Park with a woman who sounds like the alien. But she couldn't have wanted his body for herself—she was still around several hours later. My guess is that she wanted it for one of the other two. Why such a hurry if they could live outside their bodies indefinitely?'

Bukovsky interrupted: 'So you assume there was a third victim?'

'Almost certainly. Possibly a girl—if they prefer to stick to their original sexes. And now there must have been still another. You know Clapperton's body was found in the river this afternoon?'

'No.' Bukovsky hardly seemed interested. Carlsen had observed before that when Bukovsky was faced with serious decisions, his usual nervous, aggressive manner disappeared, and he became totally calm, a calculating machine surveying a thousand possibilities. After a moment of silence, he said: 'This obviously has to be treated with the utmost secrecy. If it got out, there'd be a panic. I'm going to speak to the Space Minister. What's your number there?' Fallada gave it to him. 'I'll call you back as soon as I can. Meanwhile, do you think there's any possibility of destroying these things?'

'I am inclined to doubt it.'

Bukovsky sighed. 'So am I.' He rang off.

None of them spoke for a moment. Then Carlsen said: 'I'm afraid I've got a great deal to answer for.'

'It wasn't your fault.' It was Heseltine who spoke. 'You were only doing your job. Thank God you didn't bring more back.'

Carlsen said: 'I suppose that's one consolation.'

Fallada placed a hand on his shoulder. 'Don't be too gloomy. Luck has been on our side so far. If that girl hadn't given herself away by killing Adams, they'd all be on their way back to earth by now. And if I hadn't applied my new lambda test to her body, we'd now be assuming they were all dead. Things could have been much worse.'

'Except that you think they're indestructible.'

Heseltine said: 'Come into my office. I've ordered tea and sandwiches. I don't know about you, but I'm damned hungry.'

It struck Carlsen suddenly that he was hungry too, and that part of his depression was probably due to an empty stomach.

Fallada helped himself to a cigar from the box on the desk. 'I didn't say I thought they were indestructible. There's no way of knowing. But at least there are certain things in our favour. In effect, we have three murderers loose in the community. But murderers leave a trail behind them, as we have seen.'

There was a knock at the door; a girl came in pushing a tea trolley. The ham sandwiches were freshly made; as Carlsen ate, he felt his optimism returning. He said: 'Well, I suppose the damage they can do is rather less than the road-accident rate.'

Heseltine said: 'I should hope so. The present fatality rate is about forty-nine a day.' He pressed the key of the telescreen. 'Mary, get me the City Co-ordinator, will you. It's probably Philpott today.'

When the screen buzzed, a few minutes later, they heard him say: 'Hello, Inspector. There's something I want you to do for me. You remember the girl found on the line at Putney yesterday? It turns out to be a case of murder. I want you to collect together reports of all similar deaths, from all over England. Got that? Anyone who dies suddenly, either from strangulation or without apparent cause. Get the directive out to every police headquarters in the country. I don't want any panic about it. If the press get wind of it, say it's a routine enquiry—you know, a statistics test, or something. But I want you to notify this office within seconds of getting any new report. We think this chap's a lunatic, and he's got to be caught. By the way…don't go away…he may have a woman accomplice. All right?'

He rang off. 'That's a first step, anyway. We'll have to form a separate squad to deal with it. Which means, of course, that the press are bound to get wind of it sooner or later.'

Fallada said: 'I'm not sure that would do any harm. Carlsen says that these creatures can't destroy anyone without his own consent. If we emphasised that, it shouldn't cause a panic. And we'd have public cooperation trying to track them down.'

'That's true. But I don't think it's our decision. It would have to be taken at ministerial level.' The screen buzzed as he spoke. 'Hello?'

'Hello, Sir Percy. Is Carlsen there?'

It was Bukovsky. Carlsen moved into camera range.

Heseltine said: 'Would you like to take it next door?'

Bukovsky said: 'No, it concerns you too. The P.M. wants to see us all at Downing Street as soon as possible. That includes Dr. Fallada. There's been another rather peculiar development. Could you get down there as soon as you can?'

'Me too?' Heseltine asked.

'He asked for you especially. See you as soon as you can make it.' He rang off.

Carlsen took another sandwich. 'Not until I've finished my tea.'

Whitehall was crowded with office workers on their way home. The day had turned golden and tired, and the chill had returned to the air. Carlsen reflected that any one of these people could be an alien, and his frustration sharpened for a moment into pain.

A Rolls-Royce passed them at the corner of Downing Street. Carlsen recognised one of the men in the rear seat as Philip Rawlinson, the Home Secretary. He was climbing out as they arrived at Number Ten. Rawlinson said: 'Ah, Heseltine, glad to see you here. Do you know Alex M'Kay, the Space Minister?' M'Kay was a short, bald man with a massive red moustache.

He looked at Carlsen from under raised eyebrows. 'I recognise you. You're the chap who started all the trouble, aren't you?' When Carlsen smiled embarrassedly, M'Kay clapped him on the shoulder. 'Don't worry. We'll sort it out.' Carlsen wished he shared his conviction.

Inside, a middle-aged but attractive secretary said: 'The Prime Minister won't keep you a moment. He's on the telephone.'

'No, I'm not. Bring them up.' The bulky figure of Everard Jamieson appeared at the top of the stairs. 'We'll use the Cabinet Room.'

Jamieson was even taller than Carlsen. A journalist had once said he had the face of Abraham Lincoln, the voice of Winston Churchill, and the cunning of Lloyd George. When he shook hands, his grip was so powerful that it made Carlsen wince.

'Good of you to come, gentlemen. Please sit down. He placed a hand on Fallada's shoulder. 'And unless I'm mistaken, you are the ingenious Dr. Fallada, the man they call the Sherlock Holmes of pathology?' Fallada nodded without smiling, but the compliment obviously pleased him.

There was a tray with whisky and glasses in the centre of the Cabinet table. Without waiting to be asked, M'Kay helped himself.

Jamieson sat down at the head of the table. He lowered his head, frowning at the tabletop as if in deep meditation. There was an involuntary silence, broken only by the hiss of the soda syphon. A moment later, the secretary came in and placed a sheet of paper in front of each of them. Carlsen studied it closely, decided it was upside down, and turned it round. It appeared to be a map, and the outline was vaguely familiar. But the writing was in a script he had never seen.

'No sign of Bukovsky?' As Jamieson spoke, the door opened, and Bukovsky came in, followed by a fat man in rimless glasses. 'Ah, there you are, Bukovsky. And that, unless I am mistaken, is Professor Schliermacher? How kind of you to come, Professor.' Schliermacher blushed, made a rumbling noise in his throat, then said nervously: 'It's an honour, Prime Minister.'

Bukovsky sat down and began to clean his glasses. He saw the map. 'Ah, you've got this already?'

'I had it sent from moonbase. Would you hand Dr. Schliermacher a copy? Thank you.' He looked round the table and coughed to attract M'Kay's attention; the Space Minister was mopping his brow with a handkerchief and staring out of the window. 'Now, gentlemen, I think we're all here. We can begin.' He turned to Carlsen. 'So let me start with you, Commander. Do you know what that is?' He tapped the sheet of paper in front of him.

Carlsen said: 'Is it a map of Greece?'

Jamieson turned to Schliermacher. 'Well, is it, Professor?'

Schliermacher looked puzzled. 'Yes, of course.'

'Do you know where it came from?' He was speaking to Carlsen again. Carlsen shook his head. Jamieson surveyed the faces around the table, looking for someone to answer the question. He reminded Carlsen of a headmaster with a class of sixth formers. When the silence became uncomfortable, Jamieson said: 'It came from the control room of the *Stranger.*'

There were exclamations of astonishment; Jamieson smiled around at them, evidently pleased at the effect he had created. 'The details are poor, of course. The original should tell us a great deal more.'

Rawlinson said: 'That's simply incredible.'

'But nevertheless true, as Dr. Bukovsky will confirm.'

Bukovsky nodded, without looking up from the map. Schliermacher had produced a magnifying glass from his pocket and was studying the map intently. Jamieson said: 'You realise what this means, of course?'

Rawlinson said: 'That they know the earth pretty well.'

Jamieson's face showed a flicker of irritation at being anticipated. He slapped the table. 'Precisely, gentlemen. It means that these creatures have almost certainly visited our earth on a previous occasion." The voice was vibrant and Churchillian. He looked around at them gravely. 'The only alternative I can imagine is that they have examined the earth through incredibly powerful telescopes. But I can imagine no third possibility. Can you?'

Carlsen looked across at Fallada. He could see that Fallada was baffled and for the moment unsure of himself.

Schliermacher said suddenly: 'But this is completely incredible.'

"Why, Professor?" Schliermacher was evidently so excited that he had difficulty in speaking. He tapped the map with his finger.

'You see…this is Greece, but it is not modern Greece.'

Bukovsky interrupted acidly: 'That is to be expected, surely?' He ignored the Prime Minister's stare of rebuke.

Schliermacher, stammering slightly, said: 'You don't understand me. You see, this is very strange. Look.' He leaned over Bukovsky. 'Do you know what this is?'

Bukovsky said: 'I presume it's an island.'

'Yes, an island. But it is the wrong shape. This is the island of Thera—we call it Santorin now. On a modern map, it is shaped like a crescent moon. Because about 1500 B.C. it was blown apart by a volcano. This map, was made before the volcano exploded.'

The Prime Minister said: 'You are telling us this map was made before 1500 B.C.?'

'Sure, that's what I'm telling you.' Schliermacher was so excited that he was forgetting his awe. 'But you see, there is a lot that I don't understand. This is Knossos, on Crete. This is Athens. No human being at that period could have made such a map.'

Jamieson said: 'Precisely. No human beings could have made it, but these creatures could, and did. Rawlinson, pass me the whisky. I think this calls for a celebratory drink.'

As Rawlinson pushed the tray down the table, Fallada asked quietly: 'Would you tell me what we are supposed to be celebrating?'

Jamieson smiled at him benignly. 'Gentlemen, I should explain that Dr. Fallada thinks these creatures are dangerous. And for all I know, he could be right. But I also believe that this map represents one of the greatest advances in historical knowledge of our time. And as you all know, I regard myself as a historian rather than as a politician. So I think we might be justified in raising our glasses to Commander Carlsen and the *Stranger.*' He began to pour whisky into half a dozen glasses.

M'Kay said: I think that's a damn good idea. In fact, I've already given orders for the *Stranger* to be thoroughly examined.' He turned to Bukovsky. I presume that's being done?'

Bukovsky reddened. 'No.'

M'Kay asked evenly: 'Why not?'

'Because I agree with Fallada that these creatures might be dangerous.'

M'Kay began: 'Now, look here—'

Fallada snapped: 'They *are* dangerous. They're vampires.'

M'Kay said scornfully: 'So's my grandmother.'

The others all began to speak at once. Jamieson said: 'Gentlemen, gentlemen'. His voice had a calming effect. 'I think there's no need to get excited about this.

We're here to discuss this fully, and'—he turned to Fallada—'everyone has a right to give their point of view. So let us forget our differences for a moment and drink to Commander Carlsen's health.' Fallada continued to frown as he accepted his whisky. Jamieson raised his glass. 'To Commander Carlsen and his epoch-making discovery.'

Everyone drank, while Carlsen smiled with embarrassment. Jamieson said: 'I should add, Commander, that this is only one of several maps found on the *Stranger.* I want Professor Schliermacher to take charge of the examination of this material.'

Schliermacher, his face red, said huskily: 'I am deeply honoured.'

Jamieson smiled at Fallada. 'Doctor, do you remember the story of the Piri Reis maps?' Fallada shook his head sullenly. 'Then let me tell it to you. If I remember correctly, Piri Reis was a Turkish pirate who was born at about the time Columbus discovered America. In 1513 and 1528, he drew two maps of the world. Now, the amazing thing is that these maps not only showed North America—which Columbus had discovered—but South America as far as Patagonia and Tierra del Fuego. And these countries had not been discovered at that time. Even the Vikings, who discovered North America five centuries before Columbus, never got beyond North America. But that isn't all. Piri Reis's maps also showed Greenland. That was easy enough to explain—the Vikings were familiar with Greenland. But in one place, Piri showed two bays where modern maps showed land. That seemed worth investigating, so a team of scientists made seismographic measurements in Greenland. They discovered that Piri Reis was right, and the modern maps were wrong. It wasn't land—it was a thick sheet of ice that now covered the bays. In other words, Piri Reis's-map showed Greenland as it was before the ice covered it—thousands of years ago.' He looked around the table; everyone was listening intently, even Fallada. Jamieson said: 'We now believe that Piri Reis based his maps on much older maps—maps perhaps as old as this one, or even older.' He tapped the map on the table. 'And these maps could not have been made by human beings on earth. They were not advanced enough.' He turned' to Fallada, and his gaze was almost hypnotic. 'Would you not agree that it is possible that those old maps were made by these same alien creatures that you call vampires?'

Fallada hesitated, then said: 'Yes, I suppose it is.'

'So it is possible that these creatures have visited earth on at least one, and possibly two previous occasions, without doing any harm?'

Fallada, Carlsen and Bukovsky all began to speak at once. It was Bukovsky who made his voice heard. 'What I find so difficult to understand. Surely there can be no justification in taking such risks? Even if it was only a million to one chance that these creatures are dangerous, it wouldn't be worth the risk. It would be like bringing a deadly unknown germ back to earth.'

Rawlinson said: 'I'm inclined to agree with that.'

Jamieson smiled at them, unperturbed. 'So are we all, my dear fellow. That's why we're discussing it now.'

Bukovsky said: 'Would it be possible to hear what Dr. Fallada has to say?'

'Of course!' The Prime Minister turned to Fallada. 'Please, Doctor.'

Fallada, finding all eyes on him, removed his glasses and polished them. He said: 'Well, briefly, I have established beyond all doubt that these creatures are vampires—energy vampires.'

Jamieson interrupted smoothly: 'If you'll excuse my saying so, you don't *have* to establish that. We all know what happened to that young journalist.'

Fallada's temper was visibly wearing thin. He made an obvious effort to control his irritation. 'I don't think you quite see what I mean. I have developed a method for *testing* whether someone has been killed by a vampire. Quite simply, I have developed a method for inducing an artificial life field in the body of a creature that has recently died. Now, when a body has been drained by a vampire, it won't hold a life field. It's like a burst tyre—it runs out as fast as it runs in. You see...'

He hesitated for a moment, giving Jamieson a chance to interject: 'And when did you make this discovery?'

'Oh...er...two years ago.'

'Two years! You've been working on vampirism for two years?'

Fallada nodded. 'In fact, I've written a book on it.'

It was M'Kay who interrupted this time. 'But how could you write about vampires before this happened? Where did you get your material?'

Fallada said earnestly: 'Vampirism is commoner than you think. It plays a basic part in nature, as well as in human relations. There are many predators that drain the life field of their prey, as well as eating their bodies. And even human beings know this instinctively. Why do we eat oysters alive? Why do we boil lobster alive? It's true even when we eat vegetables—we prefer a fresh cabbage to a cabbage that is a week old—'

M'Kay said: 'Oh come, that sounds total nonsense. We eat fresh cabbage because it tastes better, not because it's alive.'

Rawlinson said: 'And personally, I prefer my grouse when it's been hung for at least a week.'

Carlsen saw that Fallada's irritation was making him damage his own case. He said: 'Could I perhaps explain a little?'

Jamieson said courteously: 'Please do, Commander.'

'I've been in Dr. Fallada's lab this afternoon, and I saw the body of the girl who was found on the line at Putney yesterday. There was no doubt whatever that she'd been killed by a vampire.'

Jamieson shook his head. He was obviously impressed. *'How* do you know?'

'By Dr. Fallada's test. Her body won't hold a life field.'

'I know nothing about this girl. How did she die?'

Heseltine said: 'She was strangled then her body was thrown onto the railway line from a bridge.'

Jamieson turned to Fallada. 'And would not such violence have a similar effect on the life field?'

'To a minor extent. Not nearly to the same degree.'

'And when did this take place?'

Heseltine said: 'In the early hours of yesterday morning.'

'I...don't understand. Surely by that time, all three of these creatures were dead?'

Fallada said: I don't believe they *were* dead. I believe they're still at large.'

'But how—'

Fallada interrupted: 'I think they can take over other people's bodies. The female alien didn't really die in Hyde Park. She lured a man into the park, took over his body, then made it look like a sex crime. I also believe the other two are at large. They simply left their bodies in the Space Research building and took over other bodies.'

There was a silence. Both Rawlinson and M'Kay were looking down at the table, as if unwilling to comment. Jamieson said reasonably: 'You must admit that what you say sounds unbelievable. What *evidence* is there for these...assertions?'

Fallada said: 'It's not a matter of evidence. It's a matter of simple logic. These creatures are supposed to be dead. Yet we find bodies that seem to have been drained of life energy. That suggests they're not dead after all.'

Jamieson said: 'How many bodies?'

'Two, so far—the girl on the railway line, and the man who killed her.'

'The man who *killed* her?' Jamieson looked at Heseltine as if appealing for help.

Heseltine said: 'She was strangled by a man called Clapperton—the racing driver. Dr. Fallada thinks he was possessed by one of these creatures.'

'I see. And I gather that he is now also dead?'

'Yes.'

'And his body…is it also in…this condition?'

'We don't know yet. It's being sent to my laboratory for testing.'

'And when shall we know the result?'

Heseltine said: 'It was sent two hours ago. It may have been tested by now.'

Jamieson said: 'In that case, please find out. Here is a telescreen.' He turned and lifted a portable telescreen from the desk behind him. Rawlinson pushed it down the table to Fallada.

Fallada said: 'Very well.' There was total silence as he pushed the dialling buttons. When a girl's voice answered, Fallada said: 'Would you get Norman on the phone, please?' Half a minute went by. M'Kay helped himself to another drink. Then Grey's voice said: 'Hello, sir?'

'Norman! Did Wandsworth mortuary send a body?'

'Oh, yes, sir. The man who drowned. I've finished testing it now.'

'What result?'

'Well, as far as I can tell, sir, it's a normal case of drowning. He may have taken knock-out pills.'

'But what about the lambda reading?'

'Perfectly normal, sir.'

'No difference *whatever?*'

'None, sir.'

Fallada said: 'All right. Thank you, Norman.' He rang off. Jamieson said quickly: 'Of course, I agree that proves nothing. You *could* still be right, generally speaking, even though you are wrong in this particular case. But as I understand it, your theory now rests on a single body—the girl on the railway line?'

Before Fallada could answer, M'Kay interrupted quietly: 'I don't wish to be offensive, Doctor, but isn't it possible you've allowed your interest in vampires to…well, outweigh your judgement?'

Fallada said angirly: 'No, it is not.'

Carlsen felt it was time to support Fallada. 'I agree that this result *is* rather surprising. But I don't think it invalidates Dr. Fallada's general argument.'

Jamieson turned to Bukovsky. 'What do you think?'

Bukovsky was obviously unsure of himself. Avoiding Fallada's eyes, he said: I honestly don't know. I'm not willing to offer a judgement either way until I've examined all the evidence.'

'And you, Sir Percy?'

Heseltine frowned. 'I've the greatest respect for Dr. Fallada, and I'm sure he knows what he's talking about.'

Jamieson said: 'Of course he does. No one doubts that. We all know that he is one of our most distinguished scientists. But even scientists can be mistaken. Now, let me be frank and tell you the view that I am inclined to support—although, I should add, entirely without dogmatism.' He paused as if waiting for objections. It was a parliamentary trick; all were waiting for him to go on. 'All the evidence suggests that these are creatures from another planet or star system, who take a deep interest in life on earth. Perhaps they are scientists engaged in the study of evolving civilisations. Clearly, as a species they are far older than man, and certainly more advanced in knowledge of the universe.' He paused, regarding them from under his bushy eyebrows. Carlsen found himself listening with hypnotic fascination to the voice, with its astonishing range of expressiveness. Jamieson now dropped it to an intimate, confidential tone: 'Now, I personally find it very difficult indeed to imagine a highly evolved species who prey on their fellow creatures. I do not claim to be highly evolved, but I am a vegetarian because the killing of animals is repugnant to me. For that reason, it taxes my credulity to believe that creatures like these could be—as Dr. Bukovsky puts it—the equivalent of deadly germs.'

Fallada broke in irritably: 'Then you should have seen the body of that reporter after the woman had finished with it.' Rawlinson made a tutting noise with his tongue and shook his head. M'Kay looked at the ceiling as if he felt they were dealing with an idiot. But Jamieson seemed unoffended. He said gravely: 'I have in fact seen a photograph of that unfortunate young man. I realise that the girl destroyed him and that she is therefore, according to our laws, a murderer. But I have also heard Commander Carlsen's description of what took place, and it leaves me in no doubt that the man was intent on an act of sexual violation. What happened was in self-defence—probably of unpremeditated self-defence, since she woke up to find this man attacking her. Is that not so, Commander?'

Carlsen felt it would be too complicated to try to explain. He said: 'Basically, yes.'

Jamieson turned to Fallada. He held up his finger in a gesture that had overtones of rebuke. 'You believe these creatures are intent on destroying human beings. But is it not just as likely that they wish to help us?' Fallada shrugged, shook his head, but said nothing. Jamieson said persuasively: 'Let me explain what I mean. As a historian, I have often wondered at the suddenness with which great changes have taken place. The destiny of mankind has literally been transformed many times—by the use of weapons, by the discovery of fire, by the invention of the wheel, by the establishment of cities. And yet is it not possible that this'—he tapped the sheet of paper—'could be our answer? That these creatures could be the secret mentors of humankind?'

This time he paused, looking at Fallada as if demanding an answer. Fallada cleared his throat. He said doggedly: 'Anything is possible. I am only trying to deal with facts. And one fact I know is that these creatures are dangerous.'

Jamieson nodded. 'Very well. Then let me make a suggestion. On the whole, time is on our side. We do not have to make an immediate decision. So I suggest we leave the derelict where it is, and wait and see what happens. After all, it is unlikely to come to harm.'

M'Kay grunted: 'Except a few more meteor holes.'

That is a risk we shall have to take. Now, it is my suggestion that, after this meeting, I announce that the Space Research Institute had decided to recall the *Vega* and the *Jupiter* to earth, to allow us to study the documents discovered by Captain Wolfsen. That will delay any decisions for at least two months.' He looked at Fallada. 'If you are right, and these creatures *are* still at large, we shall probably know by the end of that time. Do you agree?'

Fallada, evidently surprised by the concession, said: 'Yes. Yes, certainly.'

'Does everyone else?'

M'Kay said argumentatively: 'I don't. I think it's a waste of time and money to recall the expedition. I think they should go on board now.'

Jamieson said diplomatically: 'And I am inclined to agree with you. But I feel that you and I are in a minority, and that the rest advise caution. So we must bow to the will of the majority.' He looked around enquiringly. Everyone nodded. Looking across at Fallada, Carlsen knew they were feeling the same thing: a strange sense of having won a tug of war because the opponent had let go of the rope. Jamieson said smoothly: 'After all, this expedition has already produced remarkable results. This map alone is, to my mind, worth the whole cost so far. So let us take Dr. Fallada's excellent advice and proceed with extreme caution. I don't think we shall have any regrets.' He stood up. 'And now, gentlemen, I think I shall make my announcement in the House. Dr. Bukovsky, I would be grateful if you would stay with me—I shall need you to help me answer questions afterwards. And

Sir Percy, I'd like a word with you about the measures you're taking to try to trace these creatures… If you'll excuse us, gentlemen…'

In the street, Fallada said slowly: 'I think I shall never understand politicians. Are they really the mindless buffoons they seem to be?'

Carlsen grunted sympathetically. 'Still, I think he reached the right conclusion.'

'He wants to bring that derelict back to earth. That would be disastrous.'

'But he's giving us time.'

Fallada smiled suddenly. His smiles had the effect of transforming his face; it ceased to be heavy and serious and became the face of a jester, with a touch of malicious humor. He laid a hand on Carlsen's shoulder.

'I notice you say "us." Do I take it that you've now become a believer?'

Carlsen shrugged. 'I have a feeling that whatever happens, we're in this together.'

2

H E WOKE UP feeling strangely sluggish and weary. His sleep had been deep, but as he came back to consciousness, he experienced a flash of memory of terrifying dreams. The bedside clock showed nine-thirty. It was a Friday; that meant Jelka had taken the children to the play school. He lay there for five minutes before summoning the energy to press the switch that opened the blinds. A few minutes later, he heard the front door close. Jelka opened the door softly, saw he was awake and came in. She threw the newspaper on the bed.

'There's a piece attacking the Prime Minister. Oh, and this came by special messenger.' She took a book bag from the table. The printed address on the label said: 'Psychosexual Institute.'

'Yes, that's Fallada's book on vampires. He promised to send me a photocopy. How about coffee?'

'Are you all right? You look pale.'

'Just tired.'

When she came in a few minutes later, with coffee and lightly browned toast, he was reading Fallada's typescript. She placed a book on the bedside table.

'I got this out of the library yesterday. I thought it might interest you.'

He glanced at the title: *Spirit Vampirism.* 'That's odd.'

'What?'

'Just a coincidence. The author's Ernst von Geijerstam. And Fallada mentions a Count von Geijerstam.' He turned to the bibliography of Fallada's book. 'Yes, it's the same one.'

'Have you read the *Times* leader yet?'

'No. What does it say?'

'Only that it's a shocking waste of the taxpayers' money to send two spaceships all the way to the asteroids and then bring them back empty-handed.'

Carlsen was too absorbed in the book to reply. She left him alone. When she returned half an hour later, he was still reading, and she could see that the glass coffee machine was empty.

'Are you hungry yet?'

'Not yet. Listen to this. This Count Geijerstam was supposed to be a crank, according to Fallada. He was some sort of psychologist, but no one took him seriously. Listen: it's a chapter called "The Patient Who Taught Me to Think." "The patient, whom I shall call Lars V, was a rather good-looking but pale ectomorph in his mid-twenties. For the past six months he had been experiencing intense compulsions to exhibit his sexual organs to women in public places. More recently, this had given way to a desire to undress children and bite them until they bled. He had not given in to any of these urges, although he admitted that he often went out with his fly open underneath his overcoat.

' "The patient's history was as follows. His parents were both gifted artists, and Lars had displayed a talent for sculpture from an early age. He entered art school at sixteen, gaining top marks in the entrance exam. At the age of nineteen, his progress had been so spectacular that he held a successful exhibition and made himself a considerable reputation. It was at this exhibition that he met Nina von G——, the daughter of a Prussian nobleman. Nina was a pale girl who looked weak but was in fact possessed of considerable physical strength. She had' enormous dark eyes and an unusually red mouth. She praised Lars and said she had always wanted to be the slave of a great artist. Within a day or so, he was hopelessly in love with her. It was many months before she allowed him to possess her, permitting him to believe that she was a virgin. Then she insisted on a strange pantomime. She lay in a makeshift coffin, dressed in a white nightdress, her hands crossed on her breasts. Lars had to creep into the room, pretending to be an intruder, then find the body, with candles burning round it. He then had to act out the fantasy of caressing the 'corpse,' carrying it to the bed, and biting it all over. Finally, he had to ravish her. During all this time, the girl agreed to remain perfectly still and give no sign of life.

' "It was clear, after he had made love to her, that Nina was not a virgin; however, Lars was now too infatuated to care. The two continued to act out extraordinary sexual fantasies. He was a rapist who ravished her in a dark alleyway, or a sadist who pursued her through the woods, tied her to a tree, and then whipped her before possessing her. After each of these occasions, Lars experienced a deep sense of lassitude, and one day the two of them slept naked, in the open, for several hours after lovemaking, to be awakened by falling snow.

' "Lars now begged her to marry him. She refused, explaining that she already belonged to another man. She referred to this man simply as 'the Count,' and said that he visited her once a week to drink a small glassful of her blood. Lars had, in fact, noticed small cuts on the underside of her forearms. She explained to Lars that she had been taking his energy, in order to be able to satisfy the demands of the Count. The only way in which she and Lars could be united was for both of them to swear total allegiance to the Count, and to acknowledge themselves his slaves.

' "In a storm of jealousy, Lars threatened to kill her. After this, he tried to kill himself by taking an overdose of a powerful drug. His family found him unconscious and sent him to the hospital. There he was detained for two weeks. At the end of this time he ran away and went to the girl's flat, intending to tell her he accepted her conditions. But she had gone, and no one knew her address.

' "Now he was subject to continual nervous exhaustion. His sexual fantasies now consisted of dreams of being mistreated by the girl and her lover, the Count. After these orgies of autoeroticism, he was often exhausted for days. His parents were deeply concerned about him, and his professor, an eminent art historian, begged him to return to his work. He had finally decided to come to me.

' "At first I assumed that this was a case of Freudian neurosis, probably involving guilt feelings about a mother fixation. The patient also admitted to having incestuous desires towards his sisters. But one episode he described made me wonder whether my approach was entirely wrong. He told me how, in the early days of the love affair, he had been working in his studio on a marble statue, and feeling exceptionally robust. The girl came into the studio, and he tried to persuade her to go away to let him work. Instead, she removed her clothes and lay at his feet until he became excited. Finally, he possessed her as she lay on the concrete floor. He fell asleep, lying in her arms. When he woke up, he realised that she was now lying on top of him, and—as he put it—sucking away his life fluid. He said that it felt exactly as though she was sucking his blood. When she finally stood up, he was too exhausted to move; but she, on the contrary, was now glowing ' with a tigerish vitality that was almost demonic.

' "I then remembered what my mother had said of my Aunt Kristin—that she could drain everyone in the room of vitality while she sat there, apparently absorbed in her knitting. I had taken this to be a figure of speech, but now I wondered if it could have any factual foundation.

' "According to the patient, his vampire often visited him in dreams, and drained his life fluid. I therefore installed him in my house and began a series of tests. Every night before he slept, I took readings of his life field and Kirlian photographs of his fingertips. For the first few nights, he showed no signs of depletion—the readings were always slightly higher in the morning, as you would expect after a good night's sleep, and the Kirlian photographs showed a healthy aura. But on the first night he dreamed of his 'vampire,' his life field became significantly lower, and his Kirlian photographs corresponded to those of a man suffering from some wasting disease…" '

Carlsen looked up. 'What do you think of that?'

She asked: 'What happened?'

'I don't know. That's as far as I've got. But as far as I can gather, his theory is that all people are energy vampires to some extent.'

Jelka was sitting in the chair by the window. She said: 'It sounds to me as if it *was* a straight-forward case of sexual hang-ups. All that stuff about lying in a coffin…'

He shook his head, staring past her. Suddenly, it seemed to him that he entirely understood the case, and that he had known about it for a long time. He said slowly: 'No…That's the interesting part of it. She *began* by worming her way into his affections.' Jelka looked at him with surprise; the phrase sounded uncharacteristic. 'Don't you see? She begins by flattering his ego, saying that she wants to belong to a man of genius—in other words, offering herself on *any* terms. Then she finds out his secret fantasies—his dreams of rape and violation. And she becomes an instrument of his fantasies until he's completely dependent on her. She begins drinking his energy, stealing his life fluid. And *then* comes the twist. When she's certain he's enslaved, she tells him that he must submit entirely —become her slave. In other words, she's completely turned the tables.'

'I've known a few women like that.' She stood up. 'Anyway, go on reading. I'm dying to find out what happens.'

A quarter of an hour later, she pushed the trolley into the bedroom. She said: 'You're looking better now.'

'Yes, I feel much better. I must have slept too heavily. Ah, that smells delicious. Toasted rolls…'

She picked up the book, which he had dropped onto the floor. 'Well, was he cured?'

He said through a mouthful of egg and bacon: 'Yes, but it's rather frustrating. He doesn't de-scribe exactly how he did it. All he says is he changed his sexual orientation.'

She sat reading as he ate. 'Yes, it *is* rather irritating. Can't you write to the author?' She looked at the title page. 'Oh, no—he must be dead. This came out in twenty thirty-two—nearly fifty years ago.'

The telescreen buzzed. She switched off the picture before answering, and used the close-up telephone. After a moment she said: 'It's Hans Fallada.'

'Oh fine, I'll talk to him.'

Fallada's face appeared. 'Good morning. Did you receive my manuscript?'

'Yes, thanks. I'm just reading it. What's the news?'

Fallada shrugged. 'None. I've just talked to Heseltine. Everything's quiet. And there's going to be a question in Parliament this afternoon about why the *Vega* and *Jupiter* have been ordered to return. So I'm ringing to warn you. If the press get on to you, claim you know nothing about it. Or say something noncommittal about the need to do these things slowly.'

'All right. Tell me, Doctor, have you actually read this book *Spirit Vampirism?*'

'By Count von Geijerstam? A long time ago.'

'I'm reading it now. He seems to believe many of the things you believe. Yet you dismiss him as a crank.'

'Yes. That book is fairly sound. But his later work is quite mad. He ended by believing that most mental illness is caused by ghosts and demons.'

'But this first case he describes—do you remember, the sculptor?—is fascinating. It would be interesting to find out how he cured him. After all, he must have worked out some kind of defence against vampirism.'

Fallada nodded thoughtfully. 'Yes, that is interesting, now you mention it. Geijerstam must be dead, of course. But he had many students and pupils. Perhaps the Swedish embassy could help.'

Jelka, who was standing by the door, said: 'How about Fred Armfeldt?' Carlsen said: 'Hold on a moment.' Jelka repeated: 'Fred Armfeldt, the man who got so drunk at your reception. He was the Swedish cultural attache.'

Carlsen snapped his fingers. 'Yes, of course. He might be able to help. A man who came to my reception in the Guildhall. I think he was from the Swedish embassy. I'll try to contact him.'

Fallada said: 'Good. Ring me back if you make any progress. I'll let you finish eating.' He had evidently noticed the breakfast tray on the bed.

Carlsen showered and shaved before he called the Swedish embassy. 'Could I speak to Fredrik Armfeldt, please?' He gave his name. A moment later, he found himself speaking to a clean-shaven young man with pink cheeks. Armfeldt said: 'How good to hear from you Commander! What can I do for you?'

Carlsen explained his problem briefly. Armfeldt shook his head. I have never heard of this Geijerstam. He's a doctor, you say?'

'A psychiatrist. He wrote a book called *Spirit Vampirism.*'

'Ah, in that case he would probably be in the Swedish writers' directory. I have that here in the office. One moment, please.' He reappeared a moment later with a large volume. He searched through it, murmuring: 'Froding, Garborg…ah, Geijerstam, Gustav. Is that the man?'

'No. Ernst von.'

'Yes, here it is: Ernst von Geijerstam, psychologist and philosopher. Born Norrkoping, June 1987. Educated at the University of Lund and University of Vienna…What do you want to know?'

'When did he die?'

Armfeldt shook his head, then looked at the cover of the book. 'As far as I can see, he's still alive. He must be…ninety-three.'

'Restraining his excitement, Carlsen said: 'Does it give an address?'

'Yes. Heimskringla, Storavan, Norrland. That is an area of mountains and lakes.' Carlsen wrote down the address.

'There's no telescreen number there?'

'No. But if you like, I can try to find out—'

'No, don't bother. That's very useful.'

They exchanged some general remarks, agreed to meet for a drink, and said goodbye. Carlsen immediately rang Fallada. 'I've just discovered that Geijerstam's still alive.'

'Incredible! Where does he live?'

'A place call Storavan, in Norrland. I wonder if I should send him a cable? He may have heard my name with all this publicity.'

Fallada shook his head; he said slowly: 'No. I think I must try to contact him. In fact, I should have tried years ago. It was sheer laziness and stupidity on my part. After all, he was the first man to recognise the phenomenon of mental vampirism. Can you give me the full address?'

Carlsen spent the remainder of the morning sitting in the sun-lounge, reading. He had intended to read Fallada's book, but he found *Spirit Vampirism* so absorbing that he was halfway through it when Jelka fetched the children from play school at lunchtime. The telescreen rang continuously: mostly newsmen wanting comments on the recall of the spaceships. After speaking to three of them, Carlsen told Jelka to say he was out.

At two o'clock, after a salad lunch, he was playing with the children in the paddling pool when Jelka came to the door. 'Dr. Fallada on the screen again.'

He went indoors, his eyes adjusting with difficulty after the bright sunlight. Fallada was on the kitchen extension.

He said: 'What are you doing for the rest of the day?'

Carlsen said: 'Nothing but reading your book.' ,

'Can you come with me to Sweden?'

He smiled with excitement. 'I suppose so. Why?'

'Geijerstam's offered to see us. And we can be in ' Karlsborg by six-thirty if we catch a plane from London Airport at three forty-two.'

'Where's Karlsborg?'

'It's a small town at the northern end of the Gulf of Bothnia. Geijerstam's arranging for an air taxi to meet us there.'

'What shall I bring?'

'Just an overnight bag. And Geijerstam's book. I'd like to read it on the way there.'

Carlsen's helicab was late; he and Fallada barely had time to exchange more than a few words before they strapped themselves into their seats on the Russian Airlines jet bound for Moscow via Stockholm and Leningrad.

Carlsen had never lost a childlike sense of delight in air travel. Now, as he watched the green fields of southern England give way to the silver-grey mirror of the sea, he experienced a rising excitement, a feeling of setting out towards adventure.

Fallada asked: 'Have you been in northern Sweden?'

'Yes. I wrote my doctoral thesis on suicide in Sweden, and spent many weeks in the north. They are a gloomy and reserved people. But the scenery is beautiful.'

A hostess offered them drinks; both accepted a martini. It was early, but Carlsen felt in a holiday mood.

He asked: 'Did you actually speak to Geijerstam?'

'Indeed. For fifteen minutes. He's a charming old gentleman. When I told him about my experiments, he became very excited.'

'How much did you tell him about…the aliens?'

'Nothing. It was too risky over the telescreen. All I could say was that I was dealing with the strangest and most complex case I had ever encountered. And he immediately invited me to come and see him. He must be fairly rich, incidentally, because he offered to pay my fare. Of course, I explained that the institute will pay. Incidentally, we are also paying your expenses. You are here officially as my assistant.'

Carlsen chuckled. 'I'll try to give satisfaction.'

They changed pianes in Stockholm, moving into a smaller plane from Swedish Airlines. Fallada remained absorbed in his book; Carlsen stared down and watched the green countryside change to pine-covered hills, then to the black tundra veined with rifts of snow. The April sun now looked pale, as if its light were filtered through ice. They were served a snack of salted biscuits and raw fish with vodka; Fallada ate abstractedly, his eyes on the book. Carlsen observed the speed at which he read and the total absorption; in the two and a half hours since they left London, he had read more than three quarters of Geijerstam's book.

The plane nosed down through misty cloud, over islands that were partly covered with snow. The airport at Karlsborg seemed absurdly small: little more than a control building and a tiny airfield surrounded by log houses. As they stepped out of the plane, Carlsen was surprised by the sharp chill in the air. The taximan who met them was not a Scandinavian type; he had black hair and a round face that reminded Carlsen of an Eskimo. He carried their bags to a six-seater helicopter in a field beside the airport; a few minutes later, they were flying low over snow-covered farmland, then over water again. Carlsen discovered that the pilot spoke a little Norwegian; he was a Lapp from the northern province. When Carlsen asked how big Storavan was, the pilot looked surprised, then said: 'About ten kilometres.'

"That is a large town.'

'It is not a town. It is a lake.'

He said no more. The scenery changed to mountains covered with forest; Carlsen caught occasional glimpses of reindeer.

Fallada read on steadily. Finally, he closed the book. 'Interesting, but definitely mad.'

'You mean insane?'

'Oh, no. Not exactly. But he believes that vampires are evil spirits.'

Carlsen smiled. 'Aren't they?'

'You saw the moray attack the octopus. Was that an evil spirit?'

'But if these aliens can live outside the body, doesn't that make them spirits?'

'Not in *his* sense. He is talking about ghosts and demons.'

Carlsen looked down at the forests that were a mere hundred feet below the aircraft. In this country it was easy to believe in ghosts and demons. There were small, dark-tinted lakes, in which the sky's reflection looked like blue stained glass. Half a mile away, on the granite hillside, a waterfall threw up a cloud of white mist; Carlsen could hear its thunder over the sound of the engine. In the west, the sky was turning from gold to red. There was something dreamlike and unearthly about the landscape.

A quarter of an hour later, the pilot pointed ahead. 'Heimskringla.'

They could see a lake, winding between mountains as far as the eye could see; a few miles to the south, another immense lake gleamed between the trees. Below and to the right, there was a small town; for a moment Carlsen assumed this was Heimskringla, then realised they were heading past it. He asked: *'Var ar Heimskringla?'* The man pointed. *'Där'* Then he saw the island in the lake, and the roof showing among the trees. As they skimmed low above the trees, they could see the front of the house, grey and turreted like a castle. Its rear overlooked the lake; in front, there were lawns and winding paths among the trees. In an open, grassy space on the edge of the lake there was a small chapel of dark timber.

The helicopter touched down lightly on the gravel in front of the house. As the rotor blades stopped moving, they saw a man coming towards them from the front door, followed by three girls. Fallada said: 'Ah, what a delightful reception committee.'

The man who advanced to meet them was tall and thin, and he walked with a vigorous, purposeful stride. Fallada said: 'Surely this can't be the Count? He is too young.'

As they stepped onto the gravel, the wind blew cold on their faces; Carlsen thought it smelt of snow. The man held out his hand. 'How good to see you. I am Ernst von Geijerstam. It is kind of you to come so far to see an old man.' Carlsen wondered if he was joking. Although the moustache was grey, and the thin, handsome face was lined, he looked scarcely more than sixty. The youthful impression was reinforced by the immaculate dress: black coat, pin-striped trousers, a white bow tie. His English was perfect and without accent.

Carlsen and Fallada introduced themselves. Geijerstam turned: 'Allow me to introduce three of my students: Selma Bengtsson, Annaleise Freytag, Louise Curel.'

Miss Bengtsson, a tall blonde, held Carlsen's hand a moment longer than necessary. Accustomed to the gleam of recognition in the eyes of strangers, he knew what she was going to say next. 'I have seen you on television. Are you not the captain of—'

'The *Hermes.* Yes.'

Geijerstam said: 'And you are here as Dr. Fallada's assistant.' It was a statement, but there was no irony in it.

Fallada said blandly: *'That* is what I shall say when I claim his expenses.'

'Ah, I see.' The Count turned and spoke to the taximan in Lettish; the man saluted and climbed into the helicopter. 'I have told him to return at midday tomorrow—unless, of course, you decide to stay longer…Would you care to see the lake before we go indoors?' The helicopter roared overhead, whipping the girls' dresses tight against their legs.

A liveried manservant took the bags. Carlsen said: 'You live in a beautiful spot.'

'Beautiful, but too cold for an old man with thin blood. Would you come this way?' He led them down a moss-grown path towards the water, which reflected the reddening sunlight.

As Fallada walked ahead with Geijerstam, Carlsen said to the blonde girl: 'The Count is a great deal younger than I expected.'

She'said: 'Of course. We keep him young.'

He looked at her in astonishment, and all three girls laughed.

They stood on the pebbled foreshore, looking across at the forest of firs and pine. The sunlight in the treetops made them look as though they were on fire. Overhead, the deepening sky was pure blue.

Geijerstam pointed. 'The chapel is older than the house. In the time of Gustavus Vasa, there was a monastery on this island. The house was built on its site about 1590.'

Fallada asked him: 'Why do you live so far north?'

'In Norrköping, they have a saying: that in Norrland, oaks, nobelmen and crayfish cease. So when I was a child, I always wanted to live here. But I found this house nearly forty years ago, when I came here to investigate the story of Count Magnus. He is buried in a mausoleum behind the chapel.'

Carlsen said: 'Wasn't he a lover of Queen Christina?'

'That was his uncle. The nephew inherited the title.' They walked along the beach, the stones crunching underfoot. 'When I came here, the house had been empty for half a century. People said it was because it was too big to keep up. But the real reason was that the people of Avaviken were still afraid of the Count. He had a reputation as a vampire.'

'Had he died recently?'

'No. He died at the battle of Poltava, in 1709. His body was brought back here. His coffin is still in the mausoleum.'

'What happened to the body?'

'In 1790, the owner of the house drove a stake through the heart and burnt it to ashes. They say that it was in an excellent state of preservation.' They were within a hundred yards of the chapel. 'Would you care to look in the mausoleum?'

The French girl, Louise, said: 'I'm cold.'

'Ah, in that case, we can look in the morning.' They crossed the lawn, passing a large ornamental pond; a skin of ice glittered on its surface. 'The monks used to keep their trout in here.'

Carlsen said: 'Do you think Count Magnus *was* a vampire—in your sense?'

The Count smiled. 'Surely there is only one sense?' He led them up the worn stone steps, into the hall. 'But the answer to your question is yes. And now, would you prefer to see your rooms? Or would you prefer a drink first?'

Fallada said decisively: 'A drink.'

'Good. Then come into the library.'

Through the far window of the library, they could see the sun dipping over the mountains. A log fire burned in the enormous grate; the firelight was reflected on copper fire-irons and on the polished leather binding of books. The German girl, Annaleise, wheeled the drink trolley onto the rug. With her plump figure and rosy cheeks, she made Carlsen think of a waitress in a beer garden. She poured Swedish schnaps into the glasses.

Geijerstam said: 'I drink to you, gentlemen. It is a great honour to have two such distinguished guests.'

The girls also drank. Carlsen said: 'If I'm not being too inquisitive, may I ask what your attractive pupils study?'

The Count smiled. 'Why not ask them?'

Louise Curel, a slender, dark-eyed girl, said: 'We learn to heal the sick.'

Carlsen raised his glass. 'I'm sure you'll make charming nurses.'

The girl shook her head. 'No, we don't study to be nurses.'

'Doctors?'

'That is closer to it.'

The Count said: 'Do you feel tired?'

Surprised by the change of subject, Carlsen said: 'Not at all.'

'Not even slightly tired by your journey?'

'Oh, just a little.'

Geijerstam smiled at the girls. 'Would you like to demonstrate?'

They looked at Carlsen and nodded.

'You see,' Geijerstam said, 'this is perhaps the quickest way to answer your question and to introduce you to my work. Would you mind standing up, please?'

Carlsen stood on the rug. Selma Bengtsson began to unzip his jacket. Geijerstam said: 'Close your eyes for a moment, and observe your sensations—particularly your sense of fatigue.'

Carlsen closed his eyes; he could see the dancing flames through the eyelids. He observed a sense of muscular fatigue, combined with a feeling of relaxation.

'They are going to place their hands on you and give you energy. Relax and allow yourself to absorb it. You will not feel anything.'

Louise Curel said: 'Would you mind removing your tie and opening your shirt?'

When the shirt was unbuttoned, they pulled it back so his shoulders were bare. The Swedish girl said: 'Close your eyes.'

He stood there, swaying slightly, and felt them place their fingertips against his skin. He could feel Louise's breath against his face. It was an exciting, slightly erotic sensation.

They stood there for perhaps five minutes. He experienced a sensation of bubbling delight, as if he wanted to laugh. The Count said: 'It could be done even more quickly if they used their lips. This is the reason that kissing gives pleasure, incidentally. It is an exchange of male and female energy. How do you feel?'

'Very pleasant.'

'Good. I think that should be enough.'

The girls helped to rebutton the shirt and replace the tie. Fallada said: 'How *do* you feel?'

As Carlsen hesitated, Geijerstam said: 'He will not know for at least five minutes.' He asked Miss Bengtsson: 'How was it?'

'I think he was more tired than he realised.'

Carlsen asked: 'Why do you say that?'

'You took more energy than I expected.' She looked at the others, who nodded.

He asked: 'So you feel tired?'

'A little. But don't forget that there are three of us, so we don't give much. And we take energy from you.'

'You *take it?*'

'Yes. We take some of your male energy, and give you our female energy in return.' She turned to the Count. 'You can explain it better.'

Geijerstam was refilling the glasses. He said: 'You could call it benevolent vampirism. You see, when you're tired, it doesn't necessarily mean you have no energy. You may have enormous vital reserves, but there is no stimulus to make them appear. When the girls give you female energy, it releases your vital reserves, exactly like a sexual stimulus. For a moment you feel just as tired as before—perhaps more so. Then your vital energies begin to flow, and you feel much better.'

Fallada said: 'A kind of instantaneous cross-fertilisation?'

'Precisely.' He asked Carlsen: 'How do you feel now?'

'Marvellous, thank you.' It was a pleasant, glowing sensation, and he was inclined to wonder how far it was due to the schnaps and the magical beauty of the sunset on the lake.

'Close your eyes for a moment. Do you still notice any tiredness?'

'None whatever.'

Geijerstam said to Fallada: 'If we took his lambda reading, you would find it had increased.'

Fallada said: 'I'd like to do full tests.'

'Of course. Nothing could be easier. I have already done them, and I will show you my results.'

'Did you ever publish them?'

'I wrote an article for it about ten years ago in the *Journal of Humanistic Psychology,* but Professor Schacht of Göttingen attacked it so bitterly that I decided to wait until people are ready to listen.'

Carlsen asked: 'How did you make the discovery?'

I first came to suspect it when I was a student, more than seventy years ago. My professor was Heinz Gudermann, who was married to an exceptionally lovely young girl. He had enormous vitality, and he often used to say he owed it to his wife. And then I read a paper that pointed out that many men have retained their vitality into old age when they were married to young women: I remember it mentioned the great cellist Casals, the guitarist Segovia and the philosopher Bertrand Russell. But the author of the paper insisted that this was purely psychological, and even then I was inclined to doubt this. Fifteen years later, when I discovered the principle of vampirism, I began to suspect that it was due to a transfer of sexual energy. I persuaded a young couple to take lambda readings before they went to bed on their honeymoon night, and then again the next day. This showed a definite increase in the energy of the life field. Next, I persuaded another couple to take readings before and after lovemaking. And the first thing I observed was that the renewal curve was similar to the curve of a hungry man eating food. Only it was much steeper. This seemed to confirm my point: that both lovers *had* eaten a kind of food— vital energy. And yet they were *both* renewed. How could this be, unless there were two kinds of energy, male and female? You see, lovemaking is a symbiotic relation, like a bee taking honey from a flower and fertilising the flower. But in those days I was more interested in the negative principles of vampirism—people like Gilles de Rais and Count Magnus. When I was in my seventies, I had a serious illness, and my nurse was a pretty peasant girl. I noticed that when she had rested her hands on me, I felt much better, but she was tired. Then it struck me that if several girls did it at the same time, it would be easier for them all. It worked. And now every day I take a little energy from my three assistants, and they take a little of mine. They keep me young.'

Fallada was shaking his head incredulously. That's really astonishing. Could it be used in general medical practice?'

'It *has* been used. You have an example here, in this house—Gustav, the footman who carried in your bags. He is from Lycksele, a small town not far from here. He was once an excellent carpenter; then a series of bereavements made him depressed and suicidal. After his third suicide attempt, he was confined in a mental home and became completely schizophrenic. Now, schizophrenia is a kind of vicious circle. The energies are low, so everything looks meaningless and futile. And because everything seems futile, you become even more depressed and exhausted.

Now, at that time I had seven young girls here for the whole summer. We brought Gustav back here—to remove him from the old environment—and began intensive treatment. This was basically the thing the Commander has just experienced. In the first few hours, the girls became very tired, but he improved noticeably. After a few sessions, he stopped taking so much energy from them. He began to manufacture his own again. Within a week he was a different man. He begged me to remain here, so I employed him, and he married the gardener's daughter. He is now perfectly normal.'

Fallada said slowly: 'If all that is true, it is one of the most amazing things I've ever heard. Can *anyone* give this energy?'

'Yes. It takes a little practice—it is easier for women than for men. But I believe anyone can do it.'

Carlsen said: 'And what if the patient becomes dependent on these energy transfusions, like a drug?'

The Count shook his head. 'That happens only in rare cases, when the patient has a criminal temperament.'

Fallada looked at him with deep interest. 'Criminal?'

'Yes. It is basically a kind of…spoiltness. Do you understand the word? Healthy people enjoy being independent. They don't like feeling reliant on others. Of course, when we are very tired or ill, we need help—as I did. But some people are more self-pitying than others. They need much more help before they are willing to make the effort to help themselves. And there are so many people who are so full of resentment and self-pity that they never reach this point. The more help they get, the more they want.'

'And you would describe that as the criminal temperament?'

'Yes. Because the real criminal has the same attitude. Perhaps he becomes a criminal because he is poor and frustrated…I am thinking of Jarlsberg, the Uppsala rapist, at whose trial I gave evidence. He once told me that when he choked and raped a girl, he was taking something that she *owed* to him. After a while, such a man begins to acquire a taste for this mixture of resentment and violence. He may commit his first rape because he is tormented by sexual frustration. But after his tenth, he no longer wants sex, but only *rape,* the sense of violating another human being. If you like, he enjoys the sense of breaking the law, of doing wrong. Burglars sometimes commit wanton destruction for the same reason.'

Carlsen said: 'You believe the vampire is the criminal type?'

'Indeed. That is the ultimate form of rape.'

A clock in the hall struck the hour. Carlsen glanced at his watch; it was seven. The girls all stood up. Selma Bengtsson said: I hope you will excuse us. We must get ready for dinner.'

'Of course, my dear.' The Count made a brief formal bow from the waist. When the door had closed behind the girls, he said: 'Please be seated.' He remained standing until they had sat down. 'In fact, I suggested to the young ladies that they might leave us alone half an hour before dinner.' He smiled at them. 'Unless I am mistaken, you believe that the aliens from the *Stranger* are vampires?'

Both stared at him with astonishment. Fallada said: 'How the devil did you know that?'

'A simple inference. It can hardly be coincidence that you bring the famous Commander Carlsen as your research assistant. We have all followed his adventures with fascination. And you tell me you want to ask my opinion about vampires. It would be strange if there was no logical connection between these circumstances.'

Fallada laughed. 'God, for a moment you had me worried.'

Geijerstam said: 'But these aliens are dead, are they not?'

'No. We don't think so.' He took out his cigar case. 'Olof, would you like to explain?' It was the first time he had used Carlsen's Christian name; it established what they had both come to feel: that they were friends as well as allies and colleagues.

Without unnecessary detail, Carlsen described his visit to the Space Research building, the death of Seth Adams, and his own encounter with the girl. At first, Geijerstam listened quietly, his hands folded in his lap. He began to nod with increasing excitement. Finally, unable to contain himself, he began to pace up and down the room, shaking his head. 'Yes, yes! That is what I have always believed. I knew it was possible.'

Carlsen was glad of the interruption; he was again experiencing the strange inner reluctance to describe what had happened when he was alone with the girl.

Fallada asked Geijerstam: 'Have you ever encountered *this* kind of vampirism before?'

'Never as strong as this. Yet it was obvious that it must exist somewhere—I say so in my book. In fact, I believe it *has* existed on the earth in the past. The legend of the vampire is not just a fairy story. But please go on. What happened to the girl?'

'She somehow walked out of the building, in spite of all the guards and the electronic alarm systems. An hour later, the other two aliens were found to be dead.'

'And the girl?'

'She was found dead ten hours later—raped and strangled.'

Geijerstam said incredulously: 'Dead?'

'Yes.'

'No! That is impossible!'

Fallada glanced at Carlsen. 'Why?'

Geijerstam threw up his hands, searching for words. 'Because—how can I say it?—because vampires can take care of themselves. That sounds absurd, perhaps...but again and again in my career as a criminologist I have noticed the same thing. People who get murdered are of a definite type. And vampires do *not* belong to that type. You must have noticed this yourself?'

'In that case, how do you explain her death?'

'You are quite sure that it *was* her body?'

'Absolutely.'

Geijerstam was silent for several moments. Then he said: 'There are two possible explanations. It is possible that this was a kind of accident.'

'What kind?'

'You could call it a mistake. Sometimes, a vampire is so greedy for energy that the life force flows the wrong way —back to the victim instead of from him. You could compare it to a glutton swallowing food the wrong way.'

'And the other possibility?'

'Ah, that is one I have never encountered. The Greeks and the Armenians insist that the vampire can abandon its body voluntarily, to create an impression of death.'

'Do you think that possible?'

'I…I believe that a vampire could exist for a *short* time outside a living body.'

'Why only for a short time?'

'Briefly—because it would require immense energy and concentration to maintain individuality outside a living body. Among occultists, there is a technique known as astral projection, which is in many ways similar.'

Fallada leaned forward. 'Do you think a vampire could take over someone else's body?'

Geijerstam frowned, staring at the carpet. He said finally: 'It *may* be possible. We know that people can be possessed by evil spirits—I have actually dealt with three such cases. And of course, possession would be the logical conclusion of vampirism, which *is* a desire to possess and absorb. Yet I have never heard of such a case.'

Carlsen said with sudden excitement: 'These cases of possession by evil spirits—did they destroy the persons they possessed?'

'In one case, he became permanently insane. The other two were cured by exorcism.'

Carlsen turned to Fallada. 'Could that be the explanation of what happened to Clapperton? If one of these things possessed him without actually killing him, he'd be aware of what was taking place, even if he couldn't resist it. They'd *have* to destroy him finally. He'd know too much about them.'

The Count asked: 'Who is this man?'

Fallada summarised the story of the girl found on the railway line, of Clapperton's disappearance and suicide. Geijerstam listened carefully without interrupting. He said: I would guess that the Commander is right. This man Clapperton was possessed by one of these creatures. He may have committed suicide to escape.'

Fallada said: 'Or was driven to it.'

None of them spoke for a moment, staring into the collapsing logs of the fire. Geijerstam said: 'Well, I will do what I can to help you. I can tell you all I know of vampires. But I am not sure whether this would be of any use in this case.'

Fallada said: 'The more we know of these things, the better. We're working against time. Suppose the other aliens on the *Stranger* managed to get back to earth?'

Geijerstam shook his head. 'That is impossible.'

'Why?'

'Because it is a characteristic of vampires that they *must* be invited. They cannot take the initiative.'

Fallada asked with a note of incredulity: 'But why?'

'I am not certain. But it seems to be so.'

He was interrupted by the sound of a gong from the hall. None of them moved. When the noise ceased, they heard the voices of the girls on the stairs. Carlsen said: 'But it's possible they may be invited. The Prime Minister of England wants to get the *Stranger* back to earth. He thinks it may be of historical value.'

'Does he not know what you have told me?'

'Yes. But he's pig-headed. He probably thinks that if we don't do it, the Russians or the Arabs might step in and take all the credit.'

'You must stop him.'

'He's given us a few months. In that time, we have to try to locate the other three aliens. Any idea where we might begin?'

Geijerstam thought for several moments, his eyes half closed. He sighed and shook his head.

'Offhand, no. Fallada and Carlsen stared at one another gloomily. 'But let us talk about it. There *must* be a way. I will do what I can. Now let us go and eat.'

The dining room was smaller than the library, but the great oak table could easily have seated forty guests. Two of its panelled walls were covered with tapestries, each about twelve feet square. A crystal chandelier, suspended from the central beam of the ceiling, was reflected in two immense mirrors, one above the fireplace and one in the opposite wall.

The girls were already seated. The manservant was pouring Moselle into the tall, green-tinted glasses.

Geijerstam pointed to the central tapestry. 'That is our famous vampire, Count Magnus de la Gardie.'

The portrait was of a powerfully built man in military dress, with a metal breastplate. The eyes stared down with the expression of a man used to command. Under the heavy moustache, the thin lips were tightly closed.

Miss Bengtsson said: 'Your English ghost writer M. R. James has a story about Magnus. We have it here in Swedish.'

'Is it accurate?'

Geijerstam said: 'Remarkably accurate. James came to this house—we have his signature in the visitor's book.' Carlsen asked: 'What did Magnus do?'

'Basically, he was a sadist. There was a peasants' revolt in Vastergotland in 1690, and the king appointed Magnus to deal with it. Magnus repressed it so bloodily that even the courtiers were shocked. They say he executed more than four thousand people—half the population of the southern province. The king—Charles the Eleventh— was angry because it meant that he lost taxes. So Magnus was banished from court in disgrace. According to the legend, it was then that' he decided to make the Black Pilgrimage to Chorazin. Chorazin was a village in Hungary where the inhabitants were all supposed to be in league with the devil. We have a manuscript in Magnus's handwriting, and it actually says: "He who wishes to drink the blood of his enemies and obtain faithful servants should voyage to the town of Chorazin and pay homage to the Prince of the Air." '

Fallada said: 'That probably explains the vampire legend—the phrase about drinking the blood of his enemies.'

'That is impossible. To begin with, the manuscript is in Latin, and it was found among various alchemical works in the North Tower. I doubt whether anyone read it for half a century after his death. Secondly, he is referred to in a manuscript in the Royal Library as a vampire.'

'Did he make the Black Pilgrimage?'

'We do not know, but it is almost certain.'

Fallada said: 'And you think that turned him into a vampire?'

'Ah, that is a difficult question. Magnus was a sadist already, and he was in a position of power. I believe that such men easily develop into vampires—energy vampires. They derive pleasure from causing terror and drinking the vitality of their victims. So he was probably a kind of vampire before he made the Black Pilgrimage. But when he decided to make the Black Pilgrimage, he made a *deliberate* choice of evil. From then on, it was no longer a matter of wicked impulses, but of conscious, deliberately planned cruelty.'

'But what did he *do?*'

'Tortured peasants, burned down houses. They say he had two poachers skinned alive.'

'Which makes it sound as if he was a sadistic psychopath rather than a vampire.'

'I agree. It was after his death that he became known as a vampire. I have an eighteenth-century account book, written by a steward, that says "The labourers insist on being home before dark, since Count Magnus was seen in the churchyard." They say he left his mausoleum on nights of the full moon.'

'And is there any evidence of vampirism after his death?'

'Some. The records of the church in Stensel mention the burial of a poacher who was found on the island with his face eaten away. His family paid for three masses to "rescue his soul from the evil one." Then there was the wife of a coach maker in Storavan who was burnt as a witch; she claimed that Count Magnus was her lover and had taught her to drink the blood of children.'

They had finished the first course; Fallada, who had been sitting with his back to the tapestry, now stood up to look at it more closely. After staring up at it for several minutes, he said: 'To be honest, I find it difficult to take the idea seriously. I accept what you say about energy vampires, because my own experiments lead me to the same conclusion. But all this is legend, and I find it hard to take it seriously.'

Geijerstam said: 'You should not underestimate legends.'

'In other words, there's no smoke without fire?'

'I think so. How do you explain the great vampire epidemic that swept across Europe at the beginning of the eighteenth century? Ten years earlier, vampires were almost unknown. And then, quite suddenly, you begin to get stories of creatures who come back from the dead and drink human blood. In 1730, there was a kind of plague of vampirism from Greece to the Baltic Sea——hundreds of reports. The first book on vampirism was not written until ten years later, so you cannot lay the blame on imaginative writers.'

'But it could have been a kind of collective hysteria.'

'Indeed, it could. But what *started* the hysteria?'

The arrival of the main course interrupted the conversation. There were small circular steaks of elk and reindeer, with fennel sauce and sour cream. They drank a heavy red Bulgarian wine, served cold. For the remainder of the meal, the conversation remained general. The girls were evidently bored with the talk of vampires; they wanted Carlsen to describe the finding of the derelict.

Geijerstam interrupted only once; it was when Carlsen was speaking of the glass column, with its squidlike creatures. 'Do you have any theory about what they were?'

'None. Unless they were some kind of food.'

Miss Freytag said: 'I *hate* octopuses.' She said it with such intensity that they all looked at her.

Fallada said: 'Have you ever encountered one?'

Her face coloured. 'No.' Carlsen wondered why Geijerstam was smiling.

They drank coffee in the library. The heat of the fire made Carlsen yawn. The Count said: 'Would you like to go to your room now?'

Carlsen shook his head, smiling with embarrassment. 'No. Your excellent food has made me sleepy. But I want to hear more about Count Magnus.'

'Would you care to see his laboratory?'

Selma Bengtsson said: 'At this time of night?'

Geijerstam said mildly: 'My dear, this is the time when the alchemists did most of their work.'

Carlsen said: 'Yes, I'd like to see it.'

'In that case, you will need your overcoat. It is cold up there.' He turned to the girls. 'Would anyone else care to come?'

All three shook their heads. Selma Bengtsson said: 'I can't even stand the place by daylight'

Fallada said: 'Do you think the Count's activities might interest me?'

'I am sure of it.'

Geijerstam opened a drawer and took out a large key. We have to go outside the house. There used to be an entrance on the other side of the hall, but the previous owner had it bricked up.'

He led them out of the front door. It was a clear moonlit night; the moon made a silver path along the water. Carlsen felt revived by the cold air. Geijerstam led them along the gravel path, towards the northern wing.

Fallada asked: 'Why did he brick it up? Was he afraid of ghosts?'

'Not of ghosts, I think—although I never knew him. The house had been empty for fifty years before I moved in.' He inserted the key in the lock of the massive door, then turned the handle. Carlsen expected a creak of rusty hinges, but it opened silently. The air inside smelt musty and was unexpectedly cold. Carlsen knotted his scarf around his throat and turned up the overcoat collar. On their left, the door that should have led into the house had been bolted to its frame with angle irons.

Fallada said: 'Was this built at the same time as the rest of the house?'

'Yes. Why do you ask?'

'I notice that the stairs are unworn.'

'I have often wondered about that. I think that perhaps no one uses them.'

As in the main part of the house, the walls were panelled with pinewood. Geijerstam led the way up three flights of stairs, halting on each landing to point out the pictures. 'These are by Gonzales Coques, the Spanish painter. As a young man, Count Magnus was a diplomatic envoy in Antwerp, where Coques worked for the Governor of the Netherlands. He commissioned these portraits of great alchemists. This is Albertus Magnus. This is Cornelius Agrippa. And this is Basil Valentinus, who was a Benedictine monk as well as an alchemist. Do you notice anything about these portraits?'

Carlsen stared hard but finally shook his head. 'The painter has given each of them a noble bearing.'

Fallada nodded. 'They look like saints.'

'Magnus was in his twenties when these were painted. I think they reveal that he possessed high ideals. And yet a mere ten years later, he was slaughtering the peasants of Vastergotland and preparing to sell his soul to the devil.'

'Why?'

The Count shrugged. 'I think I know why, but it would take'a long time to explain.' He led the way up the final flight. From the stained-glass window in the alcove, they could see the expanse of moonlit water.

The door that faced them on the top landing was covered with heavy iron bands and metal studs. Its right edge showed signs of having been forced; the wood was splintered, and there were the marks of hatchets.

Geijerstam said: 'I imagine this room was sealed after Magnus's death, and the key was probably thrown away. Someone of a later generation broke it open.' He pushed the door, and it swung open.

The room inside was bigger than they had expected. It had a strange and disagreeable odour, in which Carlsen seemed to be able to detect incense. There was another element that he found harder to place: a sickly smell. Suddenly, it came to him: the smell of a mortuary when a corpse is being dissected.

Geijerstam pressed the light switch, but nothing happened.

'It's strange. Electric light bulbs never last very long in this room.'

Carlsen said: 'You think the Count dislikes them?'

'Or there is something wrong with the wiring.' Geijerstam struck a match and lit two oil lamps on the bench. They could now see that the main furniture of the room was a furnace of brick, and a tentlike erection. When Carlsen touched this he found it to be made of black silk, the heaviest he had ever seen.

Geijerstam said: 'That is a kind of darkroom. Certain alchemical operations have to be performed in total darkness.'

On the shelves there were heavy glass bottles and containers of various shapes and sizes. There was a small stuffed alligator and a creature with a bird's head, a cat's body and the tail of a lizard. Carlsen peered at this closely, but was unable to see the joins. In the corner stood a tall, clumsy metal apparatus with many pipes leading away from it, and a heavy clay lid.

Geijerstam took down a leather-bound volume whose hinges were worn through, and opened it on the bench. 'This is the Count's alchemical diary. He seems to have had the makings of a true scientist. All these early experiments are attempts to make a liquid called Alkahest, which is supposed to reduce all matter to its primitive state. That was the first step in alchemy. When he'd obtained his primitive matter, his next task was to seal it in a vessel and put it in the athanor—that is, the furnace in the corner there. Magnus spent almost a year trying to make Alkahest from human blood and urine.' He turned over the pages. The handwriting was angular, spiky and untidy, but the drawings in the text—of chemical apparatus and various plants—showed enormous care and precision.

Geijerstam closed the book. 'On January 10, 1683, he became convinced that he had finally made Alkahest from baby's urine and cream of tartar. This next volume begins two months later, because he needed spring dew for his primal matter. He also spent two hundred gold florins on cobra's venom from Egypt.'

Fallada said with disgust: 'No wonder he went crazy.'

'Oh, no. He has never sounded more sane. He claims that he had saved the life of his bailiff's wife in childbirth, and cured his shepherd of gout, with a mixture of Alkahest and oil of sulphur. He says: "My shepherd climbed to the top of the tree beyond the fish pond." But now, look at this'—he turned to the end of the second folio—'what do you notice?'

Carlsen shook his head. 'Nothing—except that the writing gets worse.'

'Precisely. He is in despair. A handwriting expert once told me that it is the writing of a man on the point of suicide. Look: *"Or n'est il fleur, homme, femme, beauti, que la mort & sa fin ne le chace."* There is no flower, man, woman, beauty, that death does not chase to his end. He is obsessed by death.'

Fallada asked: 'Why does he write in French?'

'He was French. The Swedish court was full of Frenchmen in the seventeenth century. But now look'—he took down another folio, this one bound in black leather— 'he writes the date in code, but I have worked out the code: May 1691, the month after his expulsion from the court. "He who wishes to drink the blood of his enemies and obtain faithful servants should voyage to the town of Chorazin and there do homage to the Prince of the Air." And then the next entry is in November of 1691—six months later. And look at the handwriting.' -

Carlsen said: 'Surely it isn't the same person?' The writing had taken on an altogether different character: neater, smaller, yet more purposeful.

'But it is. We have other documents signed by him in the same handwriting: Magnus of Skåne— that is where he was born. But the handwriting changes.' He turned several pages: Carlsen recognised the headlong, untidy scrawl of the earlier volumes. 'My handwriting expert said it was a clear case of dual personality. He still performs experiments in alchemy—but now he disguises many of the ingredients in code. But this is what I wanted to show you…' He turned to the end of the volume. In the middle of an empty page, there was a drawing of an octopus. Carlsen and Fallada bent over to look more closely. This drawing lacked the anatomical precision of earlier sketches of plants. The lines were blurred.

Fallada said: 'This is inexact. Look, he shows only one row of suckers here. And he gives it a kind of face—more like a human face.' He looked up at Carlsen. 'Did these creatures in the *Stranger* look anything like that?'

Carlsen shook his head. 'No. They certainly had no faces.'

Geijerstam closed the book with a slam and replaced it on the shelf. 'Come. I have one more thing to show you.' He blew out the oil lamps, and led them back out onto the landing. Carlsen was relieved to be out of the room. The smell was beginning to make him feel sick. When they stepped out of the front door, he breathed in the cold night air deeply.

Geijerstam turned to the left and led them along the path, then across the lawn by the fish pond. The moonlight made the grass look grey.

'Where are we going?'

'To the mausoleum.'

It was dark among the trees; then the path emerged suddenly at the door of the chapel. It was built entirely of timbers and shaped like an inverted V. At close quarters, it was larger than when seen from the air.

Geijerstam turned the heavy metal ring, and the door opened outwards. He switched on the light. The inside was unexpectedly attractive. The ceiling was painted with cherubs and angels, and there were three circular brass chandeliers. The organ was small and painted in red, yellow and blue, with silver pipes. The pulpit resembled the gingerbread house of fairy stories, with a painted roof and a number of dolls that were obviously intended to represent saints.

Geijerstam led them down the northern aisle, past the pulpit, to a wooden door with an arched top. It was unlocked, and the room beyond it smelt of cold stone.

Geijerstam opened a wooden chest and took out an electric lead, with a light bulb at one end. He plugged this into a socket outside the door. 'There is no electric light in the mausoleum. When the chapel was electrified—at the beginning of this century—the workmen refused to go in.'

The bulb illuminated an octagonal room with a domed ceiling. There were a number of stone tombs and sarcophagi around the walls. In the centre of the room were three copper sarcophagi. Two of them had crucifixes on the lids; the third had the effigy of a man in military regalia.

'That is the tomb of Count Magnus.' He pointed to the face of the effigy. 'This seems to be based on a death mask—notice the wound across the forehead. But look, this is the interesting part.' He held the bulb so they could see the scenes engraved on the side of the sarcophagus. Some were military. Another showed a city with church spires. But the end plaque, nearest the feet, showed a black octopus with a human face, dragging a man towards a hole in a rock. The man's face was not visible, but he was wearing armour.

Geijerstam said: 'No one has ever been able to understand this scene. Octopuses were almost unknown in Europe at that time.' They stood there, looking at it in silence. The cold in the mausoleum was intense. Carlsen thrust his hands deep into his coat pockets and hunched his head into his collar. This was not the bracing cold he had experienced outside; there was something suffocating about it.

Fallada said: 'Very strange.' His voice lacked expression. I can't say I like this place much.'

'Why?'

'It seems rather airless.'

Geijerstam looked curiously at Carlsen. 'How do you feel?'

Carlsen started to say, 'Fine,' from force of habit, then checked himself, sensing a motive behind the question. He said: 'Slightly sick.'

'Please describe it.'

'Describe feeling sick?'

'Please.'

'Well…I've got a sort of tingling in my fingertips, and your face is slightly blurred. No, everything is slightly blurred.'

Geijerstam smiled and turned to Fallada. 'And you?'

Fallada was obviously mystified. I feel perfectly well. Perhaps Carlsen drank too much wine.'

'No. That is not the reason. I am also experiencing what he described. It always happens in here, particularly at the time of the full moon.'

Fallada said, with only the faintest touch of sarcasm: 'More ghosts and bogies?'

Geijerstam shook his head. 'No. I believe the Count's spirit is at rest.'

'What, then?'

'Let us go outside. I am beginning to find this oppressive.' He wiped the sweat from his forehead. Carlsen was glad to follow him. As soon as he stepped over the threshold, the feeling of nausea vanished. In the electric light, the colours of the organ looked gay and festive. His eyes no longer seemed blurred.

Geijerstam sat down in the front pew. 'I believe that what we just experienced in there is *not* what is usually called a ghost. It is a purely physical effect, like feeling dizzy when you smell chloroform. However, it is not chemical, but electrical.'

Fallada said with astonishment: 'Electrical?'

'Oh, I don't mean that it can be measured with a lambda meter—although I wouldn't discount the possibility either. I mean that I believe it is a kind of recording—like a tape recording.'

'And what is the tape?'

'Some kind of field—like a magnetic field. It is due to the water that surrounds us.' He turned to Fallada. 'Even you felt it to some degree, although you are less sensitive than Commander Carlsen. It was the same in Magnus's laboratory. But there it is fainter, because it is above the lake.'

Fallada shook his head. 'Have you any proof of this?'

'Not scientific proof. But more than half the people who go into the mausoleum at the time of the full moon notice it. Some have even fainted.' He asked Carlsen: 'Did you notice that it stopped quite suddenly as we crossed the threshold? These fields always have sharply defined areas. I have even pinpointed where it stops—precisely seven inches beyond the door.'

Fallada said: 'There *must* be some way of measuring it—if it's an electrical field.'

I am sure there is, but I am a psychologist, not a physicist.' He stood up. 'Shall we go back to the house?'

Carlsen said: I still don't really understand…Why *should* there be an unpleasant atmosphere? What happened?'

The Count switched off the lights and closed the door carefully. 'I can tell you what happened in the laboratory. It is all there, in the records. Magnus practised black magic. And some of the things he did are too horrible to mention.'

They walked through the trees in silence. Fallada asked: 'And the church?'

'Precisely. The mausoleum. Why should there be an atmosphere in there, when Magnus was already *dead* when he was laid there?' Carlsen felt the hair on his neck standing. 'An unscientific question, perhaps, but worth asking.'

Fallada said: 'It could have been the fear of the people who went into the mausoleum.'

'Yes, indeed—*if* anyone went in there. But for more than a century after Magnus's death, it remained locked and double-bolted. This chapel ceased to be used because everyone was so afraid of disturbing his spirit.'

None of them spoke until they were back in the house. The library lights had been switched off, but the fire illuminated the room. Selma Bengtsson was sitting on the settee.

'The others have gone to bed. I waited up to find out what happened.'

Carlsen sat beside her. 'Nothing happened. But I felt something.'

Geijerstam said: I think we all deserve a little brandy. Yes?'

She asked Fallada: 'Did you feel anything?'

I…don't know. I agree that it is an oppressive place—'

The Count interrupted him. 'But you do not believe in vampires?'

'Not in *that* kind—the kind that come back to life after they've been buried.' He sniffed his brandy. 'Vampires are one thing. Ghosts are another.'

Geijerstam nodded. 'I see your point: As it happens, I also believe in ghosts. But I do not think we are now talking about a ghost.'

'Well, a man who rises from the dead…it's the same thing.'

Geijerstam said: 'Are you sure?' He sank into the armchair. Fallada waited. ''There is an interesting phrase in the Count's journal: "He who would drink the blood of his enemies *and obtain faithful servants…"* What servants?'

Carlsen said: 'Demons?'

'Possibly. But there is no mention of demons or devils in any of the records. All we know is that when the Count came back from his Black Pilgrimage, he was a changed man…and his handwriting had also changed. You saw it yourself. Now, I have encountered five cases of multiple personality—the Jekyll and Hyde syndrome. And in some of them, the handwriting changed as they changed personality. Yet it was always basically the same handwriting—it merely changed a few characteristics, becoming stronger or weaker. In this case, there is the handwriting of a completely different person.'

Carlsen leaned forward. 'In other words, Magnus was possessed by something?'

'I think the evidence points in that direction.' He smiled at Fallada. 'If, of course, you believe that a disembodied entity could invade someone else's body.'

Carlsen said: 'And then there's the octopus…'

None of them spoke for several minutes; the only sound in the room was the burning of the logs. Fallada said finally: 'I wish I could see where this was leading us.'

The clock in the hall struck the hour. Carlsen emptied his brandy glass. Geijerstam said: 'Perhaps we should all sleep on it. We have talked enough for one day. And I think Commander Carlsen is tired.'

Carlsen had suppressed a yawn, and the effort made his eyes water. Geijerstam said: 'Selma, would you show the Commander to his room? I shall stay here for a few more minutes, and perhaps have another small brandy. Will you join me, Doctor?'

Fallada said: 'Well, perhaps just a small one…'

Carlsen said good night and followed Selma Bengtsson upstairs. The heavy carpet was yielding under his feet. The heat of the fire had induced a pleasant drowsiness. She led him to a room on the second floor. The door stood open, and his pyjamas had been laid out on the bed. It was a warm and comfortable room; the panelling on the walls was a lighter colour than downstairs. As Carlsen sat on the bed, he felt the tiredness flowing through his body. From his bag, he took a framed photograph of his wife and children, and placed it on the bedside table; this had become a habit when he was travelling. Then he went to the bathroom and splashed cold water on his face. He was cleaning his teeth when there was a knock on the door. He called: 'Come in.' He came out of the bathroom drying his hands. It was Selma Bengtsson. He said: 'I thought it was Fallada.'

'Could I just say a few words to you before you go to sleep?'

'Of course.' He pulled on his dressing gown. 'You don't mind if I get into bed?'

She stood by the bed, looking down at him. 'I want to ask you something.' Her manner was matter-of-fact, with no touch of sexuality. She leaned forward and looked into his eyes. 'Did you know you are a vampire?'

'What?' He stared at her, trying to gauge her seriousness.

'Do you think I am joking?'

He shook his head. 'No, I don't think you're joking. But I think you're probably mistaken.'

She said, with a touch of impatience: 'Look, I have been in this house for nearly a year. I know what it means to give a little energy every day. And I can tell you one thing—you have been taking energy from me.'

'I don't disbelieve you. At the same time, I find it hard to accept.'

She sat down on the chair beside the bed. "The others felt it too. We talked about it when you went out. They were feeling so tired that they went to bed. I decided I had to talk to you.'

'Yes, but…you *gave* me energy earlier this evening.'

'Quite. And that should have been enough to last you the rest of the night. Yet within an hour— when you were sitting next to me at dinner—I felt you were taking energy.'

'I don't *feel* as if I've been taking energy. I feel, worn out. Are you sure you're not mistaken?'

She shrugged. 'There is an easy way to find out. Lie down and close your eyes.'

'Very well.' He sank back on to the pillow, still aware of the powerful desire to sink into sleep. He felt her undoing the top button of his pyjama coat, and a moment later, felt both her hands laid flat against the upper part of his chest. He stiffened, there was a momentary sensation as if walking under a spray of cold water. He lay with his eyes closed, listening to a rumbling that came from his stomach. The tension vanished, and he again felt himself floating down gently into sleep. This lasted for perhaps thirty seconds. Then he became aware that he was feeling less tired. A pleasant glow was flowing through his body. He said drowsily: 'You're giving energy to me.'

'Yes, I am giving it to you.'

So far he had been totally passive, as if he were a child being breast-fed. Now he observed another sensation, the transition, he was totally awake, aware of a curious and violent hunger. He heard her say: 'Now you are taking it.' Her voice was oddly strained. He opened his eyes and looked up at her. Her face looked pale. He said: 'Then take your hands away.'

As he said it, he knew she would not respond. He was aware of something inside him reaching out, holding her. He was also aware that her resistance was low. She had no desire to withdraw now. There was an element of fear in her response, and he could feel this flowing through her fingertips, a sensation he found himself comparing to the smell of petrol. He was also aware of a duality inside himself; part of him observed what was taking place without being involved; he even felt that he could have interfered and broken the spell. The other part was pure desire, moving on smoothly like a surfer on the waves.

He reached up and grasped her wrists, pulling them away. She sank forward onto him; he could feel the warmth of her body through the thin, silky material of the dress. He kicked back the bed-clothes and pulled her down beside him. She lay there with closed eyes, her lips slightly parted. It was an intolerable temptation to lean forward and press his mouth against hers; at the same time, he was aware that the door was unlocked, and that Fallada might stop by to say good night. He slipped out of bed and locked the door, then turned off the light. There was enough moonlight in the room to show him her outline on the bed. Even with his back to her, he was aware of her, and of his will holding her down in the bed. He sat on the edge of the bed and pulled her dress up above her waist. She turned on her side, allowing him access to the buttons down the back of the dress. Carlsen was usually clumsy with buttons; now he found himself undoing them with quiet economy of movement. He unclipped the brassiere with a single movement, then peeled it off, over her head, with the dress. She was wearing only black briefs; he drew them down over her feet. As he moved onto her, he caught a glimpse of Jelka's face looking out of the photograph; she seemed a stranger. He let the pyjama top fall to the floor, then bent his head to find the partly opened mouth. As his lips touched her, the sweetness made him dizzy. Energy flowed from her in a smooth surge, sending eddies of delight through his bloodstream like tiny whirlpools. As he moved between her thighs, she moaned. The glowing warmth that flowed from her was like a drink; it produced an effect not unlike alcohol, but more exquisite than any drink he had ever tasted. At the same time, he was aware that they were not alone in their lovemaking. There was a third: the woman from the derelict. She was across the sea, but also in the bed, giving herself to him. Her lips were also slightly parted, and she was drinking the energy that flowed through him. Selma Bengtsson was not aware of her; she was only aware of her total surrender. Carlsen thought suddenly: So *that's* what it's about?

The first violent craving subsided. He kept his mouth pressed tight against hers, afraid that her moans might be heard. The esctasy rose in her, and he was aware that it was all she could bear, close to pain. At the same time, he was aware of the desire of the other woman. She wanted him to go on. Her urgent need had also slackened, but she still wanted more. She was lying underneath him, her body convulsing; she was angry that Selma Bengtsson was satisfied. For a moment, there was sharp conflict; but he refused to obey. She was urging him to take a little more. The girl was lying beside him, sinking into a sleep of exhaustion; it would have been easy to take more energy from her. At the same time, Carlsen was aware of how much he had already taken, and was appalled. He had drained off most of her vital reserves. Under normal circumstances, she could soon replace it; but in the meantime, it left her terribly vulnerable. Any sudden stress or catastrophe could thrust her into a limbo of fear and depression.

Inside his brain, he was aware of the urge, like a persuasive whisper: I don't want you to kill her. Just take a *little* more...As he refused, he was aware of the rage she was holding back; it was like trying to take the bottle from an alcoholic. He was also aware of a new element in his relation with this woman. In the Space Research laboratory, she had deliberately exercised all her seductiveness, alluring him with an irresistible essence of femininity. Now he was aware of the hardness and self-ishness below the surface. To emphasise his refusal, he turned his back on the girl beside him. The moonlight fell on the picture of his wife and children, bringing a wave of tenderness. He felt the same protective tenderness towards Selma Bengtsson. The vampire would have liked him to kill her, draining all her life force, even down to the subliminal molecular levels, and Carlsen was aware that a weaker man would have given way. It would have made no difference to her that he would be charged with murder, or that he would be of no further use. It was not that she wanted to lose Carlsen, only that her craving for life overmastered all other considerations. Carlsen felt a surge of irritable contempt, and knew instantly that she had also felt it. Immediately she became conciliatory. Of course he was right—she was just being greedy. The disappointment burned into dull rage, then was suppressed beyond the range of his awareness. For a moment, he had a frightening glimpse of a bottomless gulf of frustration, unsatisfied craving that had dragged on for thousands of centuries. At the same time, he also understood why she *had* to be a vampire. The ordinary criminal can repent, and retrace his steps towards love and human sympathy. These creatures had too much to repent; it would have taken an eternity.

He was aware suddenly that Selma Bengtsson's hand was resting against the back of his thigh, and that energy was flowing from it. The vampire was alert again, drinking it as a cat laps cream. Now, suddenly, he was aware that she was dangerous, and that if she became hostile, she could destroy him. While her attention was distracted, he closed his mind from her. He even turned back towards Selma, running his hand gently over her naked body, allowing a trickle of energy to seep through him. She stirred in her sleep and sighed; her open lips were a temptation, but he rejected it. He allowed himself to become heavy and sleepy. He reached down and carefully pulled up the bedclothes. Then he took the girl into his arms and concentrated on giving her some of his own en-ergy. The vampire lost interest; it was incomprehensible to her that anyone should give away his life force. With a deep, unconscious part of her mind, Selma Bengtsson understood what he was doing. She stirred, half opened her eyes, murmured something that sounded like 'I love you.' He pressed her against him and felt her sink back into sleep. At the same moment, he realised that the vampire was gone, and he was alone again.

The moonlight had moved around to the dressing table. He could hear the lapping of the waves in the faint breeze. He lay there, staring at the ceiling. The girl beside him was a complication. Now he understood what had been happening, and was appalled at his own ignorance, his capacity for ignoring the messages from his subconscious. For days, the vampire had been using him, sucking energy from Jelka and the children. His unconscious resistance had made this difficult. When the three girls had placed their hands on him, earlier in the evening, the vampire had suddenly become alert, sucking up the energy as it flowed from them. Subconsciously, the girls had been puzzled; it was like pouring tea into a cup, and watching the cup remain empty. At the same time, they were powerfully attracted by Carlsen. The other two would willingly have done what Selma Bengtsson had done, even though they knew—as she did—that Carlsen was an energy vampire. He filled them with a sense of mystery, a desire for surrender. If he summoned them now, using his awakened powers, they would come to the bedroom and offer themselves. He felt a stir of desire, which he instantly repressed; the vampire responded to desire like a shark to blood.

He woke up, aware of the dawn. Selma was leaning over him, brushing his mouth with her lips. He realised with surprise that her energies had recovered. She was still low, but no longer close to the danger level. And now she wanted him to take her again. He was overcome by a sense of absurdity. She aroused in him a basic tenderness, but it was a tenderness that he usually reserved for his wife and children. It struck him suddenly that her body *was* Jelka's. Both were embodiments of a female principle that lay beyond them, looking out of the body of every woman in the world as if out of so many windows.

He caressed her shoulder. 'You'd better go to your own room now. It's getting light.'

'I'd rather stay with you. Make love to me again.'

She bent down and kissed him. He shook his head. She asked: "When are you going back to London?'

'Today.'

'Then make love to me.'

'No. Lie down.'

She lay back on the pillow. He began to stroke her gently, his hand running from her shoulder, over her breast, down to her knees. He allowed his own energy to flow into her. She sighed and closed her eyes like a contented child, breathing more and more deeply. He began to kiss her at the same time. A sweetness of contentment rose in her, communicating itself to him; then he felt her drift into sleep. He lay beside her, feeling depleted but contented. He had taken nothing from her; only given back a little of the life force he had taken earlier. At least he was not yet a vampire…

There was a knock at the door, and the handle turned. He sat up, calling: *'Vem är där?'* A girl's voice said something about coffee. 'Leave it there, please.' Selma Bengtsson said sleepily: 'What time is it?'

'A quarter to eight.'

She sat up. 'My God! I must go!'

When she disappeared into the bathroom, Carlsen brought in the tray with the coffee and climbed back into bed. The lake was glittering in the morning sunlight. As he sipped the coffee, he closed his eyes, concentrating on his sensations. He felt tired; but it was no longer the strange lassitude he had experienced since he returned to earth.

Selma came out of the bathroom, now fully dressed; he thought she looked as beautiful and immaculate as if she had just dressed for dinner. She leaned over and kissed him. 'Would you mind looking outside the door to see if anyone is there?'

He did as she asked; the corridor was empty. She pressed against him for a moment, then hurried out; he closed the door quietly behind her. There was a strange relief in being alone.

He had just finished dressing when there was a knock on the door; he called: *'Stig in!'* It was Fallada.

'Good morning. What time did you get to bed?'

'About half past two. You know, I was mistaken about the Count. He's certainly no crank.'

Carlsen said: 'I never thought he was.'

Fallada stood staring out of the window. He said: 'We talked about you. He thinks your encounter with that woman might have affected you more than you realise.'

Carlsen started to speak, and experienced again the deep reluctance he had felt before. As Fallada stood, silent, he overruled it with an effort of will. 'I've got something to tell you.'

The sound of the gong vibrated up the stairs. Fallada asked: 'Can it wait until after breakfast?'

I expect so. In fact, I'd like Geijerstam to be present too.'

Fallada looked at him curiously but said nothing.

The others, including Selma, were already seated. The breakfast room faced east, and the sunlight was dazzling. Geijerstam stood up. 'Good morning. I hope you slept well?'

'Heavily.' Carlsen felt that satisfied the interests of both honesty and accuracy.

He sat between Selma and Louise. Geijerstam said: 'We are all hoping to persuade you to stay another day at least.'

Carlsen looked across at Fallada. 'It's up to Hans. I'm free, but he has work to do.'

Annaleise Freytag said: 'Oh, *please* stay a little longer.'

Reaching out for the toast, Carlsen's hand brushed that of the French girl. Instantly and without any doubt, he knew she knew about Selma Bengtsson. The knowledge startled him. At the same time, he found himself desiring her. It was not the usual masculine desire to undress an attractive girl. It was connected to the life and warmth that vibrated from her young body. He wanted to press his nakedness against hers and gently suck life from her. A moment later he realised he felt the same about Annaleise and that his desire endowed him with the power of reading her mind. Both girls knew that Selma had spent the night in his room. He even knew how they knew; Selma had left her door slightly ajar, with the light still on. Louise had passed the door at seven-fifteen, looked inside, and seen that the bed was undisturbed.

He ate his breakfast abstractedly, replying in monosyllables to questions, fascinated by this new power. He had occasionally experienced something of the sort with Jelka, when they were very intimate: a sense of being connected, so their emotions were experienced simultaneously by both. He had felt it as he held his children when they were babies. And now, he remembered, he had experienced it as a child as he stood in a garden one summer morning, leaning against a tree. In all these cases, it had been a deep, subconscious feeling that never reached the realm of conscious knowledge. Now it was more conscious and more detailed. With very little effort he could feel that Louise Curd's brassiere was tight, and the left strap was cutting into her skin. He knew Annaleise had kicked off her shoes because she liked the feeling of the deep carpet against her bare feet. Both of them were envious of Selma Bengtsson. Annaleise wanted him to stay because she wanted to remain close to him; Louise believed that he was physically attracted to her and would sleep with her if he got the opportunity. Selma's feelings disturbed him. She was in a state of almost feverish infatuation, and it was costing her an effort not to reach out and touch him under the table. She had seen the photograph, of Jelka and the children, but it made no difference. She was thinking about coming to live in London, and was wondering whether Fallada could offer her a job. She believed she would be contented to be his mistress, without demanding anything more; in fact, she hoped to supplant Jelka. There was a hard-headed, determined element about her that troubled him.

He tried to read Geijerstam's thoughts, but it was impossible. He felt no desire for Geijerstam; consequently, his mind remained closed. The same was true of Fallada. In Fallada, he could dimly sense an uneasiness; but when he tried to learn more, the contact seemed to break.

He tried to decide whether the vampire was still inside him, sucking energy through him. His experience last night had taught him how to observe her presence. As far as he could determine, she was not there. In that case, why did he desire the women who were seated at the table? The answer made his heart contract: because *he* wanted them. For himself, not for her. For a moment he struggled with a sense of panic that verged on nausea. Then he remembered that he meant to tell Geijerstam about it; the thought brought a sense of relief.

He was glad when breakfast was over; his appetite had vanished. Geijerstam said: 'I usually take a walk along the shores of the lake, or a row to the landing stage on the other side. Would you both care to join me?'

Fallada said: 'Of course.'

Selma Bengtsson asked: 'May we come too?'

'I think not, my dear. We have things to discuss. And you have your studies.'

The disappointment that streamed from her was so intense that Carlsen was tempted to intercede. As he left the room, he was aware of her eyes staring at his back, willing him to turn and smile at her; at the same time, he was aware that the other girls were observing him closely. He went out without looking back.

The air was mild and full of the smell of spring. Now the life field of the girls was no longer disturbing his equilibrium, he felt better. With relief, his senses turned outward to the sunlight, and the delight was so intense that it was almost painful.

As soon as they were among the trees, walking towards the south end of the island, he said: 'Is there somewhere we could sit down? I want to tell you something.'

Geijerstam pointed. 'There is a bench by the inlet.'

A few hundred yards away, a small stream ran into the lake. Geijerstam said: 'This flows from a spring at the top of the hill. We call it the Well of Saint Eric. According to the legend, Saint Eric spent the night praying near the hilltop, in a hermit's hut. The next day, he was leading his men into battle against the Finns. The next morning, the spring had burst from the ground—a sign that his prayer had been heard.'

A rough wooden bench, carved from a section of tree trunk, had been erected where the stream joined the lake. Geijerstam sat down; the trunk of an immense elm provided support for their backs.

Carlsen began speaking immediately, as if afraid of interruption. 'Something strange happened in the night. Miss Bengtsson came to my room.'

Geijerstam smiled, raising his eyebrows. 'And what is strange about that, my dear Commander?' From his response, Carlsen sensed that he knew already.

'Please let me finish…' Suddenly, as he had feared, the reluctance was there; it was so strong that he felt as though a hand were gripping his windpipe. His face flushed; his heart began to pound with the effort. When he spoke, his voice sounded tight and breathless. The others looked at him in surprise. He stammered out the words, determined to say them at all costs. 'I don't believe she intended to stay the night—in fact, I know she didn't, because she left her door open with the light on. All she wanted to tell me was that I'd been stealing her energy…What's, more, I didn't intend to sleep with her. I've been married for five years and in all that time I've never even kissed another woman.'

Fallada said: 'Are you all right?'

In spite of the sunlight, his teeth had begun to chatter, and his body had become icy cold. He clenched his fists and pressed them against his thighs. It was not unlike the sensation he used to experience when taking off from earth during his training as an astronaut. He continued to speak, although his voice was choked: 'Just let me finish. You see, she was right. I am a vampire. I realised that when she touched me. That damn woman's still there. But she's inside me. I'm not mad. I know that…I know this sounds strange, but even now, something's trying to stop me from telling you this.' He leaned back against the tree trunk, and the pressure brought a feeling of comfort. He breathed deeply. 'Let me alone for a moment. I'll be all right.' It took more than a minute for him to master the trembling. The knowledge that he had already told them the most important part made it easier. He wiped the sweat from his face with a handkerchief.

Geijerstam said gently: 'Don't distress yourself. Let me tell you something now. I already knew most of what you were going to tell me. I knew about it last night, when Selma said you had taken more energy than she expected. And when you told me about your encounter with the vampire woman, I knew what had happened.' He placed his hand on Carlsen's. 'I can tell you this: it is not as serious as you think.'

Carlsen said heavily: I hope you're right.'

Fallada said: 'Can you describe what happened?'

'I'll try.' As soon as he began to speak, he felt calmer. As he described it, he concentrated on accuracy in the detail, and this made it easier. He ended by speaking of his insights at breakfast.

After a silence, Geijerstam said: 'And so now you are convinced you are a vampire too?'

'Don't *you* think so?'

'No. I believe you have become aware of the vampirism that exists in all human beings. That is all.'

Carlsen had to control rising irritation. 'I could have drained away her vitality until she died of exhaustion. Is that the vampirism that exists in all human beings?'

'No. But I believe it is a possibility that exists at this point in human evolution. This creature has not turned you into a vampire. She has only awakened the seed of a new development. And it is a development that has possibilities of good as well as evil.'

Carlsen asked quickly: 'In what way?'

'To begin with, it has given you a deeper power of sympathy and insight. You *didn't* destroy Selma, did you? In fact, you *gave* her energy. You have an instinctive sense that lovemaking should involve give and take.'

There was a silence, broken only by the whistling of birds and the water breaking on the pebbles. Carlsen said finally: 'The fact remains that she's turned me into a vampire. She's given me abnormal desires that I didn't possess before—and the power to carry them out.'

Fallada and Geijerstam began to speak at once. Fallada said: 'Pardon me.'

Geijerstam said: 'You do not understand. Every man is capable of every kind of desire. Have you ever read my account of the first vampire case I encountered?'

'The young painter?'

'Yes. In fact, he was not a painter but a sculptor. His name was Torsten Vetterlund. Well, he was a man of very powerful physique and his natural inclinations were sadistic—not very much so, but slightly. This girl, Nina von Gerstein, succeeded in turning him into a neurotic masochist. You understand why?'

Carlsen nodded. Fallada said with surprise: 'You do?'

Carlsen said: 'She couldn't suck energy from a sadist.'

'Quite. The sadist wants to absorb, not to be absorbed. So she had to change his sexual orientation. And she did this by satisfying all his desires—all his sadistic fantasies—until he had become dependent on her. Finally, he was her slave, and *then* she could begin to steal his energy.'

Fallada asked: 'How did you cure him?'

'Ah, that was interesting. I noticed immediately that there was something contradictory about his symptoms. After this girl left him, he became an exhibitionist, exposing himself to women in the street. That was clearly masochism—he was enjoying the self-humiliation. But he also told me he had developed the desire to undress children and bite them. *That* was obviously sadism. Of course, many sadists have an element of masochism, and vice versa. But I became convinced that he was trying to overcome his masochism by developing his sadism. He told me about his sexual fantasies before he met Nina; they were all mildly sadistic. He told me about a prostitute he used to visit—a girl who allowed him to tie her up before they had intercourse. And the solution became obvious. I had to encourage him to develop the sadistic tendency again. He began going back to the prostitute. Then he met an assistant in a shoe shop who liked to be whipped before she made love. He married her, and they lived perfectly happily.'

'And the vampirism stopped?'

'Yes, it stopped. I cannot claim any credit for the cure. He had already started to cure himself before he came to see me.'

Carlsen smiled wryly. 'By the same logic, I should try to turn myself into a masochist.'

Geijerstam snapped his fingers; he said with sudden excitement: 'No, but you have reminded me of something. Something I had forgotten for a long time.' He stared out over the water, frowning, as they waited for him to go on. Suddenly, he stood up. 'I want to introduce you to one of my tenants.'

Fallada said: I didn't know you had any.'

'Come.' He began to stride away up the hill. Fallada glanced at Carlsen and shrugged. They followed him up a path that ran beside the stream. Geijerstam said over his shoulder: 'You remember I told you about the Well of Saint Eric? There is an old Lett woman—she lives in my cottage. She has second sight'

The path became steep, and the thick carpet of pine needles made it treacherous. The trees were so close together that hardly any sunlight was able to penetrate; After five minutes, Carlsen and Fallada were breathing heavily. Geijerstam, hurrying in front, seemed unaffected. He turned to wait for them. 'I am glad I thought of bringing you to see her. She is a remarkable woman. She used to live near Skarvsjo, but the villagers were afraid of her. Her appearance is a little—' The rest of his words were drowned by the noisy barking of a dog. An enormous animal with fur the colour of yellow clay bounded towards them. When Geijerstam held out his hand, it sniffed him, then trotted beside him as he walked on.

Geijerstam paused on the edge of a clearing. The ground was strewn with granite boulders. A small wooden cottage stood on the far side. The stream ran past it, cascading over a waterfall. Geijerstam called: *'Labrït, mate.'* There was no reply. He said to Carlsen: 'Why don't you look at the well, while I see if she is awake?' He pointed up the hill, to a small granite erection. 'That is the Well of Saint Eric. If you have arthritis, gout or leprosy, you should bathe in it.'

They climbed the steps to the well, the dog running ahead. The kiosk was built of slabs of roughly hewn granite on which the lichen looked like green velvet. The water flowed from under an immense slab that lay across the entrance. Carlsen knelt on this and looked inside. The water was perfectly clear, but so deep that it was impossible to see the bottom. He was reminded for a moment of the port glass of the *Hermes;* at the same time, with hallucinatory clarity, he seemed to see the hulk of the derelict, as if reflected in the depths of the water. The illusion lasted only for a moment. He put his hand into the water; it was freezing cold, and after a moment, it made his bones ache.

He stood up, leaning on the wall. Fallada said: 'Are you all right?'

Carlsen smiled. 'Oh, yes. I think perhaps I am going mad. But otherwise I'm all right.'

The Count appeared at the bottom of the slope. Beside him stood a woman dressed in brown. As they moved closer, Carlsen saw that she had no nose and that one eye was larger than the other. Yet the effect was not repellent. Her cheeks were as red as apples.

Geijerstam said: 'This is Moa.' He spoke to her in Lettish, introducing Fallada and Carlsen. She smiled and dropped them a curtsy. Then she gestured for them to enter the house. It struck Carlsen that in spite of her deformity, she produced an impression of youth and sweetness.

The room was large and curiously bare; it was heated by a big iron stove in the centre. A coarse woven mat covered the floor. The only items of furniture were a low bed, a table, a cupboard and an old-fashioned spinning wheel. Carlsen was intrigued by a flight of steps that ran up the wall to a railed platform; it appeared to lead nowhere.

She spoke to them in Lettish, pointing to the floor. Geijerstam said: 'She is apologising for the lack of chairs and explaining that she always sits on the floor. It is a kind of...mystical discipline.'

She gestured to the cushions near the wall. Carlsen and Fallada sat down. She leaned over Carlsen, looked into his face and placed a hand on his forehead. Geijerstam translated her words: 'She wants to know if you are ill.'

'Tell her I don't know. That's what I'd like to know.'

She opened the cupboard and took out a length of string. One end was wound around a spindle; the other end was weighted with a wooden bead, about an inch in diameter. Geijerstam said: 'She is going to test you with a pendulum.'

'What does it do?'

'You could say it is a kind of lambda meter. It measures your field.'

Fallada said: 'For some odd reason, it works. We used to have an old servant who could do it.'

'What is she doing now?'

'Measuring the correct length for a man—about two feet.' The old woman was carefully measuring the string against a meter rule, unwinding it from the spindle. She spoke to Carlsen. Geijerstam said: 'She wants you to lie down on the floor.'

Carlsen stretched himself out on his back, looking up at her as she stood over him. The pendulum, held out at arm's length, began to swing backwards and forwards. After a few moments, it began to swing with a circular motion. From the movements of her lips, he could see that she was counting. About a minute later, the pendulum returned to a backward and forward motion. She smiled and spoke to Geijerstam. He said: 'She says there is nothing wrong with you. Your health field is exceptionally strong.'

'Good. What is she going to do now?'

The old woman was lengthening the string.

'More tests.'

Again she held the pendulum over him. This time he could sense Geijerstam's tension. He watched curiously as the motion of the pendulum changed from its normal back-and-forward oscillations into a circular swing. Her lips moved, counting. She said something in a low voice to Geijerstam. When the pendulum returned to its oscillations, she lowered it onto the floor, shaking her head. She stood looking down at Carlsen, frowning thoughtfully, Geijerstam said: 'All right, you can sit up.'

'What did all that mean?'

Geijerstam spoke to the old woman in Lettish; her reply lasted for several minutes. Carlsen tried hard to follow; he had picked up a few words of Lettish when training in Riga. Now he recognised the word *'bistams,'* meaning dangerous, and the noun *'briesmas'*—danger. Geijerstam said: *'Ne sieviete?'* and she shrugged and said: *'Varbut.'* She picked up the pendulum, still speaking, and held it out over him as he sat, leaning against the wall. After a few moments, it began its circular motion. She moved across to Fallada and held it over his stomach. This time it continued to oscillate back and forth. She shrugged: *'Loti atvainojos.'* She tossed the pendulum onto the bed.

Carlsen said: 'What is she sorry about?'

Geijerstam said: 'It is puzzling, but not entirely unexpected. While Torsten Vetterlund was in the power of Nina, the pendulum registered him as a woman. I have told her this, but she is pointing out that the same length —about sixty-three centimetres—can also mean danger.'

He said: 'You mean that's the reaction she's getting from me?'

'Yes.'

He felt his stomach sink with disappointment and depression. At once he realised he was feeling sick and exhausted. In a few seconds, it had become so acute that he was afraid he was going to vomit. His forehead was prickling with sweat. As he groped his way to his feet, the dog began to growl. It was backing away, blocking the doorway, its fur bristling.

Geijerstam said: 'What are you doing?'

'I feel sick. I think I need a breath of fresh air.'

'No!' Geijerstam said it so sharply that Carlsen stared with surprise. Geijerstam placed a hand on his wrist. 'Don't you understand what is happening? Look at the dog. The vampire is back, isn't she? Close your eyes. Can't you feel that she is here?'

Carlsen closed his eyes, but he seemed unable to think or record his impressions. It was like acute delirium. 'I think I'm going to faint.' He tried to move to the door again; the dog crouched and growled, showing its fangs.

Geijerstam and Fallada were on either side of him; he realised that he was swaying. Geijerstam said: 'We must do one more test—a crucial one. Come and lie down over here.' They led Carlsen across the room. He had a sense of willingness, as if all his strength had been drained. He lay flat on his back, but immediately felt so sick that he had to turn over onto his stomach. The matting felt rough against his forehead and smelt dusty. He closed his eyes again and seemed to drift into a twilight world, a kind of black mist. At once he understood what was happening. She was there, but she was not concerned with him. She was communicating with the derelict, which still floated in the black emptiness. Now he could also sense wave after wave of ravenous hunger emanating from the wreck. The men in the spaceships had gone, and the aliens felt cheated. They were angry that they were still there; they could not understand what had gone wrong. She was finding it hard to make them understand, because she was in another world; she was conscious, they were asleep. Their agony lashed her like whips. Like an induction coil, Carlsen was recording her torment.

Through the mist he heard Geijerstam say: 'Please turn over for a moment' With an effort, he opened his eyes and twisted onto his back. He was only half in the room, and the black clouds drifted between himself and the others. He could see that the old woman had mounted the flight of steps against the wall, and that the pendulum was now dangling over his chest. It began to swing in a wide circle. He felt beads of sweat running from his armpits down his sides.

Geijerstam's voice said finally: 'You can get up now.' With a painful effort, he propped himself up on his elbows. The dog began to bark frantically. He leaned back against the wood of the stairs, afraid to close his eyes in case he was again drawn back into the world of hunger and pain. He became aware that the old woman was standing over him, holding something out. She said in halting Swedish: 'Here, take this and smell it'

From the smell he realised that it was garlic. He shook his head. 'I can't.'

Geijerstam said: 'Please try to do as she says.'

He accepted it and held it against his face. It felt as if someone were holding a pillow over his nostrils. It smelt of decay and death. He began to cough and choke, the tears running down his cheeks. Panic rose in him, a fear of choking to death. Then, quite abruptly, the sickness vanished. It was as if a door had closed, shutting out a nerve-wracking sound. He realised the dog had stopped barking.

Fallada laid a hand on his shoulder. 'How do you feel now?' He felt grateful for the genuine concern in his voice.

'Much better. Could I go outside now?' The desire for fresh air was like thirst.

They took his arms and helped him through the door. He sat down on the wooden bench, his back resting against the wall. The sunlight was warm on his closed eyelids. He could hear birds and the wind in the branches. He felt someone grasp his wrists. It was the old woman. She was sitting on a low stool, facing him, her face wrinkled, as if concentrating. Then she looked into his eyes and spoke in Lettish. Geijerstam translated: 'She says: do not give way to fear. Your chief enemy is fear. A vampire cannot destroy you unless you give your consent.'

Carlsen managed to smile. 'I know that.'

She spoke again. Geijerstam said: 'She says: vampires are unlucky.'

'I know that too.'

The old woman pressed his wrists, looking into his eyes. This time, she spoke in Swedish. 'Remember that if she is inside you, you are also inside her.'

He frowned, shaking his head. 'I don't understand.'

She smiled and stood up. She said something to Geijerstam in' her own language, then went into the cottage. She came put almost immediately and placed something in his hand. It was a small brass ring, with a piece of string attached to it.

'She says you should tie it to your right arm to protect you from evil. It is a Lett witch charm.'

Carlsen said: *'Loti pateicos.'* She smiled and curtsied.

Geijerstam said: 'Do you feel well enough to walk back to the house?'

'Yes. I feel better now.'

Geijerstam bowed to the old woman; she took his hand and kissed it As they turned back at the edge of the clearing, she was standing with one hand on the dog's head.

They heard shouts of laughter as they emerged from the trees. The three girls were swimming in the lake; Annaleise was on her back, kicking up a haze of spray. When Selma- Bengtsson saw them, she waved and called: 'Your wife tried to reach you.'

Carlsen asked: 'Did she leave a message?'

'No.'

Geijerstam said: 'Why don't you call her back? Perhaps, if there is no urgency, you could stay another day?'

'You're very kind.'

The dreamlike sensation had left him; now he was physically tired. He wanted to lie down and sleep. The idea of relaxing for another day was attractive.

In the house, Geijerstam said: 'Please use the screen in my study. That is upstairs.'

It was a small, comfortable room, that smelt of warm leather and cigars. The leather smell came from the old-fashioned settee, which was standing too close to the log fire. As he sat down at the desk, Carlsen said: 'Would you mind being introduced to my wife? She discovered your book, so she'd like to say hello.'

'It would be a pleasure.'

He was able to dial direct. Jeanette's face appeared on the screen. She said: 'Daddy! Are you on the moon?'

'No, darling. Just across the sea. Is Mummy there?'

Jelka's voice said: 'Yes, I'm here. Hello.' She picked Jeanette up and sat her on her knee. 'Are you all right?' For some reason, Jelka was never at ease on the telescreen. Her manner seemed detached and cool, like a secretary.

'Yes, I'm fine.'

Jeanette asked: 'Are you coming home today?' 'I don't know, darling. I might stay another day. I'm staying in a castle that belongs to this gentleman.' He beckoned to Geijerstam, who moved within range of the screen. Carlsen introduced him, and Jelka and Geijerstam exchanged polite comments. Jeanette interrupted:

'Daddy, what's a pryminister?'

'A what?'

Jelka said: 'Oh, yes. The Prime Minister's office wanted to get in touch with you. Unfortunately, I'd lost your address.'

He felt a stir of uneasiness, like a cold wind on the back of his neck. 'What did they want?'

'I don't know.'

'And did you find the address?'

'No. Susan's been making paper aeroplanes out of the jotting pad.'

'Then how did you get this number?'

'I rang Fred Armfeldt at the Swedish embassy. The Prime Minister's secretary's going to ring back later. I'll give him the number then.'

'No!' She looked startled at his vehemence. She asked: 'Why not?'

'Because...because I don't want anyone to disturb me.'

'But suppose it's important?'

'Never mind that.' He was aware of the irritation in his voice. 'If anyone rings, say you've lost my address.'

She looked around. 'That's someone at the door. When are you coming home?'

Tomorrow afternoon.'

When he had rung off, Geijerstam said: 'Do you have something against your Prime Minister?'

He was massaging his eyes, with his fingers; he shook his head. 'No. It's just that...' He shrugged.

'What?'

He looked up. 'Does it matter?'

'I would like to know.'

Carlsen stared out of the window, frowning. He said: 'I...don't know. I suppose I'm enjoying myself here.'

There was a knock on the door. Fallada said: 'I'm not intruding?'

'No, come in.'

Carlsen said: 'Did you leave a message with your staff about where you were going?'

Fallada said with surprise: 'Of course.' Then he frowned, scratching the end of his nose. 'Although now you come to mention it, I'm not sure I did. I meant to…Why?'

Carlsen said: 'Oh, nothing.'

Geijerstam smiled at Fallada. 'So you forgot to leave your address. And Commander Carlsen left it where it could be mislaid. So no one now knows where you are. As a psychologist, what would you say to that?'

Fallada nodded. 'Yes…you've got a point. Although if Carlsen actually left the address, it sounds more like an accident.'

'Except that I have just heard him tell his wife that she is to tell the Prime Minister's office that she doesn't know where he is.'

Carlsen and Fallada started to speak at once. Fallada said: 'That's easily explained. We both had a session with the Prime Minister two days ago. He doesn't believe these vampires are dangerous. So neither of us trusts him.'

Geijerstam stood by the window, staring out. He said slowly: 'It is my experience that when the subconscious gives us warnings, we should heed the warnings.'

Carlsen asked: 'What are you suggesting?'

Geijerstam sat on the edge of the desk, where he could look into Carlsen's face. He said: 'Do you remember the last thing Moa said to you?'

'Whatever it was, I didn't understand it.'

'She said: Remember that if she is inside you, you are also inside her.'

Carlsen said: 'Which is untrue.'

'Is it?'

'I don't know what she meant.'

'She meant that if this alien is in contact with your mind, you are also in contact with hers.'

Fallada said quickly: 'How?'

Geijerstam asked Carlsen: 'Have you ever been hypnotised?'

Fallada snapped his fingers. 'Yes! That's worth trying.'

Carlsen shook his head. Geijerstam said: 'Would you be willing to allow me to try?'

Carlsen overcame the sinking feeling; he took a deep breath. 'I suppose…it wouldn't do any harm.'

'You don't like the idea?'

Carlsen said apologetically. 'It's just that…I'm beginning to feel my mind's not my own.'

'I understand. But this is something that need not alarm you. You will remain conscious all the time.'

Carlsen asked with surprise: 'Is that possible?'

'Of course. I prefer my subjects to remain fully conscious.'

Fallada said: 'It is quite safe. I have been hypnotized a dozen times. When we were students, we used to do it as a game.'

Carlsen said: 'All right. When?'

'Why not now?'

Carlsen smiled. 'I shall probably fall asleep. I'm pretty tired.'

'That would not matter.' Geijerstam pulled a cord, drawing the curtains. He switched on the reading lamp on the desk.

Fallada said: 'Would you like me to go away?'

'Not unless Commander Carlsen would prefer it,' From a cupboard he took a metal stand; the curved top had a hook on it From this he suspended a chromium sphere on a length of string. It turned gently in the light of the reading lamp.

Carlsen, staring at it, said: 'I don't mind.'

Geijerstam turned the lamp so that Carlsen's face was in shadow. He said: 'The purpose of the ball is to fatigue your vision. Stare at it until your eyes feel tired, then close them. I want you to feel quite relaxed in your chair. I can hypnotise you only with your help. The important thing is for you to feel comfortable and relaxed.' His voice went on, speaking quietly and slowly, as he set the pendulum swinging. Carlsen allowed himself to relax deep into the leather-covered chair. Beyond the ball he could dimly see the outline of Fallada seated on the settee, the firelight reflected on his glasses. Geijerstam was saying softly: 'That's right, allow yourself to sink back comfortably, and listen carefully to what I say. Now you are thinking of nothing. Your eyes are feeling tired. Your eyelids are heavy. You would like to close them.' It was true; the light was hurting his eyes. He closed them, experiencing a sense of warm darkness. Geijerstam's voice was saying: 'Your body feels heavy and relaxed. You feel as if you are sinking into the chair. You are breathing deeply and regularly, deeply and regularly...' He was feeling the warm, comfortable sense of trust that he had experienced as a child when he was about to be anaesthetised for a minor operation. He was aware of nothing but his breathing and Geijerstam's voice. Then the voice stopped. He felt Geijerstam lift his right arm, then drop it. It was a strange sensation, like waking from a very deep sleep and lying in a warm and comfortable bed, with no desire to move. The passage of time was a matter of indifference. He would have been happy to float in this state of disconnected contentment for days or weeks.

Geijerstam's voice said 'Are you able to speak to me? Answer yes if you are.'

With an effort to overcome the heavy languor, he said: 'Yes.'

'Do you know where you are?'

'I'm in Sweden.'

'Are you one person or two?'

'One.'

'But this female vampire—is she not inside you?'

'No.'

'But she was inside you last night?'

'No.'

'Not inside you?'

'No. She was in touch with me. Her mind was in touch with mine. Like a telescreen.'

'Is she in touch with you now?'

'No.'

'Does she know where you are now?'

'No.'

'Why not?'

'She hasn't asked.'

'Would you tell her if she asked?'

'Yes.'

'Do you know where she is now?'

'Yes.'

'Where?'

'I don't know its name.'

'But you know where she is?'

'Yes.'

'Can you describe it?'

He was silent for a while. He was walking beside her, along a muddy road. It had been raining. She was wearing a brightly coloured dress, with red and yellow stripes. In the distance there were the towering office blocks of a city. Geijerstam said: 'Where is she now?'

'She is walking on a moor.'

'What is she doing?'

'She is looking for a man.'

'What man?'

'Any man. She wants someone young and healthy—someone who works in a factory.'

'Does she intend to kill him?'

'No.'

"Why not?'

'She is afraid of being caught.'

Fallada's voice interrupted: 'How could she be caught?'

'The body would give her away.'

'So what is she hoping to do?' It was Geijerstam again.

'To find a healthy man and seduce him. She will take some energy from him—not enough to kill him.'

'Then what?'

'Then she will draw energy from him—as she draws it from me.'

Fallada, who was sitting on the far edge of the desk, snapped his fingers. 'Of course! That's what they intend to do. Set up a network of energy donors!' He asked Carlsen: 'Is that true?'

'Yes.'

Geijerstam said: 'Whose body is she using now?'

Carlsen hesitated. It was almost impossible to read the alien's mind. If he tried, it would alert her. But there was another mind. He said: I think her name is Helen. She is a nurse.'

'In a hospital?'

'I...think so.'

'Is Helen dead now?'

'No. She is still in her body.'

'You mean there are two people in one body—Helen and the vampire?' Geijerstam's voice revealed his tension.

'Yes.'

Fallada said: 'What happened to the other body—the man she took over?'

Carlsen said nothing. He knew the answer was locked in the alien's mind, and that it was like an immense steel safe. Geijerstam asked him. 'Can you tell us *anything* about the other body? Anything that might give us a clue?'

Again, he was able to tell them what was in the nurse's mind. 'There is another body... But it is in the hospital.'

'A man or a woman?'

'A man.'

'Do you know his name?'

'Jeff.'

'His other name?'

'No.'

'What do you mean when you say it's in the hospital? Is it dead?'

'No.'

'Can you tell us anything about the hospital?'

'It is...on the edge of a town. On a hill.'

'You've no idea of its name?'

'No.'

'Or where it's located?'

'No.'

There was a silence. Fallada and Geijerstam were speaking, but that did not concern him. They might have been speaking in a foreign language. He was enjoying the cold breeze and the appearance of puddles in the sunlight.

Fallada said: 'What is she doing now?'

'She is sitting on a bench on the side of the road. She is watching a man.'

'What is the man doing?'

'He is sitting in his car, reading a newspaper.'

Fallada's voice said quickly: 'Can you see the number of the car?'

'Yes."

'Read it out.'

'It is QBX 5279L.'

'Are there any other cars?'

'Yes. There is a red Temeraire parked near the fence. A young couple are eating sandwiches and looking at the view.'

'What is its number?'

'3XJ UT9.'

'What is she doing now?'

'She is waiting. She is crossing her legs, pulling up the skirt. She is pretending to read a book.'

Fallada and Geijerstam spoke together again. Then Fallada said: 'Do you know what has happened to the other two vampires?'

'Yes. One has gone to New York.'

'And the other?'

'He is still in London.'

As if in a dream, the scene had changed to the Strand. He was standing at the top of the great marble steps that ran down to the river from the site of the old Savoy. The other alien was shaking hands with a short, fat man: the Chinese chargé d'affaires.

'Can you tell us his name?'

'I find it difficult to pronounce. We would say Ykx-By-Orun.'

'But what is his name now? The name of the body he uses?'

'Everard Jamieson.'

He was indifferent to their exclamations. He was more interested in watching the gleaming rocket carrier that slid smoothly downriver, hardly disturbing the smaller craft with its creamy wake.

Geijerstam was speaking to him again. In thirty seconds I am going to waken you. You will wake up feeling refreshed and rested. Now your sleep is already growing lighter. You are beginning to wake up. I will count from one to ten, and when I reach ten, you will be fully awake. One, two...'

He opened his eyes and for a moment wondered where he was. He imagined he was in bed at home and found it hard to explain why he was reclining in a chair. Then daylight flooded into the room as Geijerstam drew the curtains. He felt as though he was waking from a long and pleasant night's rest. He had some dim memory of a river and a huge silver craft, but as he tried to recall it, it faded like a dream.

Fallada was flushed with excitement. He said: 'Do you realise what you just told us?'

'No. What?'

'You said that one of these aliens has taken over the Prime Minister of England.'

He said: 'Christ!' The idea shocked him.

Fallada said wonderingly: 'Don't you remember?'

'I should have ordered him to remember everything. I forgot.' Geijerstam sat on the desk. 'You told us that one of the aliens had invaded the body of a nurse. The other is the Prime Minister.' He pressed a switch on the desk. 'Listen. I'll play it back to you.'

For the next seven minutes, he listened with astonishment to the sound of his own voice. It sounded drowsy and expressionless. He had no recollection of anything he had said. For a moment, he recalled a girl dressed in red, her hair blowing in the wind; but the memory faded immediately.

He was back in the room, seeing the world from a fixed point of view, like a man bending over a microscope.

As his voice said 'Everard Jamieson,' Geijerstam switched off the recorder.

'You see. You both knew there was something wrong with this man Jamieson. Your subconscious mind is wiser than you are.'

Fallada said: 'I still find it almost impossible to believe. I mean…he seemed so *normal* the other day. I've seen him many times on television.'

He was speaking to Carlsen. Carlsen said, shrugging: 'I agree.'

Fallada asked Geijerstam: 'Don't you think it possible he might be mistaken? That his dislike of Jamieson might have affected his subconscious judgement?'

'That is easy enough to find out.' Geijerstam laid his finger on the paper on the desk. 'You have two car registration numbers here. The car licencing department should have no difficulty in tracing them. If this proves to be accurate, then the rest is probably accurate.'

Carlsen said: 'Let's call Heseltine.'

'Good.' Fallada crossed to the desk. 'Do you mind if we call London?'

Gerijerstam said: 'Please.'

The duty sergeant answered: 'New Scotland Yard.'

'Commissioner's Office, please.'

Heseltine's secretary appeared on the screen. She said: 'Ah, Dr. Fallada. We've been trying to find you.'

'Anything urgent?'

'The Prime Minister wanted to see you.'

Fallada and Carlsen exchanged glances. Fallada said: 'Is Sir Percy there now?'

'I'm afraid not. He's at Downing Street. Can I get him to call you?'

'That won't be necessary. But I'd like to leave a message. Could you make a note of these licence numbers?' He read them out. 'I'd like to know where the owners can be located.'

'I could do that for you while you wait. Would you like to hang on?'

'No, thanks. I'll be back in London later today. I'll call you then. Would you tell Sir Percy the numbers are connected with the case—he'll know what I mean. And ask him not to mention them to anyone until he sees me.'

'Very well, sir. Where are you now?'

Fallada said, smiling: 'Istanbul.'

When he had disconnected, Geijerstam said: 'So you leave today? I am sorry.'

'I think it's important. We've got to locate this female.'

'And what then?'

Fallada shrugged. 'I don't know. Any suggestions?'

Geijerstam sat down on the settee, moving it back from the fire. For several moments he said nothing. He said finally: 'I am afraid my advice may be useless. But I will give it to you for what it is worth. The major problem is to force a vampire into retreat. Do you remember the final scenes of *Dracula?* This may sound absurd, but they show true insight into the psychology of the vampire. Once the vampire can be induced to flee, he has lost the advantage. I once defined vampirism as a form of mental karate. It depends on attack, on aggression. You see, the vampire is basically a criminal. He is like a thief in the night.'

Fallada nodded. 'Like a rapist. If the victim turned around and tried to rape *him,* he would lose all sexual desire.'

Geijerstam laughed. 'Exactly. So if you locate your vampire, do not be afraid of her. Of course, I know nothing of the powers of these aliens, so perhaps I am giving you bad advice. But I would say: try to make her afraid of you.'

Carlsen shook his head. 'The objection to that is that she might vanish again. The lengendary vampire has certain limitations—he has to sleep in a coffin full of earth and so on. These things don't seem to have any.'

Geijerstam said: 'They *must* have limitations. Your problem is to find them. For example, you say she might vanish again. But are you certain of that?'

Fallada asked quickly: 'What do you mean?'

'Think of what happened last time. The first woman disappeared from your Space Research building. Then the other two were found to be dead. You know now that they simply abandoned their bodies and found others. But, did they do it alone? Or with the help of the other vampire?'

Carlsen said: 'That's true…We've no evidence they can do it alone.'

Geijerstam said: 'And so if the three are now separated, they may be easier to deal with. Besides, you now know that you can locate her under hypnosis.'

Fallada said: 'Couldn't we persuade you to come back with us?'

Geijerstam shook his head. 'No. I am too old. Besides, you don't need me. You know as much about vampires as I do—probably more.'

There was a knock at the door. The footman, Gustav, looked in. He said: 'The young ladies want to know if you're going to join them in a drink before lunch, sir.'

'Yes, I think so. Say we'll be down in a few minutes.' He turned to Fallada. 'Before we go down, one more piece of advice. Never forget that the vampire is a criminal. That is the essence of their psychology. And all criminals get unlucky sooner or later.'

Carlsen said: 'Is that what she meant—the old woman? When she said vampires were unlucky, I thought she meant for their victims.'

Geijerstam chuckled, placing a hand on his shoulder. 'No. Not for their victims. For themselves. Look at these creatures. They lay a perfect plan to invade the earth. And at every important stage, something goes wrong. There are powers of good as well as evil in the universe.'

Carlsen said: 'I wish I could believe that.'

'You will before you are finished with these creatures.'

Carlsen wanted to question him further, but he was already on his way out of the room.

3

THE SKY WAS PURPLE WITH DUSK as the plane landed at London Airport. As be walked down the gangway, Carlsen was struck by the fragrant warmth of the air, mingled with the smell of jet fuel.

It was a strange feeling, to be back. It seemed incredible that it was only a day ago since he had left London. He felt as if he had returned from six months in space.

Fallada asked: 'How are you feeling?'

'Glad to be back. But a little depressed.'

'About Selma?'

'Yes.'

'No point in feeling guilty. It wasn't your fault. Besides, we *couldn't* stay longer.'

He said: 'It's not that.'

'What, then?'

'I wanted to stay.' Fallada looked at him quickly. 'Oh, not because I'm in love with her.' It seemed absurd, saying these intimate things as they crossed to the waiting bus, surrounded by noise, but he persisted. 'It was her vitality…' He stopped, unable to go on.

Fallada said quickly: 'Don't let it worry you.'

'It's not myself I'm worried about.'

'I know. But you've got to remember that it's just another instinctive response, like the sex drive. It can be controlled just as easily.'

But as the shuttle moved almost silently across the smooth concrete, Fallada tried to suppress his own disquiet. He understood why Carlsen should fear for his wife and children. He had seen the automatic telerecording of the death of Seth Adams; he retained an impression of instant deadly response, like a Venus flytrap closing on an insect.

In the terminal, they both made for telescreen booths. Carlsen rang Jelka; she appeared in a bathrobe. 'I'm just washing my hair. Mandy and Tom said they'd be over about nine. Will you be back by then?'

'I don't know yet. Fallada's ringing Heseltine now. I'll call you back.'

Fallada had spoken to the Duty Sergeant at the Yard; there was a message for him to ring Heseltine at home. Heseltine was chewing as he answered. Fallada said: 'I'm sorry. Have I interrupted your dinner?'

'That's all right—I was nearly finished. Where have you been?'

'I'll tell you when I see you. Did you trace the two car licence numbers?'

'Yes.' Heseltine took a slip of paper from his pocket 'One was a foreign car—Danish couple over here on honeymoon. The other's registered to a man called Pryce at Hoimfirth.'

'Where's that?'

'In Yorkshire.'

'Excellent! I think we'd better come over to see you immediately. Are you free?'

'Of course. I'm just going to have a brandy and a cigar. Come over and join me. Is Carlsen with you?'

'Yes.'

'Good. My wife's longing to meet him. Come as soon as you can.'

On the way out of the airport, they stopped at the bookstall, and Fallada bought an atlas of the British Isles. In the helicab, he opened it, searched for a moment, then gave an exclamation of satisfaction. He handed it to Carlsen, his finger pressed on the page. 'Look.'

Holmfirth, Carlsen saw, was a small town some five miles south of Huddersfield. The contour map showed high ground shaded in yellow and brown. Holmfirth was on the edge of a brown area.

'I'd guess it's less than two hundred and fifty miles from London. That means we could make it in less than an hour in a Grasshopper.'

Carlsen said: 'God forbid…Not tonight, anyway.'

'Tired?'

'Yes.' But as he spoke, he knew it was not the truth. He was afraid: afraid to go home, afraid to seek out the aliens, afraid to do nothing. But the logical part of him told him he had nothing to lose by going on.

The helicab touched down at the ramp in Sloane Square; from there, they walked the two hundred yards to Eaton Place. Fallada said: 'Incidentally, Heseltine's wife is anxious to meet you. She used to be the most beautiful deb in London—Peggy Beauchamp.' He patted Carlsen's shoulder. 'So I hope you'll control your fatal charm.'

He spoke jokingly, but Carlsen knew him well enough to sense the underlying seriousness. He smiled, clearing his throat.

They stopped at the front door of a red-brick three-storey house, whose ugly iron railings dated from the Victorian period. The door was opened by a slim, pretty woman in a green kimono. Fallada kissed her on the cheek. 'Peggy, this is Olof Carlsen.'

'I'm so glad to meet you at last, Commander.'

Carlsen had expected her to be older. He said: 'I'm delighted to meet you.' Their hands touched while he was still speaking; suddenly, without any process of thought, he was involved in her mind and feelings. He was glad the light in the hall was poor; he felt the colour rising to his face.

'Percy's gone up to his study. Have you come here to talk shop?'

Fallada said diplomatically: 'Not entirely. It shouldn't take more than a few minutes.'

'I hope not. I've just made coffee.'

She led them into the drawing-room; it was a pleasant, comfortable room, with old-fashioned furniture of the early twenty-first century.

'I'll give Percy a buzz and tell him you're here. He didn't expect you to get here so soon.'

Fallada said: 'Why don't I go up myself? Olof, stay and talk to Lady Heseltine while I go and get Percy.'

As Fallada went out she asked: 'Black or white?'

'White, please.'

'Brandy?'

'Just a little.'

Watching her as she stood at the sideboard, he experienced a confusion of feeling. The moment of insight had taught him more than he could have learned in weeks of intimacy. This power to enter the inmost thoughts of an attractive woman brought a sense of deep satisfaction. It also disturbed him; it seemed a proof that he was changing into another person.

She placed the coffee and brandy on the table. 'It's strange, but I feel as if I know you rather well. Perhaps because I've seen you on television.'

Their hands brushed as she handed him the sugar. He put it on the table and took her hand: Looking up into her face, he said: 'Tell me something. Can you read my thoughts?'

She stared back with surprise but made no effort to withdraw her hand. His insight into her thoughts told him that she was about to say: 'Of course not'; then she checked the response and allowed her mind to become receptive. At once he became aware of a flicker of communication. She said hesitantly: I…I think I can.'

He released her hand; her thoughts became remote, like a poor telephone connection. She asked: 'What on earth does it mean?'

'Did your husband tell you about the vampires?'

She nodded.

'Then you shouldn't have to ask.'

Obedient to a thought suggestion, she sat beside him on the settee. He took her hand again, placing his thumb in the centre of her wrist, and the fingers spread across the back of the hand; he knew instinctively that this would ensure the best contact. She lowered her eyes to concentrate. It was a strange sensation: to have known her for less than five minutes and yet to have achieved a more intimate contact than her husband had. She was still too confused to read his thoughts accurately, but he was clearly aware of a two-way communication. She also registered his feeling-responses. The kimono had fallen open at the neck, showing the edge of a lace-trimmed bra; without observing the direction of his gaze, she reached up and adjusted it. Then she noticed him smiling, and coloured, realising that modesty was wasted. For all practical purposes, she might as well have been naked.

For the next ten minutes they sat perfectly still. They were not communicating so much as observing. He was inside her consciousness, seeing himself through her eyes, aware of the warmth of her body. An hour ago she had taken a bath and washed her hair; he was aware of the pleasure it gave her to feel relaxed and cool, faintly scented with the bath salts. It had never struck him that feminine consciousness was so basically different from a man's When a Persian cat jumped into her lap and rubbed its head against her, purring, he had a momentary glimpse into the cat's being, and was again astonished to realise that it was so unlike his own. For a moment, he was dazzled by the thought of millions of individuals, each a separate universe, each as strange and unique as an unexplored planet.

A telescreen buzzed upstairs, then stopped. She withdrew her hand reluctantly. She said in a low voice: 'Your coffee must be cold.'

'It doesn't matter.' He sipped the brandy with pleasure.

There was a constraint between them, like two people who have just made love for the first time and are now aware of the consequences. She poured herself coffee.

'Do you think this is grounds for divorce?'

The bantering tone sounded false. He said seriously: 'I suppose it is, in a way.'

She held out her glass and touched his. 'Have you ever made love as quickly as that before?'

He said: 'Made love?'

I suppose that's what it is. Or don't you agree?'

There was an odd kind of relief in merely talking to one another, without any other communication. She sat in the armchair facing him. She said: 'I now feel no curiosity whatever about you. I know you as if we'd been lovers for years. I feel I've given myself to you and allowed you to look into all my secrets. Isn't that being lovers?'

'I suppose so.' He was feeling very tired but relaxed.

'Are you still afraid of turning into a vampire?'

It was then that he realised, for the first time, that he had experienced no desire to take her life energy. He said: 'My God!'

'What is it?'

'Now I'm beginning to understand. These things *could* be deathless, couldn't they? They could simply transfer into new bodies.'

He started to laugh. She waited for him to explain.

'It's absurd. This morning, Geijerstam told me that I wasn't turning into a vampire, I was only becoming aware of the vampirism that exists in all of us. I didn't understand what he was talking about—or rather, I thought he was talking nonsense. Now I see he was right. I wonder how he knew that?'

'He's probably more feminine than you are.'

'What do you mean?'

'It's something I've always known. Although I must admit, I'd never realised it as clearly as in the last ten minutes. I think most women know it. When a woman falls in love, it's because she wants to know a man—to get inside his skin, become a part of him. I suppose masochism's a kind of distorted form of the same thing—the desire to be absorbed, to give oneself completely and entirely. On the other hand, I suppose most men just want to possess a girl—to feel they've conquered her. So they never notice that what they really want is to absorb her...'

'That's what Fallada says in his book—he's talking about cannibalism.'

She laughed. 'He's a clever man, our Hans.'

He crossed to the window and stood looking out on the neon-lighted trees of Eaton Square. 'Geijerstam said another thing. He said he thought human beings are at a turning point in their evolution. I wonder...'

She stood beside him, and he experienced the desire to touch her. He moved away quickly.

'What is it?' she asked.

'I. .. Something in me wants to take your energy.'

She reached out for his hand. 'Take it if you need it.' When he hesitated, she said: 'I want to give it to you.' She raised his hand and placed it on the bare flesh below her throat. He tried to control the sudden voracious desire as his hand groped inside the kimono and found the naked breast. Suddenly, with exquisite pleasure, the energy was flowing into him; he was drinking it like a thirsty man. He felt her shudder and lean against him. He looked down at her face; the lips were bloodless, but it was perfectly calm. All his tiredness had left him as the force flowed from her. It was a temptation to bend down and suck the energy through her lips; some odd touch of conventionality restrained him. As he withdrew his hand, she moved dreamily across the room and sank onto the settee, closing her eyes. He said anxiously: 'Are you all right?'

'Yes.' Her voice was hardly more than a whisper. 'Tired, but...quite happy.' She looked up at him; it struck him that he had seen the same look in Jelka's eyes when she was exhausted after giving birth to Jeanette. She said: 'Go upstairs and see what Hans and Percy are doing, would you?' She was afraid that they would come down and see her like this.

'Of course.'

'Upstairs and first on the right.'

He went slowly up the stairs. He could hear Fallada's voice coming from behind the door. He knocked, then went in. 'Your wife sent me up to see where you were.'

Fallada said: 'Oh, dear, I suppose we'd better go down.'

He said quickly: 'Don't worry—I think she understands.'

Heseltine rose from behind the desk to shake hands. 'You're looking well, Carlsen. I've been hearing about your incredible adventures in Sweden. Do have a seat. Whisky?'

'No thanks. I've had a brandy.'

'Then have another.' As he poured, he asked: 'How seriously do you take this business about the Prime Minister?'

Carlsen said: 'I don't know what to reply. In a way, I know as little about it as you do. I simply heard my own voice on the tape.'

'You've no memory of saying it?'

'I've no memory of anything that happened while I was hypnotised.'

'Frankly'—Heseltine searched for words—'you see, I've been at Downing Street all afternoon. I find it frankly incredible to think—'

He was interrupted by the telescreen. He pressed the receiving button. 'Hello?'

'Sir Percy? It's Chief Constable Duckett on the line.'

A moment later a broad Yorkshire voice said: 'Hello, Perce, me again.'

'Any news?'

'Ay I think so. I've checked up on Arthur Pryce. He runs an electronics factory at Penistone—that's just across the moor from Holmfirth.'

'And the hospital?'

'That's more of a problem. There's five in the Huddersfield area, including one for geriatrics. The only one near Holmfirth is Thirlstone.'

'Thirlstone? Isn't that an asylum?'

'Ay, for the criminally insane. That's up on the moor, a mile putside the town.'

Heseltine was silent for a moment, then said: 'Okay, Ted, that's fine. Very helpful. I'll probably see you tomorrow.'

'Are you coming up yourself?' He was obviously surprised.

'It might be necessary. See you then.'

As he cleared the line, Carlsen said: 'That's the place.'

Heseltine looked at him with surprise: 'Thirlstone? How do you know?'

'I don't. But if it's a criminal lunatic asylum, it's the kind of place they'd choose.'

Fallada said with excitement: 'He's right. It hadn't struck me before we went to see Geijerstam, but these things can probably possess people without actually killing them. When I saw the way Magnus's handwriting had changed after he made the Black Pilgrimage, I suddenly realised that he was two people—in the same body.'

Heseltine interrupted: 'Who the hell's Magnus?'

'I'll explain that later. All I'm trying to say now is that an asylum for the criminally insane would be an ideal refuge for a vampire. If she's still in that area, *thats* where she is.'

'In that case'—Heseltine looked at his watch—I wonder if we can afford to wait until tomorrow.' He looked at Carlsen, then Fallada. 'How do you feel?'

Fallada shrugged. 'I'll go anywhere at any time. I'm not so sure about Olof. He's got a wife and family waiting at home.'

Carlsen said: 'No. They expect me when they see me.'

'Good. In that case…'He pressed the dialling buttons.'Hello. Sergeant Parker, please…Ah, Parker, I'm going to need a Grasshopper tonight. I have to go to Yorkshire. Are you free to take us?'

'I will be in ten minutes, when Culvershaw gets back.'

'Good. That'll be excellent. Land in Belgrave Square and give me a call when you arrive.' He cleared the line and turned to Carlsen. 'Now, Commander, if you'd like to call your wife. And after that, I'll see if I can get on to the Superintendent of Thirlstone and warn him to expect us.'

Twenty minutes later, they were watching the neon flares of the city recede into the distance behind them. As far ahead as the eye" could see, the lights of the Great North Way stretched like a giant airstrip. They were flying well below the usual air-traffic routes, at a speed of three hundred miles an hour. On the road below them, car headlights moved in a continual stream.

Heseltine said: 'Strictly speaking, I'm disobeying instructions in leaving London.'

'Why?'

'I'm supposed to be working directly under the Home Secretary and reporting every fresh development direct to his office. That's what the P.M. wanted to see me about —co-ordinating the search for the aliens.'

Carlsen asked: 'Did he have any suggestions about how to go about it?'

'No. In fact, he rather implied—without actually saying so—that he thought you and Fallada were slightly mad. All the same, we've set up an elaborate report procedure.'

Fallada said with disgust: 'And if nothing gets reported, he'll use that as evidence that there's no danger.'

They were silent for several minutes, each absorbed in his own thoughts. Heseltine said: 'Do you think there's *any* way of testing whether an individual's a vampire?'

Carlsen shook his head. Fallada looked at him in surprise. 'Of course there is. We used it on you this morning.'

Heseltine asked: 'What's that?'

'Radiesthesia—the pendulum.'

Carlsen grunted. 'I didn't get the impression it proved anything except that I'm male.'

'Ah, but you missed the most interesting part. You were asleep.'

Heseltine said: 'Would you mind explaining?'

Fallada said: 'You can use a pendulum like water-divining rods. It reacts to different substances at different lengths—twenty-four inches for a male, twenty-nine for a female. The Count said he'd used it to test whether one of his patients was possessed by a vampire—it reacted to both the male *and* female length when it was held above him. That's why he tried it on Olof.'

'And what happened?'

'It reacted for male and female. But that's not all. Geijerstam agreed it could be a coincidence, because the female length also indicates danger. So he tried testing Olof at lengths beyond forty inches—that's the length for death and sleep. Apparently there shouldn't be any reaction beyond that length, because death's an ultimate limit. As Olof lay asleep, the old woman tested him at forty inches, and got a strong reaction. Then she lengthened it to sixty-four—forty inches plus the normal male length. She got no reaction at all. So she lengthened it to sixty-nine—forty plus the female length. And the damn thing began to sweep around in enormous circles.'

Heseltine asked quietly: 'Which indicates what?'

'He wasn't sure. But he said that it *could* mean that whatever was causing the reaction was already dead.'

Carlsen felt the hairs on his neck prickle. His voice sounded oddly strained as he said: 'I don't believe that. These things are alive, all right.'

Fallada shrugged. 'I'm only reporting what Geijerstam said. I don't think these things are supernatural either.'

Heseltine said: 'That depends on what you mean by supernatural.'

'Well, dead…ghosts, whatever you want to call it.'

Carlsen experienced the now-familiar sense of despair and hopelessness, the feeling that the world had suddenly become immensely alien. He was accustomed to the emptiness of space, but even in the outer limits of the solar system, he had never lost a sense of belonging to the earth, of being a member of the human race. Now there was a frightening sense of inner coldness, as if he were moving into areas where no other human being could follow. Looking at the endless lights of the Great North Way and at the glow of some city—probably Nottingham —in the distance, he was overwhelmed by a sense of unreality that was like falling. The panic began to build up. And then, just as suddenly, it stopped. Whatever happened was too quick to be grasped by his perceptions. There was a flash of insight that made the panic seem absurd. Then the lights below seemed to become brighter; there was a sudden wave of delight, a sense of freshness. It had gone as quickly as it came, leaving him startled and puzzled. His eyes felt tired, and he closed them. A moment later, Fallada was saying: 'Wake up, Olof. We've arrived.' He realised that the Grasshopper was about to land on a deserted road and that its powerful searchlights were illuminating the tops of trees. He said: 'Where are we?'

The pilot said over his shoulder: 'A few miles south of Huddersfield. Holmfirth can't be far away.'

He looked at his watch. It was nine-fifteen; he had been asleep for half an hour.

On the road, the Grasshopper ceased to be powered by jets; rotary drive took over, and the short wings retracted; in effect, it became a large car. A few yards further on, they halted at a crossroad; one arm of the signpost pointed to Barnsley, the other to Holmfirth.

Heseltine said: 'It's still early. I think we have time to pay a visit to Mr. Pryce. Sergeant, get on to Information and find out where we can find Upperthong Road.'

The pilot dialled the computerised street guide. A map of Holmfirth flashed onto the television monitor, one of the roads illuminated in red. Parker said: 'That's lucky. We seem to be on it.'

It took less than five minutes to locate the house, an expensive bungalow of glass and fibreflex standing in a quarter of an acre of lawn; a spotlight illuminated the ornamental pond and the flower beds.

An elderly lady answered the doorbell; she looked alarmed to see three strangers. Heseltine produced his identification. 'Is it possible to speak to your husband?'

She asked: 'Is it income tax?'

Heseltine said soothingly: 'No, no. Nothing to worry about. He might be able to help us with a piece of information.'

'Just a moment, please.' She disappeared inside. Heseltine looked at the others and winked. 'It's obvious what she's got on her conscience.' Several minutes elapsed, then the woman came back. 'Come in, please.'

She led them into a curtained sitting room. A powerful elderly man in a wheelchair was seated at the table, with a cold meal in front of him. Heseltine said: 'Mr. Arthur Pryce?'

'Yes.' He seemed unalarmed; only curious.

'I...think there must be some mistake. Do you own a Crystal Flame number QBX 5279L?'

'Ay. That's mine.'

'Have you been driving it today?'

The woman interjected: 'No. He can't drive any more.'

The man said: 'Shut up, Nell.' He turned to Heseltine. 'Has it been involved in an accident?'

'Oh, no, nothing of the kind. We just want to trace the man who was driving it this morning.'

The woman said: 'That'll be Ned,'

Will you keep quiet!'

Heseltine asked: 'Who is Ned?'

The man glowered at his wife. 'Our son. He runs the business for me since I had the accident'

'I see. Could I have his address?'

The man said finally: 'He only lives across the road. What's it all about, then?'

'Nothing to worry about, I assure you, Mr. Pryce. We're trying to trace a missing person and thought he might be able to give us some information. What's the number of the house?'

The man said sulkily: 'One five nine.'

The woman, now reassured, showed them to the gate, and pointed to a house fifty yards away. 'The one with the red curtains—you can't miss it.'

The house with the red curtains looked appreciably less expensive than the other; the garden was tangled and overgrown. The car they were looking for stood in front of the garage door. When Heseltine rang the doorbell, a voice spoke from a small loudspeaker, 'Who is it?'

"The police. Could we have a word with Mr. Pryce?'

There was no reply, but a moment later, the door opened. A small, fair-haired woman was carrying a sleeping child who was far too big for her. She might have been pretty if she had looked less harassed and defeated. She peered out awkwardly from behind the head that rested on her shoulder and asked in a whisper: 'What do you want?'

'Could we speak to your husband, please?'

'He's gone to bed.'

'Could you see if he's asleep? It's fairly important.'

She looked from one to the other, evidently overawed by Heseltine's quiet air of authority. 'Well, I don't know...You'll have to wait a moment...'

'Of course.'

They watched her plod slowly upstairs, staggering with the weight of the child. Several minutes went by. Heseltine, said, sighing: 'It reminds me of my old days on the beat. I was never any good at intruding on people.' They stood staring into the hall, which contained a pram, a bicycle and a box of children's toys. Five minutes later, a man appeared at the top of the stairs. As he advanced to meet them, Carlsen could see that he was red-haired and overweight, with an unhealthy complexion. He looked worried, slightly furtive.

He seemed reassured when Heseltine apologised for disturbing him and asked if he could spare them a few minutes. He glanced up the stairs, then invited them in.

In the lounge, the sixty-inch colour television was the only illumination. The man switched the sound down, then turned on the wall light. He dropped into the armchair, massaging his eyes with his fingers. His hands were muscular and covered with coarse red hair.

Heseltine said: 'Mr. Pryce, at about eleven-thirty this morning, you were up on the moor in the car that is now outside your house.'

The man grunted but said nothing. He looked as if he had been awakened from a deep sleep. Carlsen could sense his fatigue and alarm.

Heseltine said: 'We want to know about the girl in the red and yellow striped dress...'

The man looked up quickly, then dropped his eyes again. He cleared his throat and asked: 'I haven't broken the law, have I?'

Heseltine's voice was soothing. 'Of course you haven't, Mr. Pryce. No one's suggesting that you have.'

The man asked aggressively: 'What's this all about, then?'

It was Carlsen who sensed the right approach. He had been looking at the photographs on the shelf; in most of them, the man was smiling or laughing with a group of other men. It was the face of an extrovert who disliked being made to feel guilty. Carlsen sat down on a hard-backed chair, where he could look into the man's face. 'Let me be frank with you, Mr. Pryce. We need your help, and anything you tell, us won't go beyond this room. We simply want to know what happened with the girl.'

As he spoke, he placed his hand lightly on the man's shoulder. The insight was instantaneous and unexpected, as if he had found himself listening in to someone's telephone conversation. He was in the car, and the scene was familiar, as if in a remembered dream. It was the car park on the edge of the moor; he was reading a newspaper, at first unaware of the girl who sat nearby on a bench. Then the girl was in the car.

The man said: 'What has she done?'

'She's done nothing. But we have to trace her. Where did you go when she got into the car?'

He said unwillingly: 'By the reservoir...' Carlsen had a clear, sharp glimpse of the scene: the back seat of the car, the man unable to believe his luck as she allowed his hand to move along the inside of her thigh; then the discovery that she was wearing no underwear.

'You made love. And what then?'

There was a thump from overhead. Carlsen could feel Pryce's relief to know that his wife was still upstairs, not listening at the door.

'We sat and talked. Then she suggested we should go to a hotel. So we went to Leeds—-'

Carlsen nodded. 'To the Europa Hotel. What time did you leave there?'

'Around seven.'

'And by that time she'd already left?'

The man shrugged. 'You seem to know it all anyway.' The movement caused Carlsen's hand to, fall from his shoulder; the contact was instantly broken. He stood up. Thank you, Mr. Pryce. You've been very helpful.'

As they moved to the door, Heseltine asked: 'Had you arranged to see her again?'

The man sighed, then nodded, without speaking. He heaved himself to his feet and accompanied them to the door. As he opened it, he looked direct into Carlsen's face. I suppose you blame me. But it's not often a man gets a piece of luck like that.'

Carlsen said, smiling: 'But if you'll pardon me saying so, she seems to have exhausted you.'

The man grinned; for a moment there was a flash of genuine good humour. 'It was worth it.'

As they walked back to the Grasshopper, Heseltine asked: 'Do you think it was?'

'What?'

'Worth it?'

'From his point of view, yes. She's drained his energy, but he'll recover in a couple of days. It's no worse than a bad hangover.'

'And it won't do any permanent damage?'

'If you mean do I think he'll become a vampire, the answer is no.'

Fallada asked quickly: 'What makes you say that?'

'I…I don't know. I just feel it. I can't tell you how I know.'

Heseltine looked at him curiously but said nothing.

The sergeant was studying an ordnance survey map. 'I've just been on to this loony bin over the radiophone, sir. I reckon it must be those lights you can see on the top of that hill.' He pointed into the distance.

Heseltine looked at his watch. 'We'd better get over there. It's getting late.'

Less than four minutes later, the searchlight of the Grasshopper picked out the massive grey building on the hilltop. As they approached, the lights began to go out. Fallada said: 'Ten o'clock. Bedtime for the inmates.'

The lawn in front of the hospital remained illuminated by a floodlight. As they sank quietly towards it on a cushion of air, Heseltine asked: 'Is it safe to land? Shan't we set off the radar alarms?'

'He's already switched them off, sir. I said we'd arrive around ten.'

As they touched down, the main door opened; a bulky shape stood outlined against the light from the hallway. Heseltine said: 'I think that must be the Superintendent —the man I spoke to. He struck me as a bit of a clown.' As they descended onto the grass, he said in Fallada's ear: 'Incidentally, he claims to be a great admirer of yours.'

Fallada said mildly: 'I hope the two are not connected.'

The man came towards them. 'Well, this is a great honour, Commissioner, a very great honour…I'm Dr. Armstrong.'

His bulk was immense; Carlsen guessed he must have weighed at least three hundred pounds. He was clad in a loose grey suit of a type that had been unfashionable for twenty years. The voice was fruity and cultured: an actor's voice.

Heseltine shook his hand. 'It's most kind of you to receive us so late. This is Dr. Hans Fallada. And Commander Olof Carlsen.'

Armstrong passed a fat hand across the fluffy mass of grey hair. 'I'm quite overwhelmed! So many famous guests, and all at once!' As he shook hands, Carlsen noticed that his teeth were enormous and tobacco-stained.

Armstrong led them into the hall. The smell of violet-perfumed furniture polish overlaid a ranker odour: of sweat and stale cooking. Armstrong talked all the time, the rich, mellifluous voice echoing in the bare hallway. 'I'm *so* sorry my wife's not here to receive you. She'll be green with envy. She's visiting relatives in Aberdeen. This way, please. What about your pilot? Isn't he coming in?'

'He'll stay out there for now. He can watch the television news.'

'I'm afraid this place is dreadfully untidy.' Carlsen observed that the door to his private quarters was lined with metal. 'I'm looking after myself at the moment…Ah, George, are you still there?'

A good-looking youth with a cast in one eye and a vacant stare said: 'Nearly finished.'

'Well, leave it till morning. You should be back in your quarters. But before you go, bring in some ice from the fridge.' As the man ambled out he said in a whisper: 'One of our trusties. A delightful boy.'

Carlsen said: 'What is he in for?'

'Killing his little sister. Jealousy, you know. Please sit down, gentlemen. You will have a whisky, won't you?'

'Thank you.'

Fallada noticed the open magazine by the armchair. He said: 'Ah, you've been reading my piece on vampirism.'

'Oh, of course. I've kept all four articles from the *BPJ*. Absolutely masterly! You should write a book about it.'

I have.'

'Really? How fortunate! I'm longing to read it.' He handed Fallada a tumbler half full of whisky. 'It's all so true. My wife drains me dry.' He smiled, to indicate that he should not be taken too seriously. 'Soda?'

The youth had placed a dish of ice cubes on the table. Armstrong said: 'Good boy. Now off to bed. Good night's rest!'

As the door closed, Fallada said: 'Suppose he walks out of the front door instead?'

'He wouldn't get far. This place has batteries of electronic alarms.'

'What if he let some of the dangerous prisoners out?'

'Impossible. They're locked in separate cells.' He sat down. 'Well, gentlemen, to your health! I can hardly believe you're really here!' Carlsen observed that sheer enthusiasm made^his unctuous personality rather likable. 'I hope you'll stay the night.'

Heseltine said: Thank you, but we've booked into the Continental in Huddersfield.'

'You can easily cancel.'

Fallada said thoughtfully: 'That might be an idea. We've got to come back in the morning.'

'Excellent! Then let's regard it as settled. The beds are made up in the orderlies' wing. Now, what can I do for you?'

Heseltine leaned forward. 'You've been reading Fallada's article on vampirism. Do you believe that real vampires exist?'

As he spoke, Carlsen observed the sinking feeling, as if falling backwards into a void. The voices became distant; instead, there was emptiness, the cold of space. He felt the energy draining from him, as if someone had opened a vein and allowed the blood to run. Again, he was aware of the agony and bewilderment on the derelict, and of the answering misery and tension in the alien that now sucked his energy. The room became unreal, as if a thin silver screen, like a waterfall, had been interposed in front of his eyes. He was drifting downward, like a leaf falling from a high tree. At the same time, he experienced a sexual tingle in the muscles of his belly and in the flesh of his loins. For a moment he relaxed, enjoying it, then made an effort to resist. The loss of energy ceased immediately. But now he was feeling heavy and tired. The alien was still draining his energy, now only a token amount. With mild astonishment, he realised that she was unaware of his physical proximity. Distance made no difference to them; a million miles or fifty yards: it was all the same.

He became aware of Armstrong's voice, and for a moment was frozen with astonishment at the incredible things he was saying. Then he realised that Armstrong was not actually saying them. He was speaking about one of his patients, but the inflections of the voice revealed his deepest thoughts and feelings. It seemed to Carlsen that the Superintendent of Thirlstone was some ~huge, soft-bodied creature, floating in the psychic bloodstream of his criminal lunatic asylum like a jellyfish or Portuguese man-of-war in a warm sea. His nature was multi-sexual; not merely attracted to men or women but to all creatures with a pulse of life. The disturbing thing was the deep, unsatisfied voracity of his longings. He was drawn to the inmates under his charge with an enormous, prurient curiosity. In his imagination, he had committed violations that surpassed all their crimes. One day, when his sense of reality had weakened, he might finally commit a sadistic crime. But at the moment he was all caution, with the instinct of a hunted animal.

Armstrong was saying: 'Her name's Ellen, not Helen. Ellen Donaldson. She's been in charge of the female staff for the past two years.'

Heseltine asked: 'Isn't it dangerous for women to work here?'

'Not as dangerous as you might think. Besides, women are rather good for the male patients. They're a soothing influence.'

Carlsen said: 'Could I see her?' They all looked at him in surprise.

Armstrong said: 'Of course. I don't suppose she's in bed yet. I'll ask her to come over.'

Carlsen said: 'No. I mean alone.'

There was a silence. Fallada said: 'Is that a good idea?'

'I'll be safe enough. I've met her before and survived.'

'You've met her?' Armstrong was surprised.

Heseltine said: 'He means the alien.'

'Ah, of course.' Carlsen could read his thoughts. Armstrong thought they were all slightly mad, or at least thoroughly confused. His certainty gave him a sense of superiority. His total absorption in his own desires and emotions made him incredulous of anything beyond his own limited understanding.

Fallada said: 'Why do you want to see her now? Why not wait until morning?'

Carlsen shook his head. 'They're most active in the night. It's better now.'

Heseltine nodded. 'Yes. You could be right. But listen. Take this.' He handed Carlsen a small plastic box, two inches square. He pressed the button in the centre; immediately, a high-pitched buzz sounded from the pocket of his jacket. 'If you need us, press this. We'll be with you in seconds.' He released the button, and the noise stopped.

Carlsen asked: "Where is she?'

Armstrong heaved himself to his feet. 'I'll take you.'

He led Carlsen out of the main door, along a gravel path by the edge of the lawn, through a walled garden with a lily pond, to a closed gate. He took a key from his pocket and unlocked the gate. Carlsen could see a long, low building with outside lights over each front door. "That's the nurses' quarters. Nurse Donaldson is in the one at the end, number one.'

Thank you.'

'Hadn't I better come and introduce you?'

'I'd rather you didn't.'

'Very well. The gate opens from the other side without a key. If you're not back in half an hour, we'll come and look for you.' His voice indicated he was joking, but there was an undertone of seriousness.

The gate closed behind him. Carlsen walked to the porch of the first chalet and rang the bell. A woman's voice answered through the loudspeaker: 'Who is it?'

He leaned and spoke into it. 'My name is Carlsen. I'd like to speak to you.'

He expected more questions, but the speaker went dead. A moment later, the door was opened. The woman who stood there looked at him with curiosity and without fear. 'What is it you want?'

'Can I come in and speak to you?'

'How did you get in?'

'Dr. Armstrong brought me.'

'Come in.' She stood aside and let him past. She closed the door behind him, then went to an inter-communicating screen. A moment later, Armstrong's voice said: 'Hello?'

I have a Mr. Carlsen here. Did you know?'

'Yes. I brought him. That is Commander Carlsen.'

I see.' She switched off. While she had been speaking, he had been standing near the door, looking at her. He was disappointed. For some reason he had expected her to be beautiful. The reality was oddly commonplace. She was a woman of about thirty-five, and the skin of her face was coarse. The figure had been shapely but was now beginning to spread. He noted that the hem of the green woollen dress was lopsided.

'What did you want to see me about?' Her voice had a ring of mechanical efficiency, like a telephone operator. For a moment he wondered if he had made a mistake.

'May I sit down?' She shrugged and indicated the armchair. He wanted an excuse to touch her, but she was too far away. He said: 'I wanted to ask you about the man you spent the afternoon with—Mr. Pryce.'

'I don't know what you're talking about.'

'I think you do. Show me your hand.'

She looked at him in surprise. 'I beg your pardon?'

'Show me your hand.'

She was standing, pressed back against the edge of a small table by the wall. Then, suddenly, there was contact. They were playing a game, and both knew the rules. She stood staring at him, then came forward very slowly. He reached out and took both her hands. The energy flow was like an electric spark. She swayed, and he stood up to steady her. The energy was flowing out of her, into him.

He looked down at her face; her stare was glassy. As clearly as if she had spoken, he felt the unformulated comment. He gripped her tightly by her bare arms. 'What's his name?'

She was leaning against him. 'I don't know.'

'Tell me?' She shook her head.

'I'll hurt you.' He squeezed her arms. She shook her head again. Deliberately, as if making a move in chess, he held her away from him and slapped her face. She shook her head again.

There was a knock at the door. It made him start, but she seemed to hear nothing. He said: 'Who is it?' There was another knock. He lowered the woman into a chair, then went to the door. It was Fallada. 'Are you all right?'

'Yes, of course. Come in.'

Fallada came into the room and saw the woman. He said: 'Good evening.' Then he looked at Carlsen. 'What's wrong with her?'

Carlsen sat on the arm of her chair. Her face was red where he had slapped it, and tears were running down her face.

'Nothing wrong.' He sensed Fallada's question. 'She's quite harmless.'

'Can she hear us?'

'Probably. But she's not interested. She's like a hungry child.'

'Hungry?'

'She wants me to hurt her.'

Fallada said: 'Are you serious?'

'Quite. You see, when she's possessed by the alien, she sucks energy from her victims. But she gives it all away again. She's like a woman who steals for her lover. Now, if I take energy from her'—he placed his hand on her arm—'she responds automatically. She's conditioned to giving.'

'Are you taking energy now?'

'A little, enough to keep her semiconscious. If I stop, she'll wake up.'

'Like the girl last night—Miss Bengtsson?'

'Yes. But with her, it was just a normal desire for surrender. This one is far worse. She'd like to be completely destroyed.'

'Totally masochistic?'

'Quite.'

'Wouldn't it be better to leave her alone?'

When I've found out what I want to know: the name of the prisoner who's taking her energy.'

Fallada knelt in front of the woman and raised her eyelid. She looked at him indifferently; she was interested only in Carlsen.

'Can't you read her mind?'

'She's resisting. She doesn't want to tell me.'

'Why?'

'I've told you. She wants me to force her to tell me.'

Fallada stood up. 'Would you like me to leave?'

"There's no need—if you don't mind waiting. This gives me no pleasure.' He said to the woman: 'Stand up.'

She stood up slowly, a smile nickering at the corners of her mouth. Carlsen put his arms round her. He noticed that she winced as his left hand pressed her back. He said: 'Tell me his name?' She shook her head, smiling. He pressed her back again. She gasped and writhed against him, then shook her head again.

Fallada said: 'What's hurting her?'

'I don't know.' Carlsen took hold of the zipper and pulled it down to the waist. The dress parted. The flesh of her back was scored with scratches.

Fallada looked more closely. "They're fresh. A souvenir of her lover today.'

Carlsen could feel the energy flowing through the bare flesh where his hands touched. He started to pull the dress forward off her shoulders. Fallada said: 'What are you doing?'

'If you don't want to watch, go into the other room.'

Fallada said: 'Not at all. I am a natural voyeur.'

Carlsen pulled the dress downwards, and allowed it to fall around her feet. She was wearing a bra and panties that were held at the waist by a small safety pin. Her arms now moved around Carlsen's neck. He held her close against him, feeling the warmth of naked flesh radiating through his clothes. He wanted to remove his own clothes for closer contact, but was inhibited by Fallada's presence. With one hand against her buttocks, the other on the torn skin between her shoulder blades, he pressed her tightly against him. She winced; then, as he pressed his mouth against hers, she suddenly abandoned herself. The vitality flowed into him through her lips, the tips of her breasts, and the pubic region.

Fallada cleared his throat. 'It's incredible. Her back is becoming paler...'

She freed her mouth to say: 'Now. Now.'

Fallada said: 'Are you *sure* you wouldn't prefer me to go?'

Carlsen ignored him. He did as she asked, brutally draining her energy as if intent on destroying her. He felt the glow of her body as she writhed against him, and the pressure of her arms almost stifled his breath. Her thighs and hips ground against him. Then her grip relaxed, and her knees buckled. Suddenly, her mind was no longer closed.

Fallada helped him to prevent her from falling. Carlsen picked her up and carried her into the bedroom. There was a pink-shaded lamp, and the bedsheets were turned back. He laid her on the bed. Fallada, standing in the doorway, said: 'That is the first time I have ever known a woman to reach orgasm in the upright position. Kinsey would have been fascinated.'

Carlsen pulled the bedclothes over her. Tendrils of hair were plastered over her forehead with perspiration. A dribble of saliva was running down the side of her mouth. He switched off the light and backed quietly out of the bedroom.

It was starting to rain as they left the house, a fine drizzle blown on the wind that came from the moorland. The air had the sweet smell of broom and heather. Carlsen was startled by the sensation of delight that ran through his body like electricity. And then, as if cut off by a switch, it stopped. He was puzzled, but a moment later had forgotten it.

Fallada said: 'And you still didn't find out what you wanted to know.'

'I found out enough.'

The lawn was now in darkness; they could see the shape of the Grasshopper, outlined by its phosphorescent paint. From the row of long, low buildings opposite, a man crossed the lawn towards them. Armstrong's voice said: 'Is everything satisfactory?'

Carlsen said: 'Fine, thanks.'

'Your sergeant has decided to retire to bed. You're over there, by the way, the three end rooms.' He pointed to the lighted buildings.

He inserted a key and opened the front door; the hall was now lit only by a blue night light. Heseltine was walking up and down the room. He said: 'Good, I was beginning to worry.' He told Armstrong: 'There's been an awful racket coming from upstairs—someone screaming.'

Armstrong said imperturbably: 'Many of the inmates suffer from nightmares.'

Carlsen said: 'If I described one of the inmates to you, do you think you could tell me who it is?'

'Probably. If I couldn't, the chief nurse could.'

'This is a big man—over six feet. He has a large nose—rather beaky—and red hair with a bald spot...'

Armstrong interrupted. 'I know him. That's Reeves —Jeff Reeves.'

Fallada said: 'The child killer?'

'That's the man.'

Carlsen said: 'Could you tell me about him?'

Armstrong said: 'Well...he's been in here for, oh, five years. He's rather subnormal—I.Q. of a child of ten. And he committed most of his crimes at the time of the full moon—four murders and about twenty sexual assaults. It took them two years to catch him—his mother was shielding him.'

Fallada said: 'If I remember rightly, he claimed he was possessed by the devil.'

'Or some kind of demon.' Armstrong turned to Carlsen.

'If you don't mind me asking, where did you get his description?'

'From the nurse—Ellen Donaldson.'

'Couldn't she tell you his name?'

'I didn't ask her.'

Armstrong shrugged; Carlsen sensed his suspicion that they were keeping something from him.

Heseltine asked: 'Is this man with the other prisoners?'

'Not at the moment. He becomes violent at the full moon. And since it's the full moon tomorrow, he's in a cell of his own at the moment.'

Heseltine asked Carlsen: 'Do you want to see him tonight?'

Carlsen shook his head. 'It's best to wait until tomorrow. They're less active during the daytime.'

Armstrong said: 'Would you like me to send for Lamson, the head nurse? He might be able to tell us whether Reeves has shown any signs of...vampirism.' The irony was scarcely perceptible.

Carlsen said: There's no need. He wouldn't have noticed anything—except, possibly, that Reeves is slightly less stupid than usual.'

Armstrong said: 'Then by all means let us ask. I'm intensely curious.'

Carlsen shrugged. Armstrong interpreted this as permission, and pressed a button on the I.C.S. He said: 'Lamson, would you mind coming over here?'

They sat in silence for a moment. Heseltine said: 'I still don't understand why this alien should choose a subnormal criminal. Surely she...it...could choose anybody?'

Carlsen said: 'No. To choose a criminal—particularly a criminal psychopath—is almost like moving into an empty house. Besides, this man already believed he was possessed by a devil. He wouldn't find anything strange in being possessed by a vampire.'

'But what about this nurse—Donaldson? I presume she's not a criminal?'

'It's not a matter of criminality so much as of a split personality.'

Fallada nodded. 'That's an axiom of psychology. Anyone who is at the mercy of powerful subconscious urges has a feeling of being two people.'

Armstrong said smoothly: 'If you're suggesting that Ellen Donaldson is suffering from severe personality dissociation, I can only say that I've never noticed it.'

As Fallada started to reply, Carlsen said: 'It didn't have to be a severe personality disorder. She's sexually frustrated. She has strong sexual drives and no husband. She also feels that she's no longer able to attract males. So when this creature satisfies her deepest sexual urges, she asks no questions...'

There was a knock at the door. Armstrong opened it. A powerful man with the build of a weight lifter came in. His eyes gleamed with interest and recognition as he saw Fallada and Carlsen.

Armstrong laid a hand on his shoulder. His voice was caressing as he said: 'This is my invaluable aide and chief assistant, Fred Lamson. Fred, these gentlemen are interested in Reeves.' Lamson nodded; he was obviously hoping to be introduced, but Armstrong had no intention of prolonging the interview more than necessary. Carlsen noted with amusement how Armstrong's attempt at camaraderie was spoiled by impatience and snobbery. 'Tell me, Fred, have you noticed anything different about Reeves in the past few weeks?'

Lamson shook his head slowly. 'No.'

Armstrong smiled. 'Nothing at all? Thank you, Fred.'

Lamson refused to be hurried. 'I was going to say, not in the past few *weeks*. But in the past couple of days, he's not been his usual self.'

'In what way?' Armstrong was unable to keep the impatience out of his voice.

'Oh, I couldn't really put my finger on it—'

Carlsen said: 'Did he strike you as more alert?'

Lamson massaged his close-cropped hair. 'I suppose that's it...I'll tell you one thing. The others are a bit inclined to bully him when he's quiet. But I notice they've been keeping out of his way for the past couple of days.'

Armstrong said: 'But that's because it's getting close to the full moon.'

Lamson shook his head stubbornly. 'No. I've seen *that* plenty of times. He gets all tense and nervous near the full moon. But he's different this time. It's like this gentleman says—he seems more alert.'

Fallada said: 'Have you ever seen anything like that before?'

'Can't say I have. They're more likely to go the other way.'

Armstrong said: 'But he's in solitary now?'

Well, yes, because we always put him in solitary at this time. But in my opinion, he didn't really need it this time. He just didn't strike me as... as...'

As he groped for words, Armstrong cut in peremptorily: 'Thank you, Fred. That's all we wanted to know. You can go now.'

Observing the big man's suppressed irritation, Carlsen said: 'You've been very helpful indeed. Thank you.'

'Not at all, sir.' Lamson smiled at them and went out.

Carlsen said: 'A point worth noticing. The alien doesn't wish to attract attention. But it doesn't realise that a psychopath's personality changes at the time of the full moon. And so it attracts attention, after all.'

Fallada asked Armstrong: 'Are you beginning to find it easier to believe in vampires?'

Armstrong said evasively: 'It's strange...very strange.'

Carlsen yawned and stood up. 'I think I'd like to go to bed.' Under normal circumstances, he would have been slightly overawed by Armstrong; now, able to perceive directly the underlying meanness of spirit, the vanity combined with a craving for admiration, he felt unable to control his distaste.

'Won't you have a nightcap first?'

Heseltine followed Carlsen's lead. 'We're all tired. We ought to get to bed.'

Carlsen said: 'This man Reeves. What time does he eat breakfast?'

'At about eight o'clock, usually.'

'Would it be possible to dose his food with a tranquilliser—a mild sedative?'

'I imagine so. If you think it necessary.'

'Thank you.'

He accompanied them to the door. In the hall, they met Lamson coming downstairs. Armstrong asked: 'Where have you been?'

'Just checking on Reeves, sir. What you said made me think—'

Carlsen asked: 'Did he see you?' 'Oh, he was awake, wide awake.'

They crossed the darkened lawn, Fallada walking ahead with Lamson. Carlsen said: 'It's a pity he had to do that.'

Heseltine shrugged. 'Why? It must be fairly normal— to check on the prisoners last thing at night.'

'I'm not sure…Anyway, it's too late to worry now.'

Their three rooms were next to one another. Sergeant Parker had moved their bags in from the Grasshopper. Carlsen was in his pyjamas when there was a knock on his door. Fallada came in, a bottle in his hand. 'Feel like a final whisky before bed?'

"That's a good idea.' He found glasses in the bathroom.

Fallada had removed his jacket and loosened his tie. They clinked glasses before drinking. Fallada said: 'I was fascinated by your remarks about split personalities. You really believe these things can't take over a healthy person by force?'

Carlsen, seated on the bed, shook his head. 'I didn't say that. They could probably take over anybody—by force and guile. But they'd need to virtually destroy a healthy person. That's probably why they had to destroy the early victims—like Clapperton.'

Fallada said: 'And the Prime Minister?'

'I…just don't know. It's hard to believe, and yet…there's something about him.' He frowned into his glass. 'It's something about all politicians—a kind of ability for double-think. They can't afford to be as honest as most people. They've got to be smooth and evasive.'

'Statesmanlike is the word you're looking for.'

'I suppose so. I've noticed the same thing about a lot of clergymen—the feeling they're professional liars. Or at least self-deceivers.' He suddenly became more animated. 'Yes, that's what I mean. It's the self-deceivers who'd make the easiest prey for vampires. People who won't let the left side of the mind know what the right side's doing. And *that's* the feeling I've got with Jamieson. He's the kind of person who wouldn't even know when he was being sincere.'

They sat in silence, each absorbed in his own thoughts. Fallada drained his whisky. He said: 'What are we to do if these things *are* indestructible? If there's no way of forcing them to leave the earth?' When Carlsen was silent, Fallada said: 'We've got to face that possibility. The world's full of criminal psychopaths. Every time we caught up with one, they could move on to another. Don't you agree?'

Again, Carlsen experienced the flash of insight, followed immediately by a sense of confusion, as if looking into a fog. He said: 'I don't know. I just don't know.'

Fallada stood up. 'You're tired. I'll let you get some sleep.' He paused, his hand on the door handle. 'But think about this. Isn't there any possibility of establishing some kind of understanding with these creatures? We know now they don't *have* to destroy people to get their nourishment. Look at that man Pryce. I got the impression he enjoyed giving his energy. He'd do it all over again for a chance of another afternoon in bed with that girl…It's worth bearing in mind.'

Carlsen smiled. 'All right. I promise I'll bear it in mind.'

Fallada said: 'Sleep well. I'm in the next room if you need me.'

He went out quietly. Carlsen crossed to the door and pressed the locking catch. He heard Fallada go into the room next door, then the sound of water in the wash basin. He climbed into bed and switched off the light. Fallada was right: he was tired. But when he closed his eyes, he experienced a strange sensation of duality. Part of him was lying in the bed, thinking about what he had to do the next day, and a part of him was detached, looking down on himself as if on a stranger. It was a cold, alien sensation. Then he felt his physical body sinking towards sleep, while the detached mind watched indifferently. A moment later he lost consciousness.

The awareness that returned was like floating upwards through dark water. He lay there, half asleep, surrounded by a warmth that was like the security of the womb. It was a deep, blissful relaxation, accompanied by a sense of timelessness. It was then that he realised the alien was there. She seemed to be beside him in the bed: the slim blonde girl whom he had last seen in the Space Research building. She was wearing some kind of thin garment, a gauzy material. He was sufficiently awake to think: this is impossible; this body was left behind in Hyde Park. She shook her head, smiling. Since he knew that his eyes were closed, he recognised that she was some kind of dream. Yet, unlike a dream, she seemed to possess duration and a certain reality.

Her hands reached inside the pyjama jacket, touching his solar plexus with the cool fingertips. He experienced a stir of desire. The hand tugged at the pyjama cord, then moved inside the trousers. At the same time, her mouth pressed against his; the tip of her tongue prized his lips apart. His arms lay by his side; he seemed unable to move them. Again, he tried to determine whether he was dreaming, and was unable to decide.

She was not speaking to him, but her feelings were being communicated direct. She was offering herself, telling him that he had only to take her. As her fingers moved over his body, his nerves flared into points of intensity like crystals reflecting the sunlight. He had never experienced a physical pleasure of such intensity. Again he tried to move his arms. His body seemed paralysed, inert.

He felt her head bending; the tip of her tongue ran over his neck, then across his chest. The pleasure reached an intensity that was almost painful. She seemed to be telling him: the body is unimportant; it is the mind that can experience freedom. Everything in him expressed affirmation.

It struck him suddenly that his mind, like his body, had reached a point of total passivity; his will had vanished. He was aware only of her will and its power to mould him. This produced a sudden uneasiness, a nervous withdrawal. He felt her impatience, a flash of imperious anger. Her attitude seemed to change. Instead of offering herself, transforming herself into a unified caress, she was ordering him not to be a fool. It aroused a memory he had forgotten for more than thirty years: a female cousin trying to persuade him to exchange a toy dog for a teddy bear. She had become angry and shaken him by the arms. Now, as then, the pressure aroused a sullen resistance. At the same time, he knew that if she returned to persuasion, he would give way. She held all the cards. Except one. Her own anger was impossible to control. She hated to be thwarted. He caught a glimpse of a sour abyss of frustration. He struggled to push her away. Then she was no longer caressing him but holding him tight, her mouth suddenly voracious. He had an illusion of being held by an octopus that had wrapped its tentacles around his limbs; the beak was seeking his throat. Terror burned his nerves, and he struggled violently. She held him a moment longer to prove her strength, but the murderous anger had cooled.

Although he was now fully awake, he was still unable to move. The fear had left him drained; he no longer had strength to fight. He could still experience her thoughts and feelings, and now he was able to grasp what had prevented her from killing him. His fear had aroused memories: of creatures struggling for life, drawn into the greedy vortex. Then she had remembered: for the time being, no one must die. It would wreck their plans. Even if she took over his body, it would be impossible to maintain the deception for long. Fallada would know the difference; so would his wife and children. He had to remain alive.

He became aware of a new kind of pressure. Now there was no longer someone in bed with him. He was sufficiently awake to know that there never had been. His pyjama jacket was still buttoned; the cord at the waist still tied. And the alien was no longer a woman. She had become a sexless creature, an 'it,' And it was outside him, trying to enter his body. His mental defences were closed, like hands covering his face; it was trying to force its way past the hands, to spread-eagle his will and force its way into his essential being. It was as cold and brutal as rape. He wanted to cry out, but he knew this would relax his guard.

Under the unrelenting pressure, he felt his defences yielding; the thing was forcing its way past them. He was suddenly aware of the consequences that would follow. This creature intended to enter his nervous system and sever it from his will; he would be a prisoner in his own brain, unable to move, like a fly bound by spider's silk. It needed to keep his individuality alive, but only for the sake of its knowledge. The thought of sharing his brain with the alien lent him a frantic strength. With his teeth clenched tightly together, he forced it away. This time he locked his will, as if contracting his arms and legs into the foetal position. The thing continued to cling, without relaxing its grip, hoping to exhaust him. It was aware now that there were no pretences. They were enemies; nothing could change that.

Ten minutes passed; perhaps more. His strength began to return. The alien's chief weapon was fear; yet he realised that, deep down inside, he was not afraid. He had grasped its weakness, the angry desire to impose its will that made it careless. It had the desire to be absolute master at all costs; and now it had been placed in a position where it could not destroy something it hated. As the thought passed through his mind, he felt it becoming angry again; his insight was like a taunt. It renewed the pressure, tearing frantically at his locked will. Again he resisted with the strength of desperation. After a few minutes, he realised that it was defeated again. Some instinctive biological loathing had aroused a deeper resistance. He felt a flow of power, a sense of being prepared to resist for days or weeks if necessary. He experienced a curious pride. This creature was in every way stronger than he was; its power and knowledge made him feel like a child. Yet some universal law made it unable to invade his feeble individuality against his will.

The pressure suddenly relaxed. He opened his eyes, which had been tightly closed, and noticed that the dawn was streaking the sky outside the windows. Then he was alone again. He moved his hands and realised that the bed was soaked with perspiration, as if he had suffered from a fever. His pyjamas were as wet as if he had just taken a shower with them on. He pulled the damp sheet around his neck, turned the pillow over onto its other side, and closed his eyes. The room seemed strangely peaceful and empty. A moment later he was deeply asleep.

He was awakened by the sound of a key in the door. It was the chief orderly, Lamson; he was carrying a tray. He said cheerfully: 'Good morning. It's a lovely morning. I've brought you coffee.'

Carlsen struggled into an upright position. 'That's kind of you. What's the time?'

'Eight-fifteen. Dr. Armstrong says there'll be breakfast in half an hour.' He placed the tray on Carlsen's knees.

'What's this?' Carlsen pointed to the glossy magazine on the tray. The cover looked familiar.

'Ah, I wonder if you'd mind, sir?' Lamson was holding out a pen. 'My nephew's a great admirer of yours. Would you sign your picture for him?'

'Yes, of course.'

I'll be back in a few minutes, after I've given the other gentlemen their coffee. Isn't that Dr. Fallada, the man who does the Crime Doctor programmes?'

'That's right.'

'And haven't I seen the other gentleman on TV?'

'Sir Percy Heseltine, the Commissioner of Police.'

Lamson whistled. 'Not often we get such famous visitors. Matter of fact, it's not often we get visitors at all…except relatives, of course.'

He went out, leaving the door slightly ajar; Carlsen watched him push the trolley on to the next door.

As he drank the coffee, he re-read the article. It was headed: 'Olof Carlsen—Man of the Century.' He winced as he recalled the nonstop publicity of three months ago; it had been more exhausting and nerve-wracking than his most difficult assignments in space exploration. This was one of dozens of similar articles that had appeared in the world's press; it was sentimental, with a double-page colour photograph of Carlsen with Jelka and the children.

As Lamson came back in, Carlsen asked: 'What's your nephew's name?'

'Georgie Bishop.'

He signed the photograph 'For Georgie, with best wishes,' and handed the magazine and pen to Lamson.

'He'll be real thrilled.' He looked at the photograph. 'You've got good-looking kids.'

Thank you.'

'You're lucky.' He doubled the magazine and slipped it into the pocket of his white smock.

'Do you have children?'

'No. The wife didn't want 'em.'

'You're married?'

'I was. That's all over now. We separated.'

Carlsen changed the subject. 'Have you seen this man Reeves today?'

'Oh, yes. I took his breakfast up at seven. We put the sedative in, as the doctor suggested.'

'How was he?'

'Well…I wouldn't have thought it necessary.'

Why not?'

'He was pretty quiet already.' He did a pantomime of a zombie, the eyes glazed and vacant, mouth hanging open, arms flopping loosely at his sides.

'Will it knock him out?'

'No. Just make him feel happy and relaxed. You don't want him unconscious if you're going to try hypnosis.'

Carlsen asked curiously: 'How did you know we are? Did Armstrong tell you?'

Lamson grinned. 'He didn't have to. He told me to prepare the nortropine-methidine mixture for injection. That's only used for pre-hypnosis and severe shock, and I know Reeves isn't in shock.'

'You should be a detective.'

Lamson was obviously pleased. 'Thanks.'

'How does this drug operate?'

'Induces mild paralysis of the nervous system—makes their minds go blank, if you like. After that, they're easy to hypnotise. Dr. Lyell—the man who used to be in charge of this place—used a lot of it. Dr. Armstrong says he doesn't approve of it.'

'Why not?'

Lamson shrugged and grunted. 'Says it's equivalent to brainwashing.' He looked keenly at Carlsen, decided he could trust him, and said: 'I think it's a lot of balls. Dr. Lyell didn't want to brainwash anybody. He just wanted to help people.'

Carlsen said sympathetically: 'I know what you mean.' He had already concluded that Armstrong was the kind of man who gave high-minded moral reasons for decisions that were based on laziness.

Lamson sighed. 'I'm not so sure you do.'

'No? Why do you think we're here?'

Lamson looked at him, startled. 'What?' Carlsen realised he had misunderstood the question. 'You don't mean—'

There was a knock on the door. Fallada's voice called: 'Ready to eat, Olof ?' The door handle turned.

Lamson said: 'Oh, well, I'd better get back anyway. See you later.' He stood aside for Fallada, then went out.

'Still in bed? Shall I come back?'

'No, come in.' Fallada closed the door. 'I've just been talking to Lamson.'

'He seems a good man.'

'Too bloody good.' Carlsen collected his clothes and went into the bathroom, leaving the door ajar. 'He checked up on this man Reeves last night. And I think he's given us away.'

'What makes you think so?'

For some reason, Carlsen felt unwilling to talk about what had happened in the night; it seemed too personal. 'He says Reeves is back to normal this morning.'

'Normal?'

'Semi-imbecillic'

There was a silence. Carlsen tucked his shirt into his trousers. Fallada said: 'So you think it's moved on?'

'It looks like it.' He began to shave with the electric razor. Neither spoke until he had finished. When he came out of the bathroom, dabbing after-shave on his face, Fallada was staring gloomily out of the window, his hands thrust into his jacket pockets, 'So this... creature is still one jump ahead of us?'

'I'm afraid so.'

'It may have moved back to the girl—the nurse.'

'Probably it did. And found out that we know about her too.'

'And it could be anywhere in this place—or out of it, for that matter.'

It was a statement, not a question, and Carlsen felt no need to reply. He folded his pyjamas and packed them in the bag. Fallada stared at him thoughtfully. 'I could try hypnotising you again.'

'No.'

'Why not?'

To begin with, it's too dangerous. It might try and move into *me* while I'm hypnotised. And second, it wouldn't do any good anyway. I've lost contact with it.'

'Are you sure?'

'Quite sure.'

He was glad Fallada asked no more questions.

On the sunlit lawn, Sergeant Parker was lying on his back, adjusting the vertical takeoff jets of the Grasshopper. Carlsen said: 'Aren't you coming for breakfast?'

'I ate with the medical staff, thank you, sir.'

'Did you see a woman there? Nurse Donaldson?'

'Oh, yes.' He cried. 'She asked a lot of questions about you.'

'What kind of questions?'

'"Well, like whether you were married.' He winked.

'Thanks.' As they walked on, Carlsen told Fallada: That answers your question.'

'Does it?'

'If she was possessed by the alien, she wouldn't ask questions. She'd try to be as unobtrusive as possible.'

Fallada said thoughtfully: 'True.' He smiled. 'You're becoming a Sherlock Holmes.'

Armstrong's dining room caught the morning sunlight. Heseltine was already seated at the table. Armstrong rubbed his hands. 'Good morning. What a beautiful morning. Did you sleep well?'

They both made affirmative noises.

Armstrong said: 'Lamson administered a tranquilliser to Reeves. In his coffee, of course. I also told Lamson to prepare a mild hypnoid solution. That's probably the simplest way, if you want to ask him questions—don't you think?'

Fallada said absentmindedly: 'Excellent. You think of everything.'

'I'm delighted to be of use. Really delighted.' He called into the kitchen: 'George, more coffee please.' He stood by the door, beaming at them. 'Please sit down. Don't wait for me—I've already eaten. I'll leave you now and do my ward round. George will get you anything you need.' He went out, closing the door carefully. The youth with a cast in one eye, now wearing a white coat, brought in coffee and grapefruit segments.

When they were alone, Fallada said: 'I'm afraid it's going to be a waste of time.'

Heseltine looked up quickly. 'Why?'

Carlsen said: 'It's only a suspicion. I've been talking to Lamson. He told me Reeves has changed again. He doesn't seem alert any more.' He still felt the same reluctance to talk about what had happened in the night.

Heseltine shook his head. 'So what do you suggest?'

Carlsen said: 'Let's continue as before. It can't do any harm to question this man Reeves.'

Fallada said: 'Perhaps he may still be in mental contact with the alien, as you were. He might even be able to tell us where it is now.'

'That's possible.' But even as he spoke, Carlsen knew it was untrue.

The youth in the white coat brought in eggs and bacon. During the remainder of the meal, there was no conversation. Carlsen could sense that the other two were depressed at the prospect of failure. His own feelings seemed to be strangely passive and dormant, as if exhausted by the strains of the past few days.

Armstrong returned as they were finishing the meal; he was followed by Lamson and another male nurse.

'Was there enough to eat? Good. I always start the day with a good breakfast.' Armstrong was wearing a white coat; Carlsen observed that he seemed unusually cheerful. 'I'm convinced that's the trouble with half the people in here.'

Heseltine looked at him in astonishment. 'Breakfast?'

'Or lack of it. They never acquired the breakfast habit. And the result: nervous tension, bad temper, ulcers— and emotional strain. I'm serious. If you really want to cut the crime rate in England, persuade everyone to eat a good breakfast.' He laid his hand lightly on Carlsen's shoulder. 'Eh, Commander?'

Carlsen said: 'Yes, I agree.' He realised now what was different: he no longer possessed insight into the minds of those around him. He realised it as Armstrong touched his shoulder; the contact was anonymous, devoid of intuition.

Armstrong rubbed his hands. 'Well, gentlemen, are we ready to start?'

They all looked at Carlsen; somehow, it was assumed that it was his decision. He said: 'Yes, of course,' and stood up.

'Then I would suggest that Lamson and I go in first. He'll assume it's the usual medical check-up.' He explained to Fallada: 'I check his adrenaline levels throughout the period of the full moon. If they get too high, there's danger of psychotic panic, in which case we administer tranquillisers.' He turned to Carlsen and Heseltine. 'Perhaps you'd better keep out of sight until we've injected him.'

They followed him across the hall and up two flights of stairs. Carlsen found the place depressing. It had been built around the turn of the century, when the rate of mental illness was soaring. The architecture was purely functional. The plastic walls, which had once produced an impression of light and air, were now greasy and scratched. On each landing, there were metal doors, with peeling green paint. Armstrong said: 'Those are the main wards. We keep the solitaries on the top floor, in soundproof rooms, so as not to disturb the others. Would you unlock the door, Norton?' The male nurse inserted keys into the two keyholes and turned them simultaneously; the door swung open without creaking. The walls of the corridor beyond were decorated with a plastic mosaic showing mountain scenery. Armstrong said: 'Reeves is in the room at the other end.' Carlsen observed that he refrained from calling them 'cells.'

The door at the far end of the corridor opened, and Ellen Donaldson came out; she closed it carefully behind her. She looked startled to see so many people; then, as her eyes met Carlsen's, she went pale. As Armstrong drew level with her she grasped his sleeve.

'Could I speak to you for a moment, Doctor?'

'Not now, Nurse. We're busy.' He brushed past her.

'But it's about Reeves—'

He turned on her sharply. 'I said not now.' His voice was not loud, but there was a steely undertone of command. The two orderlies exchanged glances of surprise. The nurse turned away and walked past them. Carlsen expected her to glance at him, but she walked on without raising her eyes. Her manner puzzled him. It was not the reaction of a senior nurse who has been irritably dismissed; she seemed totally subdued and without resentment.

Norton opened the door and stood aside for Armstrong to enter. Without turning, Armstrong made a peremptory gesture with his hand, ordering them not to approach. Lamson was filling a syringe from a rubber-capped bottle.

It was then Carlsen understood. Suddenly, with no possibility of doubt, he knew that Armstrong was harbouring the alien. At the same time, in the same instantaneous process of comprehension, he knew what had to be done. He reached out his hand towards Lamson, smiling. Lamson looked startled, but allowed him to take the syringe. He stepped past Norton with a single stride. Armstrong was bending over a man who lay on the bed, saying: 'Good morning, Reeves—' Before he could go on, Carlsen's left arm was around his throat, jerking him backwards. Norton shouted something. Carlsen's senses were totally calm. With a strength that surprised him, he pulled Armstrong's head back against his chest, carefully sighted the syringe, then drove it carefully through the cloth of Armstrong's jacket. He felt Armstrong wince as the point drove home; then, without haste, Carlsen pressed the plunger. Lamson had moved to the head of the bed, where he could see Carlsen's face. As their eyes met, Carlsen smiled and nodded. He had a sense of being totally in control of the situation. He counted to ten and felt Armstrong relax against him. He allowed his body to sag to the floor. Suddenly, Armstrong moved, twisting onto his face and flinging his arms around Carlsen's legs. Carlsen had made allowance for such a move; he dropped immediately, his knees striking between Armstrong's shoulder blades, pressing him to the floor. At the same time, Lamson knelt on Armstrong's thrashing legs. Armstrong struggled for a moment, then the efforts became weaker and ceased. When Carlsen turned him over, his eyes were glazed.

Heseltine, his voice unexpectedly calm, said: 'What was that for?'

Carlsen smiled at Lamson. 'Thanks for your help.'

Lamson said: 'You should have told me. I always thought there was something odd about him.'

'I daren't risk it.' He turned to Fallada and Heseltine. 'Let's get him to an empty room. I want to question him before it wears off.' He asked Lamson: 'Where could we take him?'

'Down to surgery, I should think. Hold on a minute, I'll get a wheelchair.' He went away and returned a moment later, opening a collapsible bathchair with a canvas back. 'Give us a hand, Ken.'

For the first time, Carlsen looked at the man on the bed. He seemed unaffected by the commotion. He was staring at the ceiling, his face calm. He was powerfully built and tall, but with slack, sallow skin. In spite of the breadth of his shoulders and the powerful hands, it was difficult to think of him as dangerous.

Lamson said: 'I'll take him down in the lift. I'll meet you on the ground floor at the bottom of the stairs.'

As soon as they were on the stairs, Fallada asked: 'What happened?'

'I realised the vampire had moved into Armstrong.'

Heseltine asked: 'Can you be certain of that?'

'Quite certain. I should have guessed earlier. I don't know why I didn't. Armstrong was the logical choice for the next takeover. Shifty, vain, full of sexual hang-ups.'

'How did Lamson know?'

Carlsen laughed. 'He didn't. I said something this morning that made him think we're after Armstrong. And he hates Armstrong.'

Fallada said: 'How do you know this alien is still inside Armstrong? What's to prevent it moving to someone else?'

Carlsen shook his head. 'As long as Armstrong's unconscious, it's trapped. It's subject to the same condition as Armstrong's body.'

'But are you sure of that?'

'No, but it seems to be common sense. I don't believe it can move in and out of bodies at a moment's notice. It's a fairly complicated business—like getting into a space-suit. It takes time.'

The lift arrived. Armstrong was slumped in the wheelchair, his head back against Lamson, who was pushing it. The eyes were still open.

'This way, sir.' Lamson led them into the room next to the flat. It was a small consulting room with the usual filing cabinets, reference books and bound copies of the *British Medical Journal.* Carlsen asked the orderlies to lift Armstrong onto the couch. He closed the curtains and moved the desk lamp so it shone into the staring eyes. 'Can you bring me another dose of the hypnoid drug?

Lamson looked doubtful. 'I suppose so, sir. But one's usually enough.'

'We may need it. How long does it last?'

'A dose like that—at least two hours.'

'Then we probably *shall* need more.'

As the orderlies went out, Heseltine said quietly: 'I'd rather you didn't mention this to any of your colleagues.'

Lamson nodded. 'Don't worry, sir. We understand.'

Heseltine closed the door carefully and locked it. Fallada said: 'Don't you think a second dose might be dangerous? It imposes a strain on the heart.'

'I know. But these things are more powerful than you think. It could still escape us.'

He bent over Armstrong and carefully closed the eyes. He took the electronic capsule recorder from the desk and positioned it on the small table at the head of the couch. He checked the recording level, then depressed the key. He sat on the edge of the couch, leaning forward so his mouth was close to Armstrong's ear. 'Armstrong. Can you hear me?'

The eyelids flickered, but there was no movement of the lips. Carlsen repeated the question and added: 'If you can hear me, say yes.'

The lips twitched. After a pause, Armstrong whispered: 'Yes.'

'Do you know where you are now?' Again, the question had to be repeated.

Then Armstrong's face began to pucker like a child about to cry. His voice was strained: 'I don't want to stay here. I want to go. I'm afraid. Let me go. Let me go.' The voice was almost inaudible. For several seconds, the lips continued to move, but no sound came from them.

'Where are you?'

There was a pause of more than a minute. Carlsen repeated the question several times. Armstrong's voice was choked with emotion: 'They won't let me talk to you.'

'Who won't?'

There was no reply. Carlsen said urgently: 'Listen, Armstrong, if you want us to help you escape, you've got to tell us where you are. Where are you?'

Bubbles of saliva formed on Armstrong's lips. He began to breathe hoarsely. He said: 'I'm here…'; then the sound died away into a bubbling noise. Suddenly the body twisted violently. Armstrong screamed. There was so much terror in the sound that they were all shocked. As the body thrashed wildly, all three of them tried to hold him down. It was difficult; he seemed to possess enormous strength. After a struggle, he lay still, panting, With Carlsen sitting on one of his arms, Heseltine holding the other, Fallada sitting on his legs.

Carlsen said: 'Armstrong. Can you *see* the thing that's holding you prisoner?'

'Yes.' The eyes opened, staring like a frightened horse.

'Tell him he's got to talk to us. Tell him that'

The body gave a sudden jerk and rolled halfway off the couch. Carlsen and Heseltine pushed it back. There was a knock on the door, startling them.

'Who is it?'.

'Lamson, sir. I've brought your nortropine-methidine.'

Fallada unlocked the door. 'Ah, thank you.'

'You know how to use it, don't you, sir? Wait until he's coming round before you give him another dose.'

Fallada said: 'Don't worry. We know about it.' He closed the door firmly and locked it again.

Armstrong was lying still again. Carlsen unbuttoned his cuff and pushed the sleeve up the plump, hairy arm. It refused to move above the elbow. Heseltine handed him a pair of surgical scissors from the desk; Carlsen cut the sleeve from the wrist to the shoulder. As he took the hypodermic, Armstrong sat up and twisted sideways. Carlsen dropped the syringe and grabbed him again. Heseltine helped him force Armstrong back onto the couch. Carlsen said: 'Hans, get the syringe and inject it.'

Another voice spoke from Armstrong's lips, startling them with its calm and authority: 'There is no need for that. If you let me go, I promise you to leave the earth.'

Fallada hesitated, holding the needle. Carlsen said: 'Go ahead and inject. The thing's a liar. If we don't inject, it'll be free in ten minutes.' He felt the muscles tense under his hands and used all his strength to hold down the writhing body. The voice spoke again: 'Carlsen, you disappoint me. I thought you understood.'

Carlsen resisted the temptation to be drawn into argument. He nodded to Fallada. 'Go ahead.' Fallada drove the needle into the flesh, above the trickle of blood from the previous injection, and pressed the plunger home. They sat watching the face for more than a minute. Armstrong's breathing became deeper. The eyes lost their focus, and the facial muscles relaxed.

Carlsen said: 'Can you still hear me?'

There was no reply. Heseltine said: 'Perhaps you've given him too much.'

Carlsen shook his head. He spoke close to Armstrong's ear. 'Listen to me. If necessary, we shall keep you in this state for days or weeks. Do you understand?'

'Yes.' It was the same voice, but now it was weaker, less forceful. The breathing became disturbed and spasmodic. Fallada said: 'I hope we don't kill him.'

Carlsen said: 'If we do, it can't be helped. The alien will die too. That's worth Armstrong's life.'

The voice said thickly: 'You cannot destroy us all.'

Carlsen said: 'We can try. We can send warships to destroy your space vehicle.' He leaned closer. 'And we shall pay particular attention to those yellow squids.'

Fallada looked at him with surprise but said nothing. As they watched, Armstrong's eyes closed. The face lost its strength, the flesh seemed to sag. Carlsen said: 'We have another syringe of the hypnoid drug. Will you answer our questions, or shall we inject it?'

The face was still for several moments. Then the voice said: 'Ask me your questions.'

'What is your name?'

'You could not pronounce it. You could call me G'room.'

'Are you male or female?'

'Neither. Our race does not possess genders like yours.'

Heseltine asked: 'What is your race?'

'You would call us Nioth-Korghai. But your human vocal organs will not sound our syllables.'

Fallada asked: 'Where are you from?'

'A planet of the star you call Rigel. It is not visible, even to your most powerful telescopes.'

'How old are you?'

'In your earth time, fifty-two thousand years.'

They stared at one another with amazement Carlsen asked: 'Do *all* your race live as long as that?'

'No. Only we of the Ubbo-Sathla. We are what you call vampires.'

Fallada was writing down the replies. He asked: 'And what of the rest of the Nioth-Korghai? How long do they live?'

'For about three hundred of your earthly years.'

Heseltine asked: 'How did you become vampires?'

'That is a long story.'

'We'd like to hear it all the same. Tell us.'

There was a silence for several minutes, so that Carlsen began to wonder whether the creature intended to reply. But finally the voice came again.

'Our planet is completely covered with water. And our race, as you have guessed, has the form of the creatures you call squids. But your molluscs have almost no brain. The Nioth-Korghai have a highly developed brain and nervous system. Because our bodies are so light, we can live under the greatest of pressures. Our metabolism depends on the salts of the element fluorine, which exists in large quantity in our seas, as sodium chloride exists in yours. Beneath our seas there are immense natural caves. These became our cities. They are far bigger than your caves on earth. Even the smallest of them is eight miles high.

'At the time when your planet was in the midst of the age of great reptiles, we possessed a highly evolved civilisation. But in one important respect, it was completely unlike your earthly civilisation. The human mind enjoys solving technical problems, and its noblest ideal is science. The Nioth-Korghai are interested only in what you would call religion and philosophy. Each individual wishes to understand the universe, and ultimately to become one with it. This also explains why we do not have two sexes, as you do on earth. Your bodies conduct the spark of life at the climax of your sexual excitement. But the Nioth-Korghai can receive the universal energies directly. They fall in love with the universe, not with one another. And in moments of supreme contemplation, they become pregnant through the life energy of the universe. As we learned the secrets of the universe, we also learned how to project our minds to distant galaxies. We visited your earth when the seas were first cooling. We taught the plantlike creatures of Mars to build their civilisations under water. We helped the creatures of your planet Pluto to escape to a planet of the binary star Sirius when their own world lost its atmosphere. Our greatest achievement was to help in the evacuation of more than a thousand planets in the Crab Nebula before it exploded and turned into a supernova.

'You earth creatures can have no conception of the tremendous dramas of interstellar space. Your scale is too small. But the Nioth-Korghai have watched the births and deaths of galaxies. We have seen island universes created out of nothing. You must understand that these universes are living creatures. They possess their own kind of cosmic life, on a level that cannot be grasped by biological organisms. The religion of the Nioth-Korghai teaches that the universe itself is a gigantic brain, in which the worlds we know are mere individual cells. 'Fifty thousand years ago, your earth was approaching the end of a great Ice Age, and the men who lived on it were little better than apes—you call them Neanderthals. The Nioth-Korghai decided that conditions were propitious for a great experiment—the attempt to produce a more intelligent form of life. This was during the lifetime of Kuben-Droth, one of our greatest biological engineers—'

Fallada interrupted: 'I thought you had no science?' The creature fell silent. For more than half a minute, they were afraid it had decided to end its story. Then it began again.

'We had no technology in your earthly sense. We did not need it—the sea supplied all our simple needs. But science springs from the soul and the will. Our problem was to persuade your Stone Age men to develop intelligence. No creature can be made to evolve against 'its will. We had to implant a will-to-intelligence in these creatures, and this could be done only by inhabiting their brains and making them dream. You cannot imagine the difficulties involved. For these early men could be made to experience intense pleasure, but they forgot about it a few seconds later. It was like trying to teach algebra to monkeys. Kuben-Drotb devoted more than half his lifetime to the task, but he died before we finally achieved success. It took seven hundred years to produce a man and woman whose children became the first of the new species of true men. We called them Esdram and Solayeh. They survive in your mythology as Adam and Eve.

'Now for seven hundred years, we had lived in the brains and bodies of human beings. And in some ways this was a dangerous thing to do. Their vital energies sustained us. We enjoyed the intoxication of their sensuality, although at first it disgusted us. Your world was dangerous and violent, but it was also very beautiful.

'Yet we were scientists, and we had enough self-control to know that it was time for us to leave the human race to itself. We left your earth in groups of a hundred, to return to our own star system—'

Fallada said: 'Excuse me interrupting you again, but surely Rigel is hundreds of light-years away from earth. How long did this journey take you?'

Again there was a lengthy silence, as if the creature had to prepare its answer. Then it said: 'You forget that the energies of the universe exist on many levels. On the physical level, energy cannot attain a speed greater than that of light. On our level, it can move a thousand times that speed. The journey took us less than a year.

'Our group was the last to leave. We deliberately stayed on as long as we could. Then we completed the transformation to the correct level of cosmic energy— you might call it the fifth dimension—and began our journey.

'It was on this return journey that we met with the accident. The chances against it were millions to one; it should have been impossible. When we had covered more than half the distance, we passed within a few hundred miles of a collapsing star—a black hole. These are some of the rarest objects in the universe, and none of us had ever encountered one before. They end by falling out of your universe into a nondimensional hyperspace. We decided to explore—which was a mistake. Some of us were sucked into the whirlpool. Others realised what was happening and warned the rest of us to stay away before they were also sucked in. But it was too late to escape. The force was too powerful. All that we could do was to delay our destruction. We did this by moving into orbit around the black hole. And we continued to circle around, drawn inexorably by its gravity. Some lost strength and hope and allowed themselves to be drawn in. And the rest of us continued to struggle, determined to maintain existence until the last possible moment.

'And then, after more than a thousand years, the black hole disappeared. It fell out of your space, and we were free. Yet we were now so exhausted that we lacked the strength to transform ourselves to the correct level of energy. We were free, but we were stranded in space, four hundred light-years from our own stellar system.

'It was then we began to dream of our happy days on your earth, of the flow of energy from living bodies. We began to travel slowly back towards our own system, searching for other inhabited planets like the earth. There are millions of these in the universe, and if we had been less exhausted, we could have found one without difficulty. As it was, we searched for more than a year before we found one. This was inhabited by a primitive race of animals, not unlike dinosaurs, but far bigger. Their coarse energy disgusted us, but we needed it to live. We absorbed it until we were drunk, killing the creatures by the hundred. After that, we felt less desperate; but the energy transformation was still impossible. Their lower form of energy made it even more difficult. So we moved on, looking for a planet with some higher form of life.

'It is true that we had become destroyers of life. But we had no alternative. We were like soldiers lost in the desert; we had to take whatever we could find. And we found many inhabited planetary systems. In some cases, we found creatures with the kind of life energy we needed, but they always resisted us. We had to take what we wanted by force, destroying those who were too weak to resist. On one planet of the Alnair system, we found bodies resembling those we had left behind at home, and took them over. We were gradually becoming reconciled to the state of homeless wanderers. And now we had bodies, the longing to return home was beginning to disappear. Besides, we realized that we were apparently immortal. At first, we assumed that this was some strange consequence of our ordeal in the black hole. We decided to try the experiment of living off natural foods, to see what happened. The result was that we aged at the normal rate. So it was now clear that if we wanted to stay alive, we had no choice. We had to continue to drain the vital energies of other creatures. We learned to do this without actually destroying them—in the way that human beings have learned to milk cows. This was not only more humane, but it also prevented us from destroying our own food supply. There were some among us who found even this alternative disgusting, and who preferred to allow themselves to die of old age. But the rest of us became reconciled to our new status—as vampires or mind parasites. After all, this seems to be a law of nature; all living creatures eat other living creatures.

'On a planet of the Alpha Centauri system we began to build a spacecraft. It was vast, because we wanted it to remind us of our home—the great underwater caves of our own world. More than twenty thousand years ago, we revisited your solar system. We were hoping to find beings from our own world—for we knew they intended to return here periodically to observe your progress. We were disappointed, but we stayed here nevertheless. Human beings were still hunters living in caves; we taught them the arts of agriculture, and how to build villages in the middle of lakes. And when there was no more we could do, we returned to the Alpha Centauri system and continued our explorations…'

Carlsen stood up quietly and moved to the door. The other two were so absorbed that neither of them noticed as he unlocked it and quietly closed it behind him.

In the entrance hall, he met the orderly named Norton. 'Where can I find Fred Lamson?'

'He'll be on Ward Two at this time. Hold on and I'll fetch him for you.'

Lamson came downstairs a few minutes later. Carlsen said: 'I need another dose of that hypnoid solution.'

Lamson looked startled. 'Are you sure? You know how strong it is?'

'I know. But I'd be glad if you could get it for me.'

'Okay. I'll bring it to you.'

Carlsen waited in the hall; from the surgery, he could hear the voice continuing. At this distance, its quality reminded him of voices manufactured on a computer. It also struck him that its strength had increased.

Lamson came down the stairs and held out the small cardboard box. 'There's another syringe in there. But be careful. An overdose could kill him.'

'Don't worry.'

Lamson said: 'What's he been up to?'

Carlsen slapped him lightly on the shoulder. 'If I told you, you wouldn't believe me. But you'll learn all about it later. Thanks for your help.'

He opened the surgery door quietly. There was a silence. Heseltine glanced around at him, then looked away. Apparently someone had asked a question. The curiously flat voice sounded as if it was reading from a script.

'It was necessary to adopt human bodies to make contact with your race. If you examine them closely, you will discover that they contain silicon instead of carbon.'

Heseltine said: 'In that case, why didn't you try to make contact with us, instead of disappearing?'

The answer came sooner than Carlsen expected. 'You know the answer to that. I was caught unawares and killed before I could prevent myself.'

Fallada said: 'What are you doing?' Carlsen was standing beside the couch, the hypodermic syringe poised over the naked arm. The creature stopped speaking, puzzled by the question. Carlsen drove in the needle and pressed the plunger. He withdrew the needle, leaving a drop of blood on the skin. After a silence, the creature's voice said: 'I do not understand…'

It trailed off. Fallada said: 'Neither do I. Why did you want to do that?'

Carlsen was silent for a moment, watching Armstrong's breathing. Then he said: 'Because we've got to hurry. We've got to get back to London.'

Heseltine said: 'But was that necessary? Don't you trust him?'

Carlsen snorted. 'No, of course I don't.'

Fallada asked with astonishment: 'Why not?'

'Because it told us only half the truth. I'll explain when we're in the Grasshopper. Now we'd better go. Help me lift him.'

'What do you want to do with him?'

'Take him back with us.' He depressed the capsule-release switch of the recorder and dropped the capsule into his pocket.

Sergeant Parker was dozing on the lawn, his shirt open to the waist. He sat up and stared with astonishment at the slumped figure in the wheelchair. Heseltine said: 'Help us lift him. We've got to get back to London as quickly as possible. How soon can we do it?'

'Half an hour, if we push it.'

It took them five minutes to manoeuvre the heavy body onto the rear bench seat of the Grass-hopper. Less than a minute later, they were airborne. Lamson, who had come out onto the front steps, waved to them as they rose vertically from the lawn.

Heseltine, still breathing heavily, said: 'I didn't notice any contradictions in his story.'

'It was full of contradictions. You noticed one yourself. If they assumed human bodies in order to make contact with us, why didn't they do it?'

'Surely he explained that? He killed young Adams without premeditation, then panicked—'

'Creatures like that don't panic. They calculate. Did he explain why they were all in a state of suspended animation when we found them?'

'To make the journey pass more quickly—for the same reason we sleep on aeroplanes.'

'In that case, why was it so difficult to wake them up?'

'We didn't have time to ask that. You knocked him out again.'

Carlsen said: 'There's no need to ask. The reason's obvious. They wanted us to bring them all back to earth. And when we'd got them here, they'd all die off, one by one…and we wouldn't even suspect we'd brought vampires back to earth. All we'd notice is the sudden rise in crimes of violence, sadistic murders, and so on.'

Heseltine shook his head. 'I don't know whether I'm unusually gullible, or you're unusually mistrustful. 'The question was an implied reproach.

Carlsen said: 'Look at his story again. First of all, he explains how his race helped our race to evolve. That *could* be true, although we have to take his word for it. Then he describes their accident That could be true too. It was after that I began to notice the contradictions. They became parasites on other living creatures. They stole the bodies of some squidlike creatures on another planet. And then, according to him, they tried the experiment of living off natural foods, to see what happened. That made them begin to age, so they went back to living off other intelligent creatures.'

Fallada said: 'But without destroying them. You remember, he compared their method to dairy farming—'

Carlsen said: 'You forget we eat cows as well as milk them. He was trying to convince us that they treated' their victims as fellow creatures. I don't believe it. Why do you suppose they move from planet to planet? Because they're natural predators, and they can't resist the urge to destroy their victims. When they've destroyed all the life on one planet, they move to another.'

Fallada said: 'But you've no evidence for that. It might be true, but we don't *know.*'

'I've got an instinct about it. Nothing in their behaviour leads me to trust them. The rest of these creatures are out there in space, slowly dying of hunger. Why *should* they be dying of hunger if they've learned this art of dairy farming? They'd make sure they brought enough food with them, as we do when we take a nine-month trip to Jupiter. They *couldn't* take enough food with them, because they've eaten the larder bare. And the earth's intended to be their next larder.'

Fallada and Heseltine were obviously impressed by his reasoning, yet neither was entirely con-vinced. They turned to look at the prostrate body, as if this could provide an answer. Fallada said: 'I still feel we owe them *something*. After all, they landed in this predicament after they'd been trying to help us evolve into real human beings. And according to him, they taught us about agriculture. Or do you think that was a lie too?'

'Not necessarily. Of course they wanted us to evolve. When they returned to earth twenty thousand years ago, there probably weren't more than a million human beings altogether. Even those who were little better than animals. They left us to breed and evolve, so they could come back when we'd multiplied. And now they've got a larder that could last them for ten thousand years. I'll tell you something else. He says they came to earth hoping to meet some of their own kind—'

'But surely that's common sense?'

'Is it? What do you suppose their own kind could have done for them? They couldn't help them to get back to Orion. They don't use spaceships. They convert themselves into some higher form of energy that can travel faster than light. And these creatures lost that power after they became vampires.'

'How do you know?'

'Surely it's obvious. If they hadn't lost it, they'd go back home. That's why they need a spaceship to move around now.'

'But their own people might be able to help them.'

'Do you think that likely? They've turned into galactic criminals. They probably left the earth to *avoid* their own people. They've become lepers.'

Fallada said musingly: 'It's an interesting thought. A kind of Fall...'

Sergeant Parker pointed below. That's Bedford, sir. We should be back in ten minutes. Shall I go to the Yard?'

Heseltine looked at Carlsen. Carlsen said: 'It might be better to go to the Ismeer Building. We could leave Armstrong there. We've got to keep him knocked out.' He asked Fallada: 'Does that suit you?'

'Of course. My assistant Grey can take care of that'

Heseltine said: 'And then what?'

Carlsen said: 'If I'm not mistaken, you'll find a message from the Prime Minister waiting for you. He'll be anxious to know what you're doing..'

Heseltine said: 'There *is* a message. I rang my wife this morning. The P.M. wants to see all three of us as soon as possible.'

'Good. Then we'll go and see him.'

Heseltine said doubtfully: 'He'll be more difficult to handle than Armstrong. What do you intend to do?'

'I don't know. But I'm certain of one thing. We've got to see him face to face. There's no other way.'

The policeman at the door saluted as he recognised Heseltine. A moment later, the front door was opened by a pretty, dark-haired girl.

'I believe the Prime Minister is expecting us?'

'Yes, sir. He'll be free in a moment. Would you like to wait in here?'

Heseltine said: 'I haven't seen you before.'

'I'm Merriol.' She smiled, showing small, white teeth.The accent had a Welsh lilt. She seemed scarcely more than a schoolgirl.

As she left the room, Heseltine said: 'Curious.'

'What?'

'Oh, nothing much.' He lowered his voice. 'There's gossip that Jamieson has a taste for young girls. In fact, it's more than gossip. And the latest one's supposed to be a student teacher from Anglesey.'

Fallada said: 'But surely he wouldn't bring her into Downing Street? That's asking for trouble.'

'I'd have thought so. What do you think, Carlsen?'

Carlsen had been staring abstractedly out of the window. Now he looked up, startled. 'I'm sorry, I wasn't listening.'

'It's just that it seems rather odd that this girl—' He stopped speaking as the door opened.

The girl said: 'Would you like to come this way, please?' She smiled coquettishly at Carlsen. As she ran up the stairs ahead of them, he observed with appreciation the slim bare legs under the short skirt.

She led them into the office next to the Cabinet room. Jamieson was sitting at the desk; a bespectacled man in his sixties was sorting through a tray of letters. Jamieson said: 'I think that will be all for now, Morton. Don't forget that call to the Tsar's private secretary.' He smiled at Heseltine over the top of his spectacles. 'Ah, so the wanderers return? Have a seat, gentlemen.' Three armchairs had been arranged facing the desk. 'Smoke? Throw that file on the floor—it shouldn't be there.' He pushed the cigarette box across the desk. 'I must say that I'm glad to see you. I'd begun to feel anxious. Anything interesting to tell me?'

Fallada said: 'Commander Carlsen and I flew to Sweden to consult an expert on vampirism.'

'Indeed? How...er...how very interesting.' Jamie-son's smile conveyed a mixture of politeness, amusement and boredom. He looked at Heseltine. 'Anything else?'

Heseltine glanced at Carlsen. 'Yes, sir. I'm glad to report that we have now captured one of the aliens.'

'Good heavens! Are you serious?'

The well-bred astonishment seemed so genuine that Carlsen experienced momentary doubt. He reached into his pocket, and brought out the recording-capsule. He said: 'May I?' He leaned forward, pressing the ejection button of the desk recorder. He pressed the capsule into the slot and then depressed the playback key. The controlled, unmodulated voice of the alien said: 'Our planet is completely covered with water. And our race, as you have guessed, has the form of the creatures you call squids. But your molluscs have almost no brain. The Nioth-Korghai have a highly developed brain and nervous system...'

All three of them were watching Jamieson's face. He was listening with total attention, his chin cradled in his right hand, the index finger scratching the line of the jaw. After five minutes he reached out and switched off the machine.

'That is certainly...very remarkable. How did you locate this...er...vampire?'

'The Swedish expert showed us how to do it. We've promised not to reveal the method.'

'I see. And what about the other two aliens?'

'We've traced one to New York. The other's here in London.'

'And how do you propose to locate them?'

Carlsen said: 'The first step is to broadcast that recording—to make people realise these things exist. I've arranged to be interviewed on television at ten o'clock tonight'

'What!' The bushy eyebrows were raised in surprise. 'But that would be violating our agreement.'

Carlsen said: 'When we made that agreement, you thought the aliens were dead. This changes everything.'

Jamieson slapped the flat of his hand on the desk. 'I am sorry, gentlemen, but I must categorically forbid any such thing.'

Carlsen said quietly: 'I am sorry, but you are in no position to prevent it. You are only the Prime Minister of this country—not its dictator.'

Jamieson sighed. 'Commander, you are wasting my time.' He reached out and pressed a red key on the machine. 'I have now erased the recording.'

Carlsen said: 'It makes no difference. We made copies before we came here.'

'I want those copies.'

Carlsen said: 'One has already gone to the television station.'

'In that case, you must recall it.' Carlsen stared back without speaking. He saw a flicker of doubt in the eyes that were trying to stare him down. Jamieson said, in a conversational tone: 'You are either very brave or very stupid. Or perhaps both.' As he spoke, his face changed. There was no physical alteration, and the expression remained impassive; but another personality was looking through his eyes. The gaze suddenly became hard and remote. All three of them felt the menace. It was like being in the presence of a despot with limitless powers. When Jamieson spoke, the voice was also different. It had lost the booming, assertive quality; it was depersonalised, almost metallic. There was something about its cold, totally detached quality that made Carlsen shiver.

'Dr. Fallada, I want you to call your laboratory and ask your assistant to send Dr. Armstrong over here.'

Fallada said dully: 'You knew all the time.'

Jamieson ignored him. He touched a button on the desk. The Welsh girl came in.

'Vraal, I want you to get Dr. Fallada's laboratory on the private line. He wants to speak to his assistant, Grey.' Fallada began to stand up. A look of surprise crossed his face, and he sat down again with a bump. Carlsen was suddenly aware of a languor that flowed through his body, as if someone had injected anaesthetic. He tried to force his body away from the chair; it was impossible, as if the chair had become a magnet that held him tight. When he closed his eyes, it was as if his limbs had been transformed into something massive and very heavy.

The girl pressed the key of an electronic memo-pad on the desk, then dialled a number. When a girl's voice answered she said: 'Dr. Fallada for Mr. Grey, please.' Carlsen observed the same mechanical quality in her voice.

Jamieson and the girl had both turned their eyes on Fallada. He jerked and stiffened, his face contorting for a moment. As their eyes held him, he stood up, moving stiffly, and started to cross the room. Heseltine said: 'Don't do it, Hans.' Fallada ignored him, moving in front of the telescreen. 'Hello, Norman.' His voice was hoarse. 'I want you to send Armstrong over to Ten Downing Street. Could you do that right away?'

'Yes, sir. What about the hypnoid? Shall I inject another dose?'

'No. Bring him just as he is. I want it to wear off.'

Grey said, with concern in his voice: 'Are you all right, sir?'

Fallada smiled. 'Yes, I'm fine. A little tired, that's all. Use the institute's Grasshopper.'

'Very well, sir.'

The girl reached out and pressed the cut-out switch. Fallada staggered and had to support himself on the edge of the desk. Suddenly his face had become old.

Heseltine turned to Carlsen with a painful effort. 'What are they doing to us?' His voice was thick.

'Using will-pressure. Don't worry. They won't be able to keep it up for long. It's exhausting.'

Jamieson said, in his expressionless voice: 'As long as necessary, I think.'

Fallada dropped back into his chair; his face was sweating. Carlsen felt a flash of piercing regret for exposing him to this ultimate humiliation: the use of his own body and voice at the bidding of another's will. He said: 'Don't let yourself fall asleep, Hans. So long as you fight, they can't break your resistance. The other one tried with me last night and didn't succeed.'

Jamieson looked at him curiously. "There is a great deal we have to learn about you, Carlsen. Such as how you knew about will-pressure.' He looked at Fallada and Heseltine. 'But do not be misled by his experience. He has had time to build up a certain resistance. You have not. Besides, believe me, you have no choice at all. We are making you a simple offer.'

He paused; Heseltine said: 'Get on with it.'

The voice said: 'We need your co-operation, and we can obtain it in one of two ways. We could kill you and take over your bodies. Alternatively, you could do as we ask you to do.'

Carlsen said: 'He means let them take over our bodies.'

Jamieson said: 'In case you think that might be disagreeable, let me reassure you.' He turned to the girl. 'Show the Commissioner, Vraal.'

She moved behind Heseltine's chair, and tilted back his head, her hand on his forehead. She placed the other hand on his throat. Watching Heseltine's face, Carlsen saw the momentary resistance; it dissolved, attempted to reassert itself, then collapsed completely. Heseltine's eyes closed, and he began to breathe deeply. The colour came back into his cheeks.

Jamieson said: 'That's enough, Vraal.' She removed her hands reluctantly; one of them lingered on Heseltine's shoulder. Jamieson snapped: 'I said enough.' The hand dropped. Heseltine opened his eyes drowsily and looked at Carlsen without seeming to see him.

The girl turned to look at Carlsen; her lips were moist. Jamieson said: 'No. There is no need to show Commander Carlsen. He has already experienced it.'

The wind stirred the window curtains. Jamieson sat in his chair and stared at them. The face seemed to be made of stone. There was a dreamy silence in the office. The traffic in Whitehall sounded very far away. Carlsen summoned all his energy to fight off the drowsiness. He could see that Heseltine and Fallada were on the edge of sleep. There was no sense of panic, only the warm sexual langour. Time seemed unimportant. Memories were flooding through him: stories from childhood, the field of poppies in *The Wizard of Oz,* the cottage made of gingerbread in "Hansel and Gretel." There was a feeling of total relaxation, a sense that all was well. When he tried to tell himself they were in danger, his feelings refused to respond. A golden mist of happiness drifted through his mind, blurring his thoughts.

There was a ring at the doorbell, and Carlsen realised that he had been asleep. Jamieson said: 'That should be our colleague.' He went out. A few minutes later he returned. Carlsen summoned the energy to twist around in his chair. Armstrong was there, looking grey and sick. His walk was slow and clumsy. Jamieson led him to the chair behind the desk. Armstrong looked at Carlsen, then at Fallada and Heseltine, without interest. He was breathing heavily, and his eyes were bloodshot.

Jamieson said: 'Look up at me.' Armstrong raised his eyes unwillingly. Jamieson grabbed him by the hair, making him wince, then forced his head back and stared into his eyes. Armstrong cleared his throat and groaned. For a moment, neither of them moved. Then Armstrong's face changed. The slack skin seemed to become firmer; the line of the mouth hardened. When he opened his eyes, they were clear and penetrating. He shook off Jamie-son's hand.

That's better. Thank you. They gave me three doses of that damned stuff.' He looked at Carlsen with cold anger, and Carlsen felt the impact of his will-force, like a slap in the face. Armstrong said: 'If he is to be killed, I will do it.'

The girl said: 'He is already promised to me.'

Jamieson said: 'The choice is his.' He turned to Carlsen. 'Which would you prefer? To be possessed by her? Or destroyed by him? Make up your mind quickly.'

Carlsen made another attempt to move, but their three wills were pinning him to the chair like iron bands. He experienced a sense of helplessness, of being a child in the hands of adults. It cost him an effort to speak. 'You'd be stupid to kill me. You could make use of my body, but it wouldn't deceive anybody who knew me.'

"That will not be necessary. All that we require of you is that you give your television interview this evening. You will then recommend that the *Stranger* should be brought back to earth immediately. You will say that it is stupid to delay when other countries might get there first. After that, I shall announce that you have been placed in charge of an expedition to bring back the *Stranger,* and you will leave early tomorrow for moon-base. That is all that will be required of you.' Carlsen stared back, fighting off the fatigue and a deepening sense of defeat. The voice said: 'Make your choice now.'

The girl said: 'Shall I try to persuade him?' Without waiting for a reply, she sat on Carlsen's knee and tilted back his head. It was done without coquetry, like a nurse preparing a patient for an operation. As he felt her cool hands on his skin, he was aware of the draining of his energies as they flowed into her hands. She was using her body to intensify the contact; he was aware that under the brown skirt she was almost naked. Paradoxically, in spite of his exhaustion, he felt a stiffening of desire. With her hands over his ears, she leaned forward and pressed her mouth against his. Again he experienced the drowsy delight, the desire to surrender, to allow her to take possession of his will. As she felt his relaxation, she moved, her bare arms around his neck, and the lips became moist and urgent. He felt the life being drained from him into her body; the vital forces were flowing like blood from an open artery. When he tried to move, with a final effort at protest, he felt the united force of their wills pinning him to the chair. Then, as he ceased to resist, the sense of helplessness dissolved into a glow of response. It seemed to be due to the movements of her buttocks, pressing rhythmically against him in a simulation of lovemaking. He could feel the warmth of her breasts against him, and he wanted to reach up and tear the material from her shoulders. The desire became hard and violent; he was aware of her surprise as he ceased to be passive. It was then that he realised he could use his will against her, pinning her closer and forcing her mouth against his with a strength that emanated from a source in the centre of his brain. Without moving his body, he was holding her as a bird might hold a worm. As he sucked the vital energy from her, his whole body burned with the greed of absorption.

Armstrong's voice said: 'What are you doing, Vraal? Don't kill him.'

He tightened his grip, giving himself up wholly to the pleasure of drinking the essence of her being. The intensity of the contact made his flesh burn.

He saw Jamieson grip her shoulders; he released his grip as she was torn away from him. Jamieson used so much force that she staggered against the desk and fell to the floor. Jamieson started to speak, then saw the bruised mouth and the shocked exhaustion in her eyes. His reaction was instantaneous; he turned on Carlsen, and the force of his will was like a bolt of lightning. It should have smashed Carlsen back in his chair, ending his resistance like a bullet in the solar plexus. But Carlsen's reaction had been even faster; he parried the blow, turning it aside like a boxer rolling to a punch; then, before Jamieson could recover, his own will-drive struck back, catching Jamieson in the ribs and throwing him sideways into the wall. A movement to his left made him aware of Armstrong; before he could throw up a defence, a clumsy hammer-blow of force had struck him on the side of the head. The pain irritated him into using more power than he intended. His flash of anger caught Armstrong's shoulder like a blow from the paw of a bear, breaking the bone; Armstrong sprung across the room, his head cracking against the wall. He half turned and slumped to his knees, the eyes blank and stunned.

Jamieson had dragged himself upright; he was supporting himself against the desk as he stared at Carlsen. The left eye was half closed, and blood ran down the cheek; yet it was a measure of his power that his face showed no defeat or fear. He said quietly: 'Who the hell *are* you?'

As Carlsen started to formulate an answer, he was suddenly aware that it was unnecessary. The question was not addressed to him. A voice was speaking from his lips in a foreign language that he was able to understand. It said: 'I come from Karthis.'

He was aware that it was the language of the Nioth-Korghai.

Jamieson reached into his pocket, pulled out a snow-white handkerchief and mopped the blood from his face. His voice was level and calm. 'What do you want with us?'

'I think you know that' As he spoke, he observed that the vampire who had possessed the girl was now detaching itself from her body. Although Carlsen was looking in the opposite direction, some additional sense made him aware that she was moving towards the window. He said: 'You cannot escape, Vraal. It has taken us more than a thousand years to find you. We shall not allow you to go again.' He caught her and forced her back into the room. Heseltine and Fallada were .staring in amazement at the transparent violet shape now visible against the wall. It shimmered in the light, its internal energies causing a constant motion, so that it resembled coiling smoke.

Carlsen turned to Fallada. 'I apologise for speaking in a foreign language. In our natural form we communicate by thought alone, but we can still use the ancient language of the Nioth-Korghai.'

Fallada said: I don't understand. Are you…?'

He understood the half-formulated question. 'I am an inhabitant of the world called Karthis, a planet of the sun you call Rigel. I am making use of the body of your friend Carlsen, who is fully conscious of all that is happening. You might say that I am borrowing it'

He looked at Armstrong, who was levering himself into a sitting position, then at Jamieson. 'Come. It is time for us to leave.'

Fallada and Heseltine watched with astonishment as a purple haze began to detach itself from Carlsen's body. Its glow was more intense than that of the other alien, and it seemed to be full of points of light, like sparks.

Carlsen experienced a sudden feeling of weakness, as if from loss of blood. He said: 'Wait, please.'

The purple light was hovering in the centre of the room; its intensity hurt his eyes. Now, as he watched, wavering outlines detached themselves from the bodies of Armstrong and Jamieson. In the intenser glare of their captor, they were hardly visible. Armstrong collapsed sideways, his mouth open. Jamieson dropped heavily into the chair behind the desk and stared at the girl with puzzled incomprehension, as if he had never seen her before.

Staring at the shimmering purple outlines, now visible like heat waves against the background of the wall, Carlsen experienced an upsurge of emotion that was deeper than anything he had ever known. There was a sense of awe that seemed to wrack his being, mingled with a profound pity. For the first time, he clearly understood the misery and desolation that had driven these creatures to scour the galaxy for living energy. Now he could experience their loneliness as they faced the terror of extinction. In the face of this reality, his own life suddenly appeared trivial; it seemed that every moment since his birth had been lived in a kind of insipid daydream. The perception gave him a courage born of anger. He stood up and advanced towards the light, shouting: 'Don't kill them. Let them go.'

As he spoke, the effort seemed absurd, like trying to communicate with a mountain; yet a moment later, he clearly heard a voice that said: 'Do you know what you are asking?' It was not using words, but intuitive thought-forms.

He said: 'What have they done that's so wicked? They only wanted to live. Why punish them?' As he spoke, he took another step forward into the place occupied by the light. At once he experienced again the intense flow of power, and the ability to see into the minds of those around him. This time the voice spoke from his own mouth. 'There is no question of punishment. But since it is important to see justice done, you shall be the judges.'

Using Carlsen's body, it bent and picked up the girl, setting her gently in the hard-backed chair behind the desk. Her eyes opened, and she stared at Carlsen in alarm and surprise. He bent over Armstrong, grasping both his shoulders; the healing power flowed from his fingers, causing the bone to knit. He stepped across to Jamieson, who flinched away as he reached out; his hand touched the swollen and discoloured cheekbone; as he watched, the bruising dissolved and the swelling disappeared.

The alien returned to Carlsen's chair and looked from one to the other. 'Are you prepared to pass judgement on these creatures who intended to destroy you?'

There was a silence, and Carlsen could read the thoughts and feelings of everyone in the room. In Armstrong and Jamieson, guilt and fear were being transformed into hatred, an instinctive desire to join the hunters. The girl was detached and bewildered. Only Fallada and Heseltine were attempting to be impartial. Fallada said: 'How can we judge?'

'Listen and decide.' The voice was gentle and patient. 'For more than two hundred years I have been on your earth, awaiting the return of the Ubbo-Sathla. And for more than a thousand years our people have searched for them among the galaxies. Our task was more difficult than searching for a single grain of sand in all the deserts of the world.'

The words were less important than the images that accompanied them. The alien was project-ing its thoughts and feelings into their minds, so that they grasped something of the immensity of space and the infinity of its worlds.

'It was just over two thousand years ago that one of our expeditionary forces discovered the remains of the planet B.76 in the Vega system. It had exploded into fragments. We knew that the planet had been inhabited by a race of highly developed beings called Yeracsin—to you they would look like balloons made of light. These creatures were lazy, but harmless and nonaggressive. There-fore we became curious about the catastrophe that had destroyed their world. Our first assumption was that it was some natural accident. And then, as we examined the fragments, we discovered signs of an atomic explosion. It was then that we began to suspect that the planet had been destroyed to cover up some appalling crime, as your human criminal sometimes set fire to a house. Further ex-amination convinced us that the planet had been the scene of a mass murder—the murder of a whole species.' His eyes turned coldly on the flickering shapes against the wall. It seemed to Carlsen that they were fading. 'Then the hunt began. We made a systematic search of all local planetary systems for any evidence that might point to the identity of the criminals. We discovered that evidence in your own solar system, where another planet had been blown to fragments.'

Fallada said with surprise: 'The asteroids?'

'In our language, it was called Yllednis, the blue planet. When we had last visited your solar system, Yuednis was the home of a great and ancient civilisation of creatures like ourselves—intelligent molluscs. And Mars was also inhabited by a race of humanoid giants who were learning to build cities. Now Mars had become a waterless desert, and Yllednis had exploded into a thousand rocky fragments. Yet your earth, with its highly evolved Mediterranean civilisation, was untouched. Why should that be, unless these criminals regarded it as some kind of base? It was then we began to suspect that these criminals were the Lost Ones—the name we gave to the scientists who van-ished on their way back to our galaxy fifty thousand years ago. At first this seemed impossible—for the Nioth-Korghai, like the human race, is physically mortal. But when we visited your earth and studied its racial memories, it was no longer possible to doubt. The criminals were creatures like ourselves, members of the Nioth race, in whom the impulse of protection towards weaker races had been perverted to a kind of sadism...' Carlsen could feel the surge of irritable contempt that ema-nated from the flickering shapes against the wall. The voice of the alien continued evenly: 'Your mythology of spirits and demons is full of memories of the Ubbo-Sathla, the space vampires. And since they had spared your planet, it was clear that they intended   to return here one day. Of course, we continued our search throughout the galaxies, hoping to prevent further crimes. But your galaxy alone contains over a hundred thousand million stars. And so our efforts brought no results—until now.'

The voice ceased. Again Carlsen experienced the waves of anger and frustration that flowed from the aliens. The silence lengthened. The voice said: 'Well? Is there anyone who still believes they should be allowed to go free?'

The eyes turned on Jamieson. Jamieson coloured and cleared his throat 'Of course not. It would be criminal stupidity.'

Fallada said: There's one question I'd like to ask.' He spoke nervously, his eyes on the car-pet. 'You said their impulse of mercy had been perverted into a kind of sadism. But couldn't it be unperverted?'

Jamieson said irritably: 'Talk sense, man.'

Fallada said doggedly: 'I want to know whether these things are *entirely* criminal.' He stared at Jamieson from under bushy eyebrows. 'Most people have got *some* good in them.'

The alien said: 'Only they could answer that question.' He looked across at the vampires. 'Well?'

Fallada said: *'Can* they speak?'

'Not without the use of a body. But they have six to choose from.'

Carlsen felt suddenly weak and sick; it took him a moment to realise that the alien had left his body and was hovering above his head. The nerves of his stomach tensed as he saw one of the wavering shapes floating towards him. Then reassurance flowed into his brain. He relaxed, allowing the shape to blend into his body. For a moment he experienced a sensation of nausea, as if he had been forced to swallow some disgusting fluid. Then it passed and was replaced by a savage exultation. A coarse vitality tensed all his muscles. It was the alien that had possessed Jamieson: the leader. The voice that spoke through his mouth had a harsh undertone of emotion.

'I will speak, although I know it is useless. No one here is concerned with justice. But I would like to point out a simple fact. The Nioth-Korghai, like the human race, are mortal. We of the Ubbo-Sathla have achieved a kind of immortality. Is it nothing to have discovered the secret of living forever? You will say that we have achieved it by destroying lives. That is true. But is it not also a law of nature? All living creatures are murderers. Human beings feel no compunction about killing the lower animals for meat. They even eat the flesh of newborn lambs. And the cows and the sheep eat grass, which is also alive. Dr. Fallada here has studied vampirism. He will tell you that is the basic principle of nature. If that is so, then in what way are we guilty?'

Fallada said: 'Are you denying that you destroy for pleasure?'

'No.' The voice was calm and reasonable. 'But since we have to kill to survive, is there any reason why we should not take pleasure in it?'

Carlsen was less concerned with the words than with the power that accompanied them. It surged into his consciousness like an electric current, producing a vision that brought a sense of ruthless delight. Human beings *were* trivial, irredeemably trivial; personal, self-obsessed, lazy, stupid, dishonest; a race of feeble-minded drifters, hardly better than imbeciles. If the law of nature was extinction of the weak, survival of the strong, then human beings were asking to be destroyed. In the essence of their being, they were victims.

Heseltine cleared his throat. 'But surely…cruelty springs out of weakness, not strength?' He spoke hesitantly, without conviction.

The vampire said reasonably: 'No one has a right to speak of weakness or strength who has not experienced total despair. Can you imagine what it is like to struggle for a thousand years against this possibility of extinction? After that, we saw no reason to accept death while there was still a chance of life. Do you condemn us for that?'

He was speaking to Heseltine and Fallada, but it was Jamieson who answered. He said: 'You condemn yourself. You have just said that murder is a law of nature. You intended to murder us. Is there any reason why we should not murder you?'

'If you had the power, that is what I would expect of you.' There was no sarcasm in the voice. 'But the Nioth-Korghai do not believe that murder is a law of nature. They believe in higher laws.' He tilted his head back, without looking directly at the ball of light. 'That is why I want to know what you intend to do with us.'

Again the voice communicated without words. 'That will be decided on Karthis.'

'But we cannot return to Karthis unless you give us the energy of transformation.'

'That will be given to you.'

'When?'

'Now, if you want it.'

Carlsen experienced the explosion of incredulity and delight. It ceased a moment later as the alien left his body. He tried to look toward the light, but it hurt his eyes. He glimpsed the pain on Heseltine's face, then covered his face with his hands. It made no difference; the light seemed to be inside him, filling him with joy and terror. He was aware that the energy flowed from the being in the centre of the room, yet came from some Other source in the universe. This in itself struck him as a revelation. The normal limitations of his mind had dissolved; he understood suddenly that all human knowledge is secondhand and drained of its content of reality. Now he was able to glimpse the reality directly, and the ecstasy was unbearable. His fear was mitigated by the knowledge that he was only a spectator; this force was flowing for the aliens. He opened his eyes and looked at the vampires. They were absorbing the energy, gulping it, bathing in it; and it flowed through them, their shapes solidified; their colour deepened and their outlines became firmer until they resembled physical bodies, seething with an inward force like coiled smoke. As he watched, they ceased to absorb; instead, they began to radiate energy, like the being in the centre of the room. This lasted only for a moment; patches of darkness formed in the light. Then he understood. He wanted to shout a warning, to advise them to retreat and begin all over again. Then, with a suddenness that shocked him, they had vanished; it was as if three electric light bulbs had simultaneously burned themselves out.

The room became dim and strangely silent. Fallada's voice said: 'What happened?' Carlsen was amazed that he could speak.

Jamieson shouted: 'Wait Don't go yet' Carlsen looked up and understood why the light was fading. Although it remained suspended in the same place, the Nioth-Korghai gave an impression of receding, as if hurtling into the distance. Carlsen experienced a feeling of loss that was as acute as pain. It was reality that was fading, and his thoughts tried to hold it back. Then he knew it was impossible; its business on earth was finished. As they watched, it shrank to the size of a pinpoint, hovered coldly, like a star in the dawn sky, then vanished. At once the room seemed to become cold and dull, as it filled with a snowy twilight. The usual dreamlike unreality, which he had always taken for normal consciousness, was back again.

Jamieson expelled a shuddering sigh of fatigue, and touched a button on the desk; the windows opened automatically. The sound of Whitehall traffic filled the room; the warm air smelt of summer. For several minutes no one spoke. Heseltine was leaning back in his chair, his eyes closed. Fallada was slumped forward, his chin against his chest, although his eyes were open. The girl had dropped onto a reclining chair in the corner and was breathing through her open mouth. Carlsen closed his own eyes and ceased to resist the rising fatigue. As he did so, he experienced a stab of sexual excitement, and a momentary image of bare thighs. He opened his eyes and looked at Armstrong, who was staring intently towards the girl. By glancing out of the corner of his eye, Carlsen could see that she was lying with parted knees; her dress had slid up her thighs. Carlsen closed his eyes again. There could be no doubt about it; he was tuning in to Armstrong's excitement. He shifted his attention towards the girl and knew that she was asleep. His mind caught the confused images of her dreams. He turned his attention to Jamieson and immediately realised that he was less exhausted than he pretended to be. Jamieson possessed remarkable inner powers of endurance and the tough, unreasoning stubbornness of the man who loves power. He was looking at Carlsen and Fallada and wondering how he could persuade them to remain silent…

The buzzer on the desk startled them all. Jamieson snapped: 'Hello?' and his voice had a note of suppressed hysteria. The secretary's voice said: 'The Minister of Works to see you, sir.'

Jamieson said: 'Not now, for Christ's sake.' He made an effort to control himself. 'Make some excuse, Morton. Tell him something's come up unexpectedly.'

'Yes, sir.'

Jamieson shook himself and sat up, looking from one to the other. He cleared his throat. 'I don't know about you, but I need a drink.' He looked and sounded like a man who has exhausted himself from vomiting. Carlsen was interested to observe that this was acting. For Jamieson, it was a matter of policy to hide his thoughts. 'Merriol, get the whisky out, will you?' Carlsen could sense Armstrong's disappointment as she pulled down her dress and stood up.

Armstrong laughed nervously. 'I've never needed one so much in my life.'

Jamieson nodded approvingly. 'I think you behaved admirably, my dear chap.'

Armstrong accepted the compliment modestly. 'Thank you, Prime Minister.'

Carlsen met Fallada's eyes. Both were aware of what was happening. The situation called for responses beyond the normal range of daily emotions; Jamieson and Armstrong were 'normalising' it.

The girl placed the whisky decanter on the desk, and a tray of glasses. Jamieson slopped whisky into six glasses, unashamed of the shaking of his hand. He raised the tumbler to his lips and drained it, then set it down again, breathing heavily. Carlsen accepted a glass from the tray; whisky dripped from its bottom onto his leg. The drink tasted raw and unfamiliar, as if he were drinking petrol. It came to him that he had not entirely lost the sense of a deeper reality. It was as if he had become two persons; one looking out through his eyes at the world around him, the other looking at it from a different position, as if slightly to one side. And the tension between the two endowed him with the power to fight against the dream.

Jamieson drank his second drink more slowly. He said: 'Well, gentlemen, we have all been through a strange ordeal. Thank God it is now over.'

Heseltine said: 'But what happened to the vampires?'

Carlsen felt Jamieson's flash of alarm. Jamieson said: They have gone. That is all that concerns us.'

Fallada asked Carlsen: 'Do you know what happened?"

'I think so.'

Armstrong said: 'Does it matter?' He was following Jamieson's lead.

Fallada ignored him. 'Why did they all vanish?'

Carlsen tried to find the right words. He could understand, but it was difficult to express. 'You could say it was a kind of suicide. They'd forgotten.'

Jamieson said: 'Forgotten what?' His curiosity overcame his fear of losing control of the situation.

'That we all take energy from the same source. It's like stealing apples from the larder when you have the run of the orchard.'

Fallada said: 'But what *happened* to them?'

'He gave them all the energy they wanted, the energy they needed to get back to their own star system. He was speaking the truth when he said they wouldn't be punished. Their law knows nothing about punishment. But he warned them they'd be judged. He was trying to warn them what to expect. As the energy flowed into them, they ceased to be vampires. They became gods again—because that's what they were originally. And now they could judge for themselves whether they were right to become vampires. They passed judgement on themselves—and condemned themselves to extinction.'

Jamieson said: 'You mean they *could* have lived and returned to their own planet?'

'Yes. It was entirely up to them to decide.'

Jamieson said: 'They must have been insane...'

'No. Just totally honest, incapable of self-deception. As vampires, they'd become experts in the art of self-deception. Then they faced the truth and knew what it involved. Self-deception is to pretend that freedom is necessity.'

He was aware that his words were stirring up a deep uneasiness in Jamieson, a self-doubt that could turn into panic. Jamieson said: 'According to the Christian religion, no sin is unforgivable.'

'You don't understand. They could have told themselves that they weren't really to blame, or that they'd make up for their evil by doing good. But they'd become too conscious to indulge in self-deception. They suddenly understood what they'd done.'

Fallada said: 'So they had to die?'

'No, they didn't have to. It was their choice. You once described the body of someone who'd been killed by a vampire as a tyre with a thousand punctures. They were the same. That's why they disappeared.'

Heseltine asked: 'What about the others—in the *Stranger?*'

'They'll be given the same choice.'

Jamieson said: 'And some of them may choose to live?'

His eyes held Carlsen's, and Carlsen was surprised by the anxiety that communicated itself. He felt the disgust vanish, replaced suddenly by pity. He said: 'I don't know, of course. But I think it is possible.'

'You have…no way of finding out?'

'No.'

Jamieson looked away; Carlsen could sense his relief. Big Ben began to strike the hour. They all listened, counting the strokes: midday. As the last sound died away, Jamieson stood up. He seemed filled with a new vigour.

'And now, gentlemen, if you don't mind…I think we all need time to rest and recover.' As Carlsen rose to his feet, he went on quickly: 'But before we leave this room, can I take it that we are all agreed on the need for silence? For the time being, at any rate?'

Fallada said doubtfully: 'I suppose so.'

Jamieson said: 'I am not asking for my own sake. Or for the sake of Dr. Armstrong or Miss Jones. This is something that concerns us all equally.' Carlsen could feel his confidence returning as he spoke. Jamieson leaned forward, placing his fingertips on the desk. '*If* we told this story, some people would believe us. But I can tell you this with confidence: the great majority would think we were insane. They would lock us up in the nearest lunatic asylum. And frankly, I think it would be our own fault. For why *should* anyone believe such an incredible story?'

Fallada said: 'Why should anyone disbelieve it?'

'But they would, my dear doctor. And the Opposition would be the first to imply that we were all mad, or inventing the whole thing for sordid personal motives. I would feel bound to offer my resignation—not because I feel in any way ashamed of my part in this matter, for which I hold no responsibility, but because I would feel I was endangering my party. If that happened, then the Commissioner would also be expected to resign. In short, we would be inviting scandal and mud-slinging. It would damage every one of us.'

Carlsen was observing Jamieson's mental processes with amusement. When he had started to speak, he was concerned only to persuade them to keep silent; within a few sentences, he had convinced himself that his motives were totally disinterested. With wry self-mockery, Carlsen realised that his pity had been misplaced. He said, with apparent concern: 'But is it fair to put our own interests first and keep these things a secret from the world? Surely people have a right to know?'

'That, Commander, is an abstract question. As a politician, I am a pragmatist. I tell you, quite simply, that we would make our lives intolerable. There is also the moral question. I am the Prime Minister of this country. It is my business to do my best for Great Britain. This affair would turn into a scandal that would damage us in the eyes of the world. Have any of us a right to take that risk?' As Heseltine began to speak, he held up his hand. 'Let me tell you frankly that what has happened this morning has left me with, a sense of profound unworthiness. I can say in all sincerity that I shall spend the remainder of my life pondering its significance. When I think of the peril that has been averted, I feel as though I were standing on the edge of a deep abyss. We have faced that peril together and, by the grace of God, we have somehow triumphed. I feel that this has bound us all close together. And, I may add, I shall make it my business to ensure that you all receive the recognition that is due for your services. I think that you will find that your country will not prove ungrateful.' He poured himself the last of the whisky and smiled at Heseltine. 'May I take it that I have your agreement, Commissioner?'

Heseltine said: 'Whatever you say, Prime Minister.'

'Commander Carlsen?'

Carlsen said: 'When you put it that way, how can I help agreeing?'

Jamieson looked keenly at Carlsen, scenting mockery; Carlsen's gravity reassured him. He turned to Fallada. 'Doctor?'

Fallada said: 'And my book? Am I supposed to suppress that?' He was having difficulty keeping his voice level.

'Your book?' Jamieson looked puzzled.

'The Anatomy and Pathology of Vampirism.'

'Good heavens, no! What an extraordinary idea! The book is obviously an important contribution to science. I shall see personally that it receives the full backing of the British Medical Association. No, no, Doctor, the book must certainly be published. And I have no doubt that it will earn you a knighthood."

Fallada said irritably: 'I don't think that will be necessary.' He stood up. Jamieson pretended not to notice his annoyance.

Heseltine said: 'And what about the *Stranger?*'

'Ah, yes. The *Stranger.*' Jamieson frowned, shaking his head. I am inclined to think that the sooner we forget about that, the better.'

Fallada went out, slamming the door. As Carlsen started to follow, Jamieson gave him a conspiratorial smile. 'Have a word with him, Commander. He's understandably upset. But I'm sure he can be persuaded to see our point of view.'

Carlsen said: 'I'll do my best, Prime Minister,'

He caught up with Fallada outside the front door. Fallada looked around angrily, then relaxed as he recognised Carlsen. Carlsen said: 'Don't let it upset you, Hans.'

'It doesn't. It bloody well disgusts me. He's not a man so much as a reptile. How does he know my book's important when he hasn't even read it?'

'It's important, whether he's read it or not. So what does it matter?'

Fallada grinned, suppressing his irritation. 'I don't know how you can take it all so calmly.'

Carlsen placed a hand on his shoulder. 'It's not difficult. We've both got more important things to think about.'

4

EXTRACT FROM *Mathematicians and Monsters: The Autobiography of a Scientist* by Siegfried Buchbinder
(London and New York, 2145)

I WAS PROBABLY AMONG THE FIRST to hear Carlsen use this famous phrase (time-reversal). This was in the spring of 2117, and it came about in this manner.

During the second year of his visiting professorship at M.I.T., Professor Fallada became a frequent visitor to our house on Franklin Street. This was partly because of his friendship with my father (who was then head of the Psychological Section of Space Research), but mainly because my sister Marcia and Fallada's attractive wife Kirsten had become inseparable companions. Fallada was more than fifty years his wife's senior, but the marriage seemed an exceptionally happy one.

One warm April evening, the Falladas had been invited to our house for a barbecue. Around nine o'clock, Kirsten Fallada rang my mother to ask if she could bring a guest; naturally, my mother said yes. Half an hour later, they arrived with a man we all recognised as the famous Commander Carlsen. Only that morning, a national news magazine had reported that Carlsen had turned down a sum of nearly two million dollars for his book on the space vampires. For more than two years, his whereabouts had been a secret; *Universe* magazine reported that he was living in a Buddhist monastery in the Sea of Tranquillity area of the moon. And now the legendary figure strolled onto our patio and began to talk about the art of frying reindeer steaks…

Even then, when he was approaching eighty, Carlsen was a big man, well over six feet tall. At a distance, you would have taken him for fifty; you had to get close up to observe the fine wrinkles around the eyes and mouth. My sister Marcia said he was the most attractive man she had ever met.

It is unnecessary to say that I spent the evening in a state of tongue-tied hero worship. Like all schoolboys, I wanted to be a space explorer. I should add that most of the family shared the emotion; it was like having Marco Polo or Lawrence of Arabia to dinner.

For the next couple of hours the conversation revolved around general topics, and we all relaxed. I was allowed a mug of home-made beer with my chicken. When nobody was looking, I sneaked to the barrel and refilled it. Towards midnight my mother told me to go to bed; when she told me a third time, I went around the table saying good night. When I got.to Carlsen, I stood staring at him, then blurted out: 'Could I ask you something?' My mother said: 'No, go to bed,' but Carlsen asked me what it was. 'Do you really live in a monastery on the moon?' Dad said: 'That's enough, Siggy. Do as your mother says.' But Carlsen didn't seem offended. He smiled and said: 'Why, no. As a matter of fact, I've been living in a lamasery at Kokungchak.' 'Where's that?' I asked (ignoring my father's head-shaking). 'In the central highlands of Tibet.' So there it was. The secret that any journalist would have given his eyes for—handed out to a twelve-year-old schoolboy. And still I wasn't satisfied. 'Why don't you come and live here at Cambridge? Nobody'd bother you.' He patted me on the head and said: 'I may at that.' Then he told my father: 'I'm going back to Storavan, in northern Sweden.'

At this point I sat and listened, and nobody told me to go to bed. Now the ice was broken, and Carlsen didn't seem to mind answering questions. My sister Marcia took up the questioning (as a child she was known as Keyhole Kate because of her insatiable curiosity). She asked him what he'd been doing in Tibet; he said he'd gone there to escape the publicity after the vampire story appeared in *Universe* magazine. *[The Killers from the Stars: The True Story of the* Stranger *Incident* by Richard Foster and Jennifer Geijerstam—26 January, 2112, later expanded into the .book of the same title.] My father asked whether trying to escape publicity didn't produce the opposite effect. Carlsen said that was true, but it hadn't always been true. When the vampires were destroyed [in 2080], he needed time to be alone and think. Fallada needed time to rewrite his book. If the full story had been published then, their lives would have become a hell of nonstop publicity. Whatever happened, they had to avoid that.

At some point, I switched on my portable tape recorder; then I fell asleep behind the armchair. My father carried me up to bed. The next morning, Carlsen had gone. But my recorder was still running under the armchair. And I still possess the recording of the conversation. Most of what was said appeared later in Carlsen's book *The* Stranger *Incident.* But that book ends with the story of the recovery of the *Stranger* and its landing on the moon. Carlsen went on to discuss his life in Storavan and his work on vampire theory with Ernst von Geijerstam; this ended with von Geijerstam's death in a skiing accident at the age of 105. Carlsen was convinced that von Geijerstam would have died anyway. His 'benevolent vampirism' prolonged his life, but only by slowing down the normal metabolic change. The problem, Carlsen said, was not merely to slow it down, but to *reverse* it.

This idea was apparently new to Fallada, who says at this point: 'It is a physical impossibility to reverse time.' Carlsen replies: 'Time in the abstract, yes. But not living time. In our universe, time is another name for metabolism—or process. In our bodies, this process ticks on, like the hour hand of a clock, gradually burning away our lives. But every time we concentrate, we slow this process—that is why scientists and philosophers tend to live longer than most men. Benevolent vampirism increases the length of human life because it increases the power to concentrate. The Space Vampires acquired a kind of immortality by concentrating for a thousand years on avoiding destruction in a black hole. But they failed to recognise the meaning of their discovery. They thought they had to keep on absorbing life energy to keep alive. They were wrong. It only stimulated them, like a glass of whisky.'

My father interrupts: 'But if they'd grasped the meaning of their discovery, would *that* have made them immortal?'

'No. Because they still hadn't realised that the true solution lies in time reversal. I should have realised it that day in Downing Street. [He apparently is addressing Fallada.] All that power flowing from the Nioth-Korghai…[words inaudible here; someone is throwing logs on the fire].

Fallada asks: Then why were the Nioth-Korghai mortal?'

'Because they had pursued a line of development that involved abandoning their bodies. That made them subject to absolute time. The body protects us from absolute time. Which means that we have less freedom of movement, but more possibility of control. Our physical time can be reversed. Not permanently, of course. But for a split second, as you might halt a stream for a moment, or as the wind can hold back the tide…'

Fallada: 'Are you telling me that this supersedes my theory of vampirism?'

Carlsen: 'On the contrary, it completes it.'

My father: 'But is there any evidence that we could achieve time reversal?'

Carlsen: 'I have done it.'

At which point, you would expect someone to ask how or when. Instead of which, my mother asks: 'Would anyone like coffee?' and my sister says: I'll make it…' The conversation then returns to matters of vampirism and victimology—the title of von Geijerstam's last book. At which point, the tape capsule runs out.

This was the only occasion on which I spoke to Carlsen. After the decision of the World Court to protect his privacy against journalists, he retired once more to Storavan. Five years later, I wrote to remind him of that evening, and to ask if I could call and see him when I came to Europe. He replied, courteously but firmly, that his researches had reached a crucial point, and that he was unable to receive visitors.

I saw him only once more—in his coffin. I arrived in Stockholm the day after his death was announced, and immediately hired a private plane to take me to Storavan.

His third wife, Violetta, received me kindly, but told me it would be impossible to invite me to stay. But she allowed me to join them at dinner—Carlsen's family seemed to be enormous—and then conducted me into the mausoleum behind the chapel. This was an octagonal room containing a number of stone sarcophagi. These, apparently, were the tombs of von Geijerstam's ancestors. [Editor's note: Buchbinder is mistaken; the tombs are those of the de la Gardie family.] Von Geijerstam's body was not among them; his last request had been that it should be sunk, in a granite coffin, in the middle of the lake. In the centre of the room stood four copper sarcophagi. Mrs. Carlsen told me that one of these contained the ashes of Queen Christina's lover, Count Magnus. Next to this, on a stone platform, stood the sarcophagus of Olof Carlsen. The lid had been pulled down to reveal his face. I was amazed to see that he looked no older than when I had last seen him. If anything, he looked younger. I placed my hand on the sunburned forehead. It was cold and had the slackness of death; yet the mouth looked firm, as if he were pretending to be asleep. He looked so lifelike that I overcame my misgivings and asked Mrs. Carlsen if the doctor had performed a lambda test. She said he had, and that it indicated a total cessation of all normal metabolic change.

Mrs. Carlsen—a Catholic—knelt to pray. I also knelt, as a mark of respect, feeling awkward and somehow dishonest. The stone slabs were cold, and after a few minutes, I began to experience the discomfort that I used to feel in our local Episcopalian church as a child. Mrs. Carlsen seemed so absorbed that I was ashamed to move. I rested one hand on the stone platform and leaned forward so that I could see Carlsen's face. And then, as I stared at the profile, I felt a strange calm that seemed to spread over my body like the effect of a drug. At the same time, I experienced an absurd sense of joy that brought tears to my eyes. I cannot explain the sensation; I can only record it. I was certain that the place contained some supernatural influence, an influence for good. The sense of peace was so profound that it seemed to me that time had ceased to flow. All discomfort vanished, although I remained kneeling for more than half an hour. As Mrs. Carlsen locked the door of the chapel, I said: 'I find it hard to believe that he is dead.'

She said nothing, but I thought she looked at me strangely.